"With echoes of the Lost Boys in Nancy Farmer's THE HOUSE OF THE SCORPION and even SLUMDOG MILLIONAIRE, this is a tightly woven tale of a boy's will to survive, the power of story, and the bonds of friends tied together in the hope of a better day."
—*BookPage*

"Sheth's lush prose creates a vivid portrait of slave labor without losing the thread of hope that Gopal clings to."
—*Publishers Weekly*

"Kashmira Sheth gives a name to the pernicious practice of child bondage in her unforgettable portrait of Gopal, a boy enslaved in a grueling factory job in India. And she shows the power of storytelling to inspire acts of kindness and courage in even the darkest of situations."
—Patricia McCormick, author of the National Book Award Finalist SOLD

"BOYS WITHOUT NAMES is not a heartbreaking story, even if there are moments that break the heart. Instead, it is a story about growing up, about learning and relearning the meaning of family. And it is a story about strength, the way it is inside of each of us as we move steadily on our way. This is one of the best books I've read this year."
—Jacqueline Woodson, author of the Newbery Honor Book AFTER TUPAC & D FOSTER

KASHMIRA SHETH

BOYS without NAMES

Balzer + Bray
An Imprint of HarperCollins*Publishers*

For my uncle and aunt,
Rohit and Susan Trivedi

Balzer + Bray is an imprint of HarperCollins Publishers.

Boys without Names
Copyright © 2010 by Kashmira Sheth

www.harpercollinschildrens.com

        Library of Congress Cataloging-in-Publication Data
Sheth, Kashmira.
   Boys without names / Kashmira Sheth.—1st ed.
     p. cm.
   Summary: Eleven-year-old Gopal and his family leave their rural Indian vil-
lage for life with his uncle in Mumbai, but when they arrive his father goes
missing and Gopal ends up locked in a sweatshop from which there is no
escape.
   ISBN 978-0-06-185762-1
   [1. Bombay (India)—Fiction. 2. India—Fiction. 3. Sweatshops—Fiction.
4. Missing persons—Fiction.] I. Title.
PZ7.S5543Bo 2010   2009011747
[Fic]—dc22   CIP
                                           AC

Typography by Carla Weise
13 14 15 CG/OPM 10 9 8 7 6
❖

First paperback edition, 2011

one

"We stay, we starve," my father says. Baba's tone is as firm as my grip on my mother, Aai's, wrist.

"Baba, you want us to move to Mumbai?" I ask. I feel giddy with excitement and fright, as if I've climbed to the very top of a coconut tree.

"Yes, Gopal."

Aai's forehead wrinkles, making lines in her large red *bindi*. "We can't leave our *desh*, the land of our forefathers," she whispers.

I feel the opposite pulls of Aai's worry about moving and Baba's fear of staying.

I envy the twins, Sita and Naren, who are outside with their friends without a care in the world. They're just six years old and too young to understand everything. I'm eleven, and for the last three years Baba and

Aai have told me about our troubles.

Baba rolls his eyes. "In the village all we will have is this mud-wall and palm-frond-roof home. In the city—" His eyes rest on Aai's round face, and his expression softens. "We have lost our farm and we will never get it back. There's so much work available in the city and it pays well," he pleads. "We won't go hungry there."

Aai turns away from Baba and nervously wraps the end of her sari around one finger. "It will be so lonely without our family and friends."

I've never seen Aai so scared. I put my arm around her. "Don't worry, we will all be together."

She shakes her head.

"The city is filled with people." Baba's impatience sharpens. "Surely we will become friends with some of them." He takes a deep breath. "If it weren't for the moneylender, I'd go by myself to Mumbai, but I can't leave you behind. He will come after you."

Baba turns around and looks out the window. Aai is silent.

Baba is right. If he left, the moneylender would harass Aai and might force me to work for him. Besides, Aai, Naren, Sita, and I would miss Baba so much. It is better for us to go together.

Unlike Aai, I don't think of Mumbai as a monster, and I am not afraid to go there. One of my friends, Mohan, visited the city last year. He says that the city is the home of film stars, cloud-reaching buildings, markets that are bigger than our village, mirror-shiny cars, double-decker buses, and dozens of languages. It would be so exciting to see all the things that are in the store windows, to watch people, and to learn different tongues. He even taught me a couple of new words they use in the city. One is *khajoor*, which means stupid, and other is *bindaas*, which means carefree.

Like many other villagers, we have lost our land and can't grow crops. But there are no other jobs in the village as there are in the cities. And we're poor. As poor as the *pipul* tree is bare in the autumn. In the past few months, the hunger has settled permanently in our stomachs.

When we still had our land, we grew *bajra* and onions on it. I love *bajra* bread with freshly dug onions dipped in salt and pepper. When Aai made spinach and potatoes or spicy fish with rice, we had a feast. And there was always something growing around the woods, like the sweet *gorus-chinch*, mangoes, or guavas I picked.

Baba always worked hard and paid the bills on time, but it all changed in the year of good rain two monsoons ago, when everyone had a bumper crop of onions. The price of onions tumbled, and Baba couldn't pay back the money he had borrowed to buy seeds and fertilizer. Last year, besides working on the farm, Baba worked at a quarry splitting stones, and Aai carried luggage for tourists at the nearby hill station of Matheran. But after we paid the interest on our debt, there was barely enough left to keep five bellies from growling.

Then Naren came down with a cold. Aai had to stay home to look after him. For a week she gave him warm milk with turmeric and tea with ginger, but his cold turned into a nasty cough and high fever, and we had to take him to a doctor. The doctor's visit and the medicine were expensive. The pills were each a quarter of the size of a *gorus-chinch* seed, but they cost Baba almost one month's income. We had to borrow more money. At the end of last year, Baba sold the farm to pay the lender.

We all cried the day we sold our farm—even Baba did. He didn't speak a word for a week. And yet, selling the land has done no good because the debt keeps multiplying. And now there is no farm to feed us. The debt is like hunger in our bellies. The interest we pay is like the food we eat—just enough to get by. The debt and hunger never leave.

Baba moves away from the window and breaks the silence. He stands in front of Aai. "I will find work as soon as we get there. You can do the same. Think of our children. Do you want them to rot here?"

"But our village, our—"

He cuts her off. "With or without us, the village will still be here."

"We will visit," I say.

Aai twists the end of her sari around her finger tightly. "It might take a long time."

Baba rolls his eyes and points to the ground. "Why do

4

you want to come back, anyway? There is nothing here but lumpy soil and clumpy roots! Even when the harvest is good, it harms us. Mumbai is the place for us. They call it *maha nagari*, grand city, for a reason."

Does Baba never want to return to the village? I ball up my hands in fists at his words to hide my sadness and anger.

"Don't forget, it is called *mayavati nagari*, make-believe city, too," Aai says.

Baba paces back and forth in our small mud-walled home. In one corner is our kitchen with the wood-burning clay stove, pots, and dishes. In another corner, we keep our sets of clothes folded neatly in a stack on top of a cardboard box. We sleep in the far corner, where our blankets are piled.

I see Baba's hands, clasped together behind his back. They are raw, red, and scabby. His hands were rough but healthy when he only worked on the farm. But the hard work of splitting stones in the quarry has given him a hunched back and worn-out fingers.

He puts a blistered palm on my shoulder. "Sit down."

I let go of Aai's hand and sit on a mat on the floor. She sits next to me.

Baba kneels down. "Listen, both of you."

The mat is unraveling at the edges and I pick a thread and tug it. It frays a bit more.

Baba holds Aai's gaze. "As long as we stay here, there's no way we can pay our debt. I want to get out of here."

"Without paying?" Aai's voice is shrill.

"We've been paying off our debt for almost two years, and yet we owe more than ever. When I saw the moneylender last time he said, 'Bring your son with you. He can work and help you pay off the debt.' Do you know what that means? He will have Gopal by the throat for who knows how long. Gopal is smart, and we must send him to school so he has a future. I don't want my son's lungs filled with dust and his life to be wasted like that. I won't allow it."

Now I know why Baba's breathing is so labored at night, heavy and gasping.

"Baba, but how—"

"It is shameful and wrong to go without paying the money we have borrowed, but we have paid the moneylender many times over. If we stay here he will own us. I see no other way out." Baba stares at the floor.

A tear rolls down Aai's cheek.

Baba wipes it away with a fingertip.

Aai reaches to me and before I know it, I am enveloped in the folds of her sari. It has gone through many washes and is soft and smells of Aai. She extends her other hand to Baba. "If there is no other way then we will go. But I will miss . . ." A sob soaks the rest of her sentence. Baba and I hold her tight.

"When do we leave, Baba?" I ask.

"Tomorrow, before the sunrise, quickly and quietly. And don't tell a soul."

Aai's eyes are wide. "So soon? We don't have money to buy the tickets for Mumbai."

"We do."

Aai and I look at each other. We know who gave Baba the money.

Only a few weeks ago, Jama, Aai's brother, showed up wearing new clothes, shiny leather sandals, and a wristwatch. He brought a blue marble with white and navy swirls for Naren and a red plastic hair clip for Sita. Then Jama slipped his hands in his cotton bag and pulled out a notebook and a slim pencil for me. On the cover of the notebook in gold letters SHREE TOOLS, INC. was printed. "That is where I work," Jama said.

That evening he tried to convince Aai and Baba to move, saying, "I work hard in Mumbai, but I don't have to toil until my bones ache. Besides, the children will get a much better education there. You can stay with me."

Baba wanted to go, but Aai refused. Later Baba and Jama must have talked alone and made plans.

"Did Jama give you the fare money?" I ask Baba to make sure.

"Yes."

"How will we find his home?"

Baba takes out a piece of paper from his pocket and hands it to me. "Gopal, this is Jama's address. He told me if we get off at Dadar it is a short walk from there. Any of the shopkeepers will help us."

❧

Aai starts to make *roti* for our trip while Baba goes to the market for jute sacks. I sit cross-legged in front of Aai to tell her I feel as sad as she about leaving my friends and our village. I want to promise her I will study, work hard, and bring her back for a visit, but before I open my mouth, Sita and Naren saunter in.

"What are you making, Aai?" Naren asks.

Sita rolls her eyes. She has picked that up from Baba. "Can't you tell it is *roti*?" When she comes closer her eyes widen with surprise. "So many!"

My chance to talk to Aai is ruined, because I don't want the twins to find out we are leaving. They will run out and tell their friends. I get up to leave. "*Mi jato,*" I tell Aai as I grab the notebook Jama gave me.

"*Sambhalun ja!*"

Aai tells me to be careful, which means she knows I'm going to my favorite spot. "*Ho,*" I reply.

"Where are you going? Can we come?" Naren shouts. But I am out the door and don't look back.

Without thinking, I start walking toward the homes of my friends, Mohan and Shiva. I do want to talk to them one last time before we leave, but Baba said not to tell a soul about our move. Can I do that? Once I speak to Mohan and Shiva, they will know from my voice that I am hiding something. If they ask me questions, I won't be able to keep our secret. It is better to avoid them.

I turn around and walk in the opposite direction to the edge of the pond. I stop by the *gorus-chinch* tree.

There are some fruits left, so I pick a handful of pods and settle on the limb of a nearby *nimba* tree that arches over the pond.

The light shines through the leaves onto my notebook. The shadowy sunshine is cool and I have a view of the world through curtains of lacy leaves, but the world can't see me.

Aai thinks it is dangerous to sit on a branch above the water, but I can't stay away from it. Sitting here, I used to dream of being a king, a pirate, a pilot, a cricket player, and even a magician. Every year when branches were crowded with small, white, fragrant flowers, I would pretend to be the Mogul king Akbar sitting in my garden that extended all the way beyond the pond and into the woods. I haven't dreamed like that in a long, long time. Now I come here to think about how to get rid of our troubles, to get away from Naren and Sita, to write in my notebook about my plans, and to watch the birds, trees, and pond.

Today, swollen green beads of *nimba* fruits have replaced the flowers; in a couple of months they will be bigger and ripe.

I open my notebook on my lap and flip pages. On one page I have written, *What can I be today? An innocent man who is ordered never to return to his land and sneaks back in disguised as a magician?* Underneath is a picture of a bearded magician, dressed in flowing robe. Even though it is a pencil drawing I know the beard is silver and the robe is red.

I turn the page. There's a story about a boy who loves stories and opens up a bookstore so he can read all the books he wants to. The store is small but the line of customers extends all the way out into the street.

Suddenly, a flock of parrots fly above the pond, making a ruckus.

I realize I have not written a single story about my village, friends, and neighbors—about my life—so I hold my pencil between my thumb and middle finger and find a blank page. Furiously, I write. I describe not only the trees, pond, and birds, but also the clumpy soil, the fluffy clouds moseying along, and the meandering path into the woods. I draw Mohan with his crooked smile and Shiva throwing a stone, because his stones always traveled farther than mine.

On another page I write how one day walking home from school, I fell and skinned my knee. I was six years old and started to cry. Mohan stayed with me and Shiva ran ahead to tell Aai. She came rushing and carried me home. I scribble about Mohan's and Shiva's families, our school, and my teacher, Mr. Advale, who thinks I am smart, and about the horses and the tourists I have met in the summer. I write about all the fun Mohan, Shiva, and I had even though we worked all day carrying luggage for the tourists. As we climbed the Matheran Hill the sun floated up from a misty horizon like a red balloon. Sometimes we rode horses, and we always chased monkeys. When we watched a swift flutter its wings, take off from a hill, and soar above us, it made us happy.

I hope next summer maybe Aai, the twins, and I can come back to the village. Then, like the last two years, Mohan, Shiva, and I can work in Matheran together. I know that unless we pay off our debt we can't return. Once more, sadness washes over me.

When I look up I realize more time has gone by than I thought, and I have a kink in my neck.

There is so much more to write and there is no way I can put it all down. Frantically, I write some more. *I won't be here to eat the fleshy yellow fruit of the* nimba. *Will they have* gorus-chinch *in Mumbai? I will miss these trees, leaves, pond, sounds, soil.* Tears trickle down my cheeks.

I wish I had a camera like the tourists in Matheran. I would take pictures of the *nimba* tree, our home, Mohan and Shiva, and the hills that surround our village. I wish I had colors and brushes; I would paint the forest, the pond, and birds.

Unlike regular *chinch*, which is sour and strong, *gorus-chinch* is sweet and mild. I bite the pink pods and suck on the fleshy part until I am down to the pebbly seed. I spit it out. It plops in the water, sending up a tiny spray. Soon, the water in the pond stills.

As I eat the last *gorus-chinch* my heart feels the same as my mouth, sour and sweet at the thought of leaving our village. School has just started, and my friends will wonder where I am.

I have sat on the *nimba* branch for a long time, and

the evening has fallen softly between the branches. The chirping of the birds has vanished, but the light of the moon shines through the leaves of the *nimba*. Even though I want to write more, it is time to go home. I close my notebook and sit for a few more seconds. When I climb down I go as slowly as I can because this is the last time I will do that. I want the bark to imprint on my palms just as it has imprinted on my heart.

The pond shimmers with moonlight. I look up. The sky is clear and the stars are packed together like people crowded in the temple courtyard at festival time.

I stand at the edge of the pond sucking on the last black seed of *gorus-chinch*. I'm ashamed that we have to leave in secrecy, without paying off our debt. It is not right. Baba knows that too. But he doesn't want me to split stones in the quarry like he does. I don't either. In Mumbai, I can get a good job after high school and won't have to starve.

Still, not paying the debt bothers me. The interest may be high, but we did borrow money and we must repay it. It is Baba's debt, but if I do well in the city, I will return the money with interest. That is the only right thing to do.

The bright moon lights the path. I take the long way back, passing the homes of my friends, Mohan and Shiva. Even though Baba didn't want me to, maybe I should see them and say good-bye.

I think of Shiva's baba, who killed himself last year

because he couldn't pay his debt. Like Baba, he was an onion farmer. If we stayed, Baba might do the same. The thought of life without Baba sends shivers through my heart. We must go. Someday we will return to the village and I will see my friends again.

I keep on walking.

two

When I return home everyone is waiting for me. Sita puts her hand on her hip. "It is dark outside. Where were you?"

"You're not Aai. I don't have to tell you."

"But you do have to tell her."

"Only if she asks me."

Sita and I look at Aai. Her eyes are moist. Was she cutting an onion? "Let's eat," she says, giving each of us a *roti* with some pieces of onion. I peel back the thin top layer of the *roti*, stuff my onion pieces evenly under it, and cover it back up. That way each bite has onion in it. It is not as good as having *ghee* on the *roti*, but better than eating it plain.

"Can you do the same for me?" Naren asks.

"Here, take this," I tell him. I exchange mine with

him and stuff the other one with onion pieces.

"Don't you want to eat it like us?" Naren asks Sita.

"No. My way is better."

She is cross with me because I didn't tell her where I went. If it were any other day I would tease her and make her laugh, but today I am out of jokes.

"Tomorrow we leave early and travel by train," Aai tells us all after supper.

"Where are we going?" Sita shrieks.

"To see Jama."

"I love Jama!" Naren says. "Do you think he will have more presents for us?"

"Maybe."

"Aai, can you put the red clip in my hair tomorrow?" Sita asks.

They are loud and can't stop bouncing. Baba gives Aai a sharp look—maybe he is afraid our neighbors will overhear our plans.

"If you both lie down I'll tell you a story," I say to the twins.

"You never finished the one about the marble. I want to hear that one," Sita says.

They both stretch out in one corner. I cover them with a blanket Aai has made by sewing patches of her two old saris together. My mind is so full of thoughts about our moving that I would rather tell them a story that I don't have to make up as I go along. But the

15

marble story will quiet them down.

"One day, a little boy went for a walk looking for a treasure. He didn't want silver or gold or money and jewels. All he wanted was something beautiful. He meandered into a forest where trees as tall as ships filled the land. Before long the boy saw something glint. It was under a pile of dirt, so he kneeled down to remove it."

"Not dirt. You told us the marble was under the *gorus-chinch* leaves," Naren reminds me.

I wish he would relax and fall asleep. "Sorry, under the *gorus-chinch* leaves. So he bent down and picked up the glinting thing. It was a marble. The most beautiful one he had ever seen."

By this time Naren is up on his elbow. He shakes his head. "You have it all wrong. First the boy had to remove the leaves to see the marble."

I give him a stern look, but his wide eyes shine like a pair of dark stones. I sigh. "I forgot. Yes, first he removed the leaves and then he picked up the marble."

"All wrong."

Sita rolls her eyes. "Just listen quietly."

"But Gopal doesn't know it. Don't you remember? Once he removed the marble he saw a hole?"

Why does Naren have to memorize every word and interrupt me? I wish I had read a story from one of my books. That way there would have been no arguments. "I've made up the story, so I can change it if I want to," I say.

"No, no, no. You can't change it if it is the same story. Are you telling the same marble story or not?"

"Well, I am."

"Then—"

Baba kneels down beside Naren and Sita. "It is late and I want you both to sleep. Gopal will finish the story when we get to Jama's house."

The twins look disappointed but they don't argue with him. I am relieved Baba got me out of this story telling.

When Naren and Sita are asleep Aai takes out her cotton bag to begin packing. Besides my clothes, the only things I must bring to Mumbai are my books. My book about the life of Buddha is almost new, but the *Akbar and Birbal Stories* looks like our frayed rug. Last year I collected the sticky *nimba* sap and used it to glue the pages back. These two books are like old friends—friends I don't have to part with

I hand the books to Aai. She unfolds her sari, packs the cracked mirror and my books in it, and refolds it gently. She lays them at the bottom of the bag. Then she slips in our extra clothes and tucks in a comb, black ribbon, and a sliver of a soap wrapped in paper. On top she puts my notebook and her faded old sari.

"This way it's right there, if you need it."

I give Aai a hug. "Thank you. There will be a lot to write about on our travels."

"And once we get to Mumbai you will have even more."

Aai is right. The city will be filled with people, shops, buildings, roads, buses, cars, noises, and even bookstores. "I—I can't believe tomorrow night we will be at Jama's." My voice crackles with excitement.

Baba brings two jute bags that the grocery shop owner has sold him. They're large and must have held wheat, because a few grains tumble out as Baba and I shake them. Unlike the soft cotton bag, the jute bags are rough and scratch my fingers. Aai packs two bowls in one of the jute bags. We have three aluminum plates, one knife, and two spoons, and she packs them, too. On the very top, she puts three onions and a round container full of *bajra roti* she has made. It will be our food while we travel.

"What's the other bag for?" I ask Aai.

"For the rug, blankets, and pillows."

"We can't pack them until tomorrow. We have to get up early, so let's go to bed," Baba says.

I stretch out next to Naren. My thin blanket is too small for me, but in the warm weather it doesn't matter. In the winter I will have to curl up to be able to fit under it. Maybe by the time winter comes, we'll have enough money to buy a new one that is bigger, thicker, and warmer.

While we packed I was calm, but as soon as I lie down my heart quickens as if I have been running a race. I don't remember ever being this thrilled and scared, even when I started school or went to Matheran for the first time. And then I have a terrible thought. What will the moneylender do once he finds out we are gone? Will he burn our hut in revenge? Will he find out where we are and come after us? Will he send someone to beat up Baba?

Now I know why Baba didn't want to tell anyone about our leaving. This way when the moneylender asks our friends and neighbors they can tell him they don't know where we are.

Still, our friends will be sad when they don't see us tomorrow. I know I would be if one day Mohan or Shiva and their families suddenly vanished. If we had told them about our move, said our good-byes, and hugged them, it would have been better. But that is not possible. Deep down in my chest I feel pain as if one of the *gorus-chinch* seeds is rattling in my heart.

three

It is still dark when I wake up and look out the window for the last time. Baba stands behind me with his hands on my shoulders. "It is such a shame. . . ." Baba gets choked up.

I didn't realize he feels just as bad as Aai about leaving our village. Something moist and sad is stuck in my throat, too. I cough to clear it. "We will be back, Baba."

Aai comes and stands next to me. I put my head on her shoulder and close my eyes. The three of us are silent, but I feel better. "We must leave soon," Baba says.

I kneel down next to the twins. "Naren, Sita, get up."

Usually I have to wake them up two or three times, but not today. They both bolt up as if they were already awake and were waiting for me to call them.

"How many days do you think we will stay with

Jama?" Naren asks Sita as we wash up.

"We'll stay there exactly for a month," she declares.

I hand them *nimba* twigs. "Hurry up and brush your teeth or else we will miss the train."

"Then we will just go tomorrow." In the moonlight I can't see Sita's face well, but I can imagine her rolling her eyes.

Sita doesn't know about our debt. If we don't leave today Naren or Sita will tell their friends we are going to Mumbai, and if the moneylender finds out, he will stop us. "Let's see if I finish brushing first or you do," I say.

Sita and Naren get busy. By the time we rinse our mouths Aai is ready and has tied up the top of one jute bag with string.

"I want to talk to all of you before we leave," Baba says, scowling. It worries me. I try to remember if I did anything wrong.

"What, Baba?" I ask. Naren and Sita stare at him.

"In the city there will be a lot of traffic and many people."

"How many?" Naren asks.

"You always interrupt. Just listen," Sita says.

Baba puts his hand up. "In the city you must not fight about little things so you can pay attention. You must stay close to us. Be careful and don't let anyone know our names, where we come from, or where we're going. I don't want strangers to find out that we're new in the city."

"Does Gopal have to do all these things?" Naren asks.

21

"Yes, all of you. Do you understand?" Baba asks us as he stuffs the pillows in the second jute bag.

"I do," I reply.

"Naren and Sita?"

They nod. "*Ho*, Baba."

I fold blankets and Baba puts them on top of the sack. Aai picks up the tattered rug. "Jama will have rugs. Do we need this one?" I ask.

Baba agrees with me. "We must travel light. Why carry more weight?"

"Better take it," she insists.

Baba and I exchange a glance that says, *Why is she so stubborn?* But we pack the rug anyway.

"Can you put this clip in my hair?" Sita asks Aai.

"Not now. Just take it with you."

"I want you to put it in my hair."

Aai looks at me. "Gopal?"

I smooth Sita's hair with my fingers, gather it up, and fasten it with the clip. Some of the curls around her face escape and settle on her forehead.

"Don't forget your marble, Naren," she says.

He pats his pocket. "It is right here."

Baba picks up the sack with pans and dishes. "Let's go."

"Shhhh," Aai whispers as we walk out the door. She carries the cotton bag and I take the other jute bag with bedding.

The station is a good four kilometers away, so it will

take at least an hour to reach it. We move at a quick pace so we can be out of our village before daylight comes. "I want to—" Naren says.

Baba puts his finger on his lips.

Naren knows something is wrong because he holds my hand and whispers in my ear. "Why can't we talk, Gopal?"

I shake my head.

When we pass Mohan's house, Baba glances at me. I can't decide if I want to slow down and hope Mohan is up and sees me, or run down the lane so he doesn't. I clamp down my jaw and walk along with my family as we go as fast as the twins' short legs can.

No one spots us on the way to the station.

Baba has kept the ticket money ready. "Two full and three half tickets to Dadar Station," he tells the ticket master.

The man counts the money. "This is not enough. Did you know that there was a fare increase on the first of the month?" The man points to the sign that says so.

Baba looks at the man like he has hit him over the head with a pan.

I read the notice. "Baba, it is true. The price went up only four days ago! Now what are we going to do?"

Baba looks down as he tries to hide his disappointment.

We huddle to the side. One by one, the people behind us get their tickets.

The train whistles and I know it will be here soon. If

23

we don't get on this train, we'll have to go back home and then everyone will know we were trying to leave. If the moneylender finds out about it, he might go to the police to complain. Baba might end up in prison. My heart sinks slowly as if it has landed in a muddy hole. Sweat beads form on my forehead. A man comes rushing through. "One for Thane," he says in his out-of-breath voice to the ticket master.

I notice that the price of going to Thane is less than going to Dadar. "From Thane can we go to Dadar?" I ask the man.

"Yes, yes," he replies as he walks away.

The platform vibrates under my feet. The train is almost here.

I count in my head. "Baba, we have enough for us all to go to Thane."

"Then how will we find Jama? He told us to go to Dadar."

"That is our only way. From Thane we can find a way to go to Jama's place."

Baba hands the money to the ticket master and buys the tickets, just as the train slows down.

four

We have second-class tickets, the cheapest fare. Aai boards the train first, then Naren, Sita, and I. Once I get in, Baba hands me the luggage, piece by piece. He is the last one to get in. We turn into the corridor that goes through the entire car and is lined with windows. On the other side of the corridor are compartments. Each one of them is fitted with long wooden benches that face each other with windows at the end.

The first two compartments are full. Baba goes to the third one and we follow him. While he slides our luggage under the bench Aai cushions the seat with the tattered rug from home and instantly it becomes our space. She sits in the middle with Naren and Sita on either side. Baba sits on the other side of Naren by the window, and I on the other side of Sita. I am on the aisle and the corridor separates me from the window on my right.

I like the way Aai, Baba, and I protect Naren and Sita, but sometimes I envy the twins. As long as they are near I never get to sit by Aai and whisper to her. Even when Aai is not there, the two of them are always together like a pair of *gorus-chinch* seeds nestled in the same pod. I know I'll miss my friends and I feel guilty about not saying good-bye to them, but the twins have no such worries. First, because they don't understand that we're leaving our village and may not return, and second, because they are each other's best friend and will always be together.

People pour in. The bench across from us gets filled up with three men and two women. One of the men is large and takes up more room than Baba and Naren combined.

Even with the furiously whirling fan above, sweat trickles down my back. I get up and try to open the window across the aisle, but it seems to be stuck. It needs more force. I take a deep breath and apply all my strength and still can't move it an inch. At the moment I turn around to sit down, someone skinny with thick, black hair plops down on my seat. Aai opens her mouth to say something, but it happens so fast that her words never come out.

"I was sitting here," I tell him.

"Were you?" he asks.

"Yes. I just got up to open the window."

"You get up, I sit down."

Baba leans over and shows the man our tickets. "These are our seats."

"Good man, there is nothing like 'your seat' or 'my seat.' We're all travelers and sit where we find a place, and when our station comes, we move along. You're not taking this seat anywhere and neither am I."

"True, but my son was sitting there."

"*Was* is not the same as *is*, is it? Haven't you heard about the law, 'the land belongs to the one who farms it'? There should be another law: 'the seat belongs to the one who occupies it.'"

"That's not—I mean, you can't just take my seat. It's not right," I say.

The man laughs. His teeth are even and clean. "Right or wrong, I don't know. It doesn't matter. I take this train every week and always find a seat. But I don't claim it as my own. Do what you want to do, you won't be able to move me from here." He shrugs and looks straight ahead as if I don't exist.

"*Bhai*," Aai says tenderly. "We are fellow travelers and space is scarce. We don't mind sharing. We will move a bit and you move a little too, and make room for my son."

As soon as Aai calls him *bhai*, brother, the man's expression changes from smug, smirky, and superior to soft, sheepish, and sorry. He wiggles and draws his legs together. Baba, Aai, and the twins all do the same, so there is enough room for me to squeeze in. I'm not as comfortable as I was before the man took half of my space, but it is better than standing the entire trip.

The man slides his bag underneath the seat. "Do

you want me to open the window?" he asks me after he straightens up.

"Sure."

When he gets up I think about scooting over to claim the space back. Aai smiles. "Don't," she whispers.

He turns the knob away and pushes the window open. "It was locked," he says as he sits back down. "Did you see how I unlocked it?"

I wonder why he is giving me lessons in window opening. He doesn't sound arrogant, though. "Yes," I reply.

The train starts, and as it picks up speed, the breeze filters in. I don't feel so suffocated and sweaty anymore. Naren and Sita fall asleep, resting their heads on Aai. Two of the men across from us have dozed off and one of them snores loudly. The women whisper in a language I don't understand.

Outside, trees, huts, and people zip by. For a while, it is fun to watch. I should have kept my notebook out to write, but I am so cramped that it would be difficult. Even if I did, the man next to me would be able to read every word. That is something I don't want.

The man takes out a pack of cards with a blue cloud pattern and asks me if I want to play. I do, but I am ashamed that I don't know how to play real cards. I have never had a complete deck, so Mohan, Shiva, and I used to combine our decks and make up our own games. Sometimes we had two kings of hearts and no queen, and other times we had only one nine. It was fun, because each time our decks changed, our rules changed. But I don't know any proper games.

"Watch this," he says, getting a clipboard out of his bag, "I am going to play solitaire."

He lines up seven cards facedown on the clipboard resting on his lap. He lays one card faceup on the first one and the rest of them facedown. There is a pattern to his arranging, because he puts a faceup card on the second one and the rest of the five facedown. When he is done setting up his game, he still has cards left in his hands and checks them against the open cards. He lines up king, queen, jack, and so on, red on black and black on red. I find it very interesting.

"Did you get it?" he asks.

"A little."

He stops, looks up, and asks, "What's your name?"

"Gopal."

I name him Card-Man. He teaches me the game and I like him, but I remember Baba's warning. "Be careful in the city and don't let anyone know our names, where we come from or where we're going. I don't want strangers to find out that we're new in the city."

Somehow, I think Card-Man knows we're going to Mumbai for the first time without our telling him. He hands me the deck and glides the clipboard toward me. "Now you play."

The cards are monsoon-grass smooth and slide off my hands. I play one game of solitaire. Then I gather up the cards. Card-Man is looking out the window with a steady gaze. It reminds me of how Naren becomes still before he falls asleep. When I hand him back the cards and the clipboard he slips the cards in his pocket, the clipboard in his luggage, and closes his eyes.

I must have also fallen asleep because I wake up just as the train slows down and comes to the stop called Kalyan.

The noise on the platform is like a million buzzing bees punctuated by whistling birds and barking wild dogs. Naren and Sita are awake and hungry. Aai opens the aluminum container of *roti* spread with the last of the pickles. First, she offers them to Card-Man.

He takes one *roti* and bows to Aai. We each take one too. The shouts of vendors are loud. A boy younger than I pokes his head through the window and asks, *"Ek chai?"* to the Card-Man. They seem to know each other.

"Six."

The boy looks puzzled.

The Card-Man points at us. "For my family."

I look at Baba and Aai in horror. We probably don't have money and even if we did, we wouldn't want to waste it on tea. But as quick as he sat down on my seat, the man pays the boy and begins passing the tea glasses to us.

"We're grateful for the *chai*," Baba says.

"And I am grateful for the *roti*. You can get tea any-place but not such delicious homemade sweet *bajra roti* and pickles."

The tea is steaming hot and I sip slowly. I haven't even finished half of it when the train whistles. The twins are still blowing on their tea to cool it. I panic. "How are we going to give the boy the glasses back?"

Card-Man puts his hand on my shoulder. "Enjoy it and don't worry about the glasses. He will collect them later."

"Does he travel on the train?"

"Not officially."

The train goes forward before it stops again. I'm puzzled and so are the twins. "Why isn't the train moving, Baba?" Naren asks.

"I'm not sure."

"We have a red signal. Until it changes, we can't move," Card-Man explains.

"When will that happen?" Naren asks.

"As soon as you finish your tea."

"How will they know I've finished it?"

Card-Man laughs. "Just enjoy it."

The reddish-brown tea, the color of our moist farm soil, is strong and sweet. I feel so refreshed after drinking it that I wonder if I will be able to fall asleep again. Finally, the boy who sold us the tea comes around and we hand him our glasses. He collects them in a carrier that holds many glasses. I get up and stand in the corridor to watch him. Since there is no platform, he puts his two carriers on the floor of the car and jumps to the ground. Then he picks up the metal carriers. Someone closes the door behind him.

I wonder if the boy goes to school or if this is all he does. If his family is very poor, then he must work to help his family. Maybe he just works in the morning before school starts. This thought makes me feel better.

The boy waits between the two sets of tracks. A few minutes later, I hear a rumble. The boy's hair flutters in the wind. A fast train whizzes by. Its massive wheels could grind anything that came in its path. A chill passes through me. This boy must do this every day and very carefully or else.

"Or else" is too scary to think about.

After the fast train passes, ours gets going. "We have a green signal," Sita cries.

"You're a smart girl," Card-Man says.

The *chai* boy is still waiting between our train and the next set of tracks. I take my seat. "Why is he not going back?" I ask Card-Man since he seems to have all the answers.

"He is waiting for the slow train that comes from the opposite direction. It will stop like ours and he will get on. Then he will go to his tea stall to refill his carriers with fresh glasses of *chai* for the next train."

"He owns a tea stall?" I ask.

"No. He works for someone."

I just hope he doesn't have to do this all day long, every day.

Baba dozes off. Naren and Sita want Aai to tell them a story, so she does. "Once in a forest, there lived a timid rabbit. She was afraid of getting lost, so she stayed close to her home by a banyan tree. One day a storm swept through the jungle. The wind hissed and howled. The trees swayed. Their trunks and branches cracked and whipped. Then something fell smack on top of the rabbit's head. It startled her. '*Oui maa!*' she exclaimed. 'A part of the sky must have fallen on my head.'"

"But it hadn't. Silly rabbit," Naren says.

"Don't talk in the middle," Sita says, "or else I'll seal your lips with *nimba* gum."

"Where're you—"

The big man sleeping across from us opens his eyes and gives the twin a stern look. They both fall quiet. Aai continues. "Just then a twig above her snapped. 'The sky is falling! The sky is falling! Run, run, run,' the rabbit said, scampering as fast as her little legs could take her."

Aai used to tell me stories while I helped on the farm, and it made the weeding and harvesting go faster.

I have heard this story many times over, and my mind wanders off.

Outside, the land flies by. We are far away from our village and our neighbors. Mohan and Shiva must have left for school. If they don't see me at school they might come by on their way back to see me. How will they feel when they find out we have left? They won't know where we have gone for sure, but it wouldn't be hard for them to guess, since Jama lives in Mumbai. Where else would we go? I wonder if they might be a little jealous like I was when Mohan visited Mumbai with his older brother.

Maybe they would be mad at me. When Shiva's father died he was so angry he wrote *Baba* in the dirt and spit on it several times. Then he cried like a baby. I don't want to make my friends sad and upset. I wish I could have written them a note explaining why we had to leave. Then they would have understood. But I didn't do that and now if they are angry with me, they might write my name and spit on it, too.

I just hope Baba and Aai find good, steady work in Mumbai so I won't have to worry about anything except my studies. Maybe Baba will find a job like Jama and will have money to buy new clothes for all of us and I can get books to read. I won't have a *nimba* tree by the pond, but the books will help me do the same—get away from everyone. Maybe we might go see a movie and meet a film star. What would I say if I met Shahrukh Khan?

As the train slows down, so do my thoughts. The next station is Thane. Card-Man hands the deck of cards to me. "They're yours," he says.

"But . . ."

"No problem," he says. "Keep them and play with your brother and sister. And if they don't want to, you can always play solitaire like I taught you." He winks at me.

"Are—are you . . ." I am so shocked that I don't know what to say. This stranger has taught me a game and now is giving me his deck of cards. "Thank you," I mumble.

I slip the cards in the cloth bag on top of my notebook after Baba takes out our luggage from under the bench. Aai wakes up the twins just as we pull into the platform. As soon as they get up I fold the rug and hand it to Baba. Quickly, he stuffs it in one of the bags.

"*Chala, chala,*" Baba says as he rushes toward the door carrying the jute sacks.

I follow him with the cotton bag. When the train stops, there are people waiting to get on the train, and they charge forward. "*Thahro*, wait," Card-Man shouts at them. Baba gets down first, then Aai. Card-Man picks up Naren and Sita and hands them to Baba. He helps me pass the luggage down to Baba. Finally, I get off. Some people have wiggled past me and others are clamoring up the steps. I check to make sure we have everything.

On the platform a sea of people surround us. Aai holds Naren's and Sita's hands, and we are all wide-eyed. Unlike the small, empty station near our dusty village, Thane station is filled with moving people—women dressed in colorful saris and dresses, men running to catch the train, vendors shouting their wares. The smell of fried food and hot tea mixes in the air with Marathi, Hindi, and many other languages.

A group of women dressed in expensive clothes walk past us. They're wearing gold necklaces and bangles. A young girl has a bag on a wheel. Sometimes I used to carry these kinds of bags in Matheran, but I could never wheel them, because streets in Matheran are not even and smooth like this platform. There is a long bridge that passes from one side of the station to the other, spanning several platforms. The bridge is filled with pedestrians crossing in a hurry. We move to a side near a stall selling magazines and newspapers. I wonder if Jama has magazines and books at his home.

"You stay here. I'm going to find out how we get to Mumbai," Baba says to us, and hurries off.

When I look up to thank Card-Man, he has disappeared. I peek through the window and wave at him to get his attention. There are many more people jammed in that compartment than before and it is hard to see him. Finally when he looks at me the train blows a whistle and moves forward. I shout, "Thank you, thank you!"

"Who are you shouting 'thank you' to?" Naren asks.

"The man sitting next to us who bought us tea, helped us get off the train, and gave me a deck of cards to play with."

"He gave you cards?" Naren's eyes sparkle. "If we meet him again I will say hello to him."

I ruffle his hair. "*Khajoor!* In the city there are so many people you won't ever see him again."

"Don't call me stupid." He stomps his feet. "If he lives in Mumbai and we get there, we might see him. And when we do, I am going to talk to him."

"You do that," I say, just to shut him up.

"I will," Naren says, folding his arms across his

chest. "You should too."

"I'll do what I want to do." I turn to Aai. "Do you see Baba?" I whisper.

She shakes her head.

Naren scans the platform. "What if Baba doesn't come back? What if he gets lost?" He tugs at my hand.

I look at Aai and we both burst out laughing. "Why are you laughing?" Naren asks.

"Because you think we will meet that stranger in this big city and you think we will lose our own baba because we don't see him at the moment."

"It isn't funny," Naren says.

"No." Sita stomps her foot.

Aai kneels down and takes them both in her arms. "Your baba will be back any minute." She takes out two pieces of rock sugar from a cloth pouch and gives one to each of them to suck on. I want one too, but if we had enough Aai would have given one to me. It is not fair being the oldest. I avoid meeting Aai's eyes because I don't want her to see that I am hurt.

And I don't want to see her eyes telling me that she is sorry.

five

Slowly the platform begins to drain of people and Baba walks back to us. His face has this strange look, as if someone has promised him a singing bird and handed him a rusty cage. Aai, Baba, and I huddle together to figure out what we need to do.

"I don't know who to ask how to get to Jama's house. People here are all in a hurry," Baba says.

"Let's get out of the station first," Aai says.

I pick up the cloth bag; Baba picks up the ones with cooking utensils and bedding. Aai holds the twins' hands and we walk toward the exit.

Naren starts to go through the gate, but a ticket checker in a white uniform puts his hand out. "You should keep the tickets ready when you're going through the gate."

Baba puts his bag down, sticks his hand in his back

pocket, and pulls out the tickets.

Outside the station, horns blare and the cars and rickshaws fly by. The air is heavy with the smell of petrol and thick with dust. I look up to see where the sun is, but all I see is a hazy light and above it a gray mass just hanging there.

I wonder how far we have to travel to get to Dadar.

Baba takes out a crumpled piece of paper with Jama's address. He shows it to a rickshaw driver. "Do you want a ride?" he asks Baba.

"No, I want to know how far this place is."

Someone else gets in that rickshaw and the driver takes off without answering. Baba stares at the back of the rickshaw with wide eyes and open mouth.

We move to the other side, where yellow and black taxis are waiting. He hands the piece of paper to a driver. "Is it close by? Can we walk?" he asks, while the man reads the address.

"If you start walking now you will get there before sunrise," the man answers. Baba's face turns dark as he takes a step backward. He seems to have shrunk since we got off the train. The man thinks this is a joke and laughs, exposing his brown, stained teeth. "Huh, huh, huh."

So far, I haven't seen anything in the city I like.

"We're tired," Sita cries.

"We're thirsty," Naren pipes in.

"Wait for a few minutes with Aai until Gopal and I find someone who can help us," Baba says.

Aai and the twins sit with our luggage on the station's footpath while Baba and I shuffle between people. The street we are on is crowded not only with pedestrians, but also with vendors and shoppers. Some vendors are selling from carts, others from baskets, and some have spread their things on the footpath, so it is a challenge to walk without bumping into someone or something.

It is way past noon, and the day has heated up. As we go through the market, we ask people how to get to Jama's place. One man wearing old-style *dhotar* and a long shirt doesn't even look at Baba when he shows the man Jama's address. He walks on. Others shake their heads after glancing at the address. It seems like everyone is in a hurry to get somewhere.

"There are people standing in a bus line across the street. We can ask them. At least they won't walk away," I tell Baba.

Baba and I wait to cross the street but there is no break in the traffic. People get to the other side while we wait, and wait, and wait. Baba grips my hand tightly as a motorcycle zooms too close to us. I watch others to see how they cross the street. Some step up boldly and hold their hand out to stop the traffic, others dash when there is the slightest opening. A couple of times the traffic backs up and comes to a crawl. That is the time some people zigzag between cars, bicycles, motorcycles, trucks, buses, and rickshaws. No matter what, everyone gets to the other side, unlike Baba and I. If we want to live in the city we must learn how to weave through the traffic.

I move a little forward when there is a break and pull Baba along. He is slow and by the time we go a bit forward, someone blares the horn so loud that Baba jumps back.

His grip on my hand tightens. "I don't think we can go across, Gopal."

"If we can't cross this side street how are we going to tackle a big one? Come," I say, inching closer to a group of people. A few more people stand behind us. When the people ahead of us begin to move forward, I pull Baba. "Hurry."

"That was clever of you," Baba says when we get to the other side.

He shows the piece of paper to a man waiting in the bus line. The man reminds me of Jama because he is wearing a new pair of sandals and a shiny watch. "Catch the bus number thirty from the Marathon Chowk. Remember to get off at Dadar," he says.

"Where is that bus stop?" I ask.

He points with his hand. "Walk that way. It is hardly a ten-minute walk."

A bus arrives and the people rush forward.

By the time I thank him he is on the bus.

I stand with my mouth agape. It doesn't matter if the passengers are fat or skinny, tall or short, old or young, men or women. They rush to board the bus, just like the other passengers did to board the train.

While we walk toward the Marathon Chowk, a number 30 bus passes by. Baba shakes his head. "Look at that, Gopal. The passengers are stuffed in there like *bajra* in a bag."

"Maybe it wouldn't be so crowded early morning or late evening."

"You might be right. We don't have enough money for all of us to travel, so I will go by bus and bring Jama here. I don't know how long it will take me to get to Dadar, find Jama's home, and return with him. It will be evening in a few hours, and I don't want to leave you in the dark alone."

"That means you can't go until tomorrow. Where will we sleep tonight?"

Baba doesn't reply. I don't think it is going to be easy to find a place to sleep and he knows that. Baba reaches for my hand. "Let's cross back." His grip tightens when we step onto the curb but he doesn't hesitate when I pull him across.

On the way back I notice the vegetable vendors selling summer squash and cabbages. My stomach growls a few times. I read the names of the stores out loud so Baba can also know what they say. Lakshmi Auto Parts, Sagar Electronics, Urban Tailors.

Close to the station, we stop at Deepak Food Store. In the front, the man has arranged glass bottles full of rainbow-colored hard candies. They must taste better than the plain rock sugar. My mouth waters. When Baba asks the store owner if there is place for a traveler, he says, "Not if you don't have money." His face is clean-shaven and his bald forehead reflects the light of a naked bulb that hangs above him.

Baba points across the street. "My family is waiting by the station and we have two other young children, so if you can tell us about a place where we can spend a night, I will pray to God to bless you."

A man paying for groceries turns around. "You better pray for your own family. Looks like you can use it," he says to Baba.

No one has insulted Baba like they have in this city. I want to stuff the man's mouth with rocks.

I am not the only one. The store owner takes the customer's money and as soon as the customer leaves, he says, "There're some people who think showing sympathy will cost them a rupee." Then he asks me, "Have you eaten?"

I shake my head.

He tells us. "I'll give you some lentils and rice. That's all I can do."

"We're grateful for that." Baba's voice trembles.

"You're like thousands of others who pour into Mumbai and its suburbs looking for a better life," the store owner says, opening up an old newspaper. "This place is big, but not big enough for everyone."

"Thousands of others? I don't understand," Baba says.

The store owner picks up a page of newspaper, tears

it in half, and rolls each into a cone. He fills one with rice and the other with lentils. "Yes. Every single day people from Bihar, Bengal, Gujarat, Karnataka, Assam, Madhya Pradesh, and other states come to this city wanting a good life. We can't feed and give homes to everyone," he mumbles.

"But we are willing to work and not live on charity," Baba protests.

"I know, but don't you realize that there're too many people like you looking for work?"

He packs some salt, red pepper, and turmeric in small packages. He puts it all in a plastic bag and hands it to me. Baba takes out some money. "Today, you're my guest. You don't need to pay," the owner says.

Baba bows. "I pray to God to keep your family happy and healthy." I bow too.

"We better get back to Aai and the twins. I'm sure they are scared," I tell Baba.

"Yes," he replies. "We have wandered enough for the day."

Aai, Sita, and Naren are huddled on the footpath. "What did you bring?" Sita asks as soon as she sees my bag.

"Look what the man gave us," I say, showing the packages. "There's rice and lentils and spices."

"What else?"

"Isn't this a lot? He gave it for free."

"But how will we eat it?" Sita asks.

I am annoyed with her. We got all these groceries and she is still whining about food. Before I tell her to stop complaining, she says, "We have no stove to cook rice and *dal*."

"What about the *rotis* you made, Aai?" I ask.

"There're only two left. What difference does it make once we get to Jama's house? Did you find out how to get there?"

"I'll take a bus tomorrow morning and bring him here," Baba replies.

Aai's face tenses up and her *bindi* is wrinkled with worry lines. She doesn't say anything, though. Baba takes out the money he has squirreled away in his pocket. "Let's get some food, Gopal," he says.

"Don't go too far," Aai calls after us. I turn around and wave at her before we round the corner. Aai's face is still scrunched up as she holds Sita's hand. Naren is crouched by them. Maybe it would be better if I stayed with them, but Baba has asked me to go with him and I can't say no.

Baba and I plod along, trying to avoid banging into people. Luckily, we don't have to cross the street. Nearby there is a handcart selling snacks and we return with two packages of hot, fried *pakoras*. Then he takes out a pan from the sack and walks away to get water. I open one package and we each take one *pakora*, except Aai. She waits for Baba to return.

The *pakoras* are made with potatoes, chickpea flour

called *besan*, and spices. Once, a tourist in Matheran bought me one for carrying his bags. This one is spicier.

Baba returns with water, and it tastes good to have a few sips of it. By the time Baba and Aai start to eat, one package is finished and the twins are waiting to eat more.

"Gopal?" Baba holds out the open package to me.

I hesitate because I want to make sure Baba and Aai had enough.

Baba hands me a big, fat *pakora*. "One more, for me."

I feel pretty full after I finish that one and drink some more water. Aai says, "One thing nice about *besan* is that when you drink water, it expands in your stomach."

As soon as my stomach is satisfied, I feel sleepy, but there are so many people walking by us, I don't think I can fall asleep. Aai spreads the tattered rug on the edge of the footpath for the twins. I sit with my back against the station wall and watch.

The evening is warm, the fumes are heavy, and the noise has thickened. The hazy gray cloud hangs low. It is dark now and the lamps light up the area. I look up but can't see a single star. The lovely moon that shone so brightly over the pond last night is hidden behind the layers of smog.

Even with my family here I am scared. We should have been at Jama's house by now and we are not. This place is full of people and so much is going on, and yet I feel I am not part of it. It is like they are all in a movie—real but not real. Was this the right thing to do? Before I left our village, I thought the stars might change our luck in Mumbai, but here the stars can't see us and we can't see them.

"Will you tell us a story?" Naren asks me.

"Even an old one is fine, if you are tired," Sita says, patting my arm.

I don't want to, but Aai smiles at me, which says to me, *Please, tell them a story.*

I can't say no to her. "How about a Birbal story?"

Naren shakes his head. "You didn't finish the marble—"

I don't feel like making up a story. "I'll tell that one when we get to Jama's house. If you don't want to hear this one—"

"We do," Sita says. "And we will keep quiet." She stares at Naren to make sure he understands the rule.

I tell them a story that I have memorized from my book. That way I don't have to think. I begin, "A long time ago the Mogul king Akbar ruled India. He had nine special people in his court and he called them *navratna*, nine jewels. They were his advisors and his friends. One of his *navratna* was a man named Birbal. Birbal was smart, funny, and he wasn't afraid to speak the truth. Akbar thought Birbal was the smartest and the wisest man in his kingdom.

"Akbar's other advisors were jealous of Birbal because he was the king's favorite, so they made a plan to get rid of Birbal. They bribed Akbar's barber. The barber told the king, '*Shahanshah!* Birbal delights us all and makes us laugh. We all love him dearly. Just think how much your forefathers would enjoy him if he went to heaven and entertained them!'"

"They didn't like him. They wanted him to die," Naren blurts out.

"Shhh," Sita whispers.

I ignore them and continue. "Akbar knew his other advisors were behind his barber's strange request, but he was sure Birbal would outsmart them. 'Excellent idea,' Akbar said. 'Let's send Birbal to heaven.'

"In the full court that evening Akbar told Birbal about how he should go to heaven to entertain Akbar's ancestors. 'I'd love to,' Birbal said. 'Please give me a few days to finish my work here.'

"On the day Birbal was ready to ascend to heaven, Akbar took his advisors and the barber to the cemetery. After everyone waved good-bye to Birbal, he walked to his funeral pyre in the distance and climbed up on it. When smoke came out of it Akbar turned to the others. 'Well, there goes my friend, and I will miss him greatly. But my ancestors will be happy.'

"The barber bowed deeply. 'They will be, *Shahanshah*!'

"Two months went by and no one mentioned Birbal. One evening in the court the guards announced that Birbal had come from heaven to visit them.

"Everyone's faces were shadowed with a dark cloud except Akbar's; his brightened with delight. 'Let him come in, let him come in,' he said, getting up from his throne to greet his dear friend.

"Akbar asked Birbal about his father and mother, about his grandfather and other family members. 'They are all well, except for one thing,' Birbal said.

"Akbar asked, 'Tell me, what do they need?'

"Birbal stroked his beard. 'As you can see, they don't have a barber there.'

"Akbar's laughter filled the courtroom. 'Then I must send mine,' he said. The barber's color faded and he trembled."

The twins are fast asleep. I cover them with a blanket.

"You picked a good story to tell. When they know the end they relax and doze off," Aai says to me.

"Is your *kahani* done?" a voice from my left asks.

I turn and see a girl my age sitting cross-legged. Even in the dim light her smile is bright. I am surprised because I didn't think anyone else was listening to my story. "Yes. This is the end," I tell her.

"But I thought Birbal had died."

"No, no. Birbal had dug a tunnel from his house to the cemetery. He climbed down from the pyre before the fire could burn him. Then he didn't leave his house for two months."

"You never mentioned that," she says with a confused look.

49

"I know. My brother and sister have heard this story so many times that I don't need to."

"*Tum acchi kahani sunate ho,*" she says.

I smile. Her compliment that I tell a good story fills me with happiness. By now the footpath has filled up and I can't tell if the people sleeping next to the girl are her family or not. Without a family and a home, it would be so scary to live in this city. I'm fortunate to have Baba, Aai, Naren, and Sita with me. And tomorrow we will be at Jama's home.

I stretch out on the pavement. In the village, sometimes we slept outside our hut in the open, but here it is different. Strangers walk by us; they have homes and they know we don't. I am ashamed to be sleeping here and wish I could tell them we have a place to go. I can't do that, but tomorrow when these people walk home they won't see us.

The traffic thins out as the night descends. In the daylight the city is overwhelming like a crowded fair, and at night it is forbidding like an enemy's camp. Many people line up on the footpath like us. Some have old rugs or blankets, and some have put down pieces of cardboard or tarp to lie on. The girl who listened to the story has a piece of fabric spread out. There are a few who use nothing. No one walking, especially the people with fancy clothes and a home to go to, seems to pay any attention to us. I guess half the city sleeps outside. The concrete is hard to lie on and I miss the mud floor.

The voices seem to move away as I get drowsy.

I wake up with a scream when something hits me hard in the stomach. I double over with pain. "Why are you sleeping here?" a voice blares at me. I open my eyes and see black shoes too close to my face.

six

"What happened, Gopal?" Baba asks.

I manage to look up at the man with the black shoes. He is dressed in a khaki uniform. A policeman.

"Is this your family?" he asks Baba. In the dark, it is hard to see his features, but his mustache is thick and bushy.

Baba is sitting up by now and so am I.

"You can't sleep here," the policeman barks.

There're other people doing the same thing on both sides of us. Why is he only bothering us? Maybe other people have paid him to sleep here and we haven't.

"We just arrived from our village yesterday and have nowhere to go. Let us sleep here tonight. I have two small children," Baba pleads, pointing at Sita and Naren.

The policeman stares at us and waits. Aai is up too. She puts her finger on her mouth, signaling me to be quiet.

Baba joins his palms together as if he is praying. "Please, show mercy. Where can we go in the middle of the night?" The policeman doesn't budge. I think he's waiting for a bribe.

"We poor people have no money," Baba says. His face is pinched with pain. I hate what this place has done to Baba. He would never have talked like that in the village. I wish we could just go back this instant and never return.

The policeman taps his foot. My insides knot up, getting ready for another kick. But it doesn't come. "If I see you here tomorrow night, you will have a place to sleep. The jail," he says, and walks away.

It takes me a while to fall back to sleep.

I usually wake to the sounds of water wheels going *kichood-kichood*, the chirping of the birds, and the soft footsteps of Aai and other women sweeping the yards. This morning, all I hear is honking horns, shouts of vendors, and hundreds of shoes hitting the pavement.

We wash up at a faucet outside the station where other people are cleaning up. For breakfast Baba and I get three cups of tea for us all to share. We split two leftover *rotis* among us because they won't keep for much longer, and we have little money, so it is wise to save it.

"I am going to take the bus to Jama's house now,"

Baba says as soon as he finishes his tea.

Aai pulls the loose end of her sari tightly around her. Ever since we arrived in the city, her forehead is pinched with worry, but now panic spreads over her face.

"Can't we all go together?" Naren asks.

I know we don't have enough money for all of us to travel.

"No. Sita and you stay here with Aai and Gopal. The buses are too crowded," Baba says. "I will bring Jama and then maybe we can take a rickshaw back to his house. It will be fast." His voice is full of forced excitement.

The twins jump up and down. Yesterday they were worried, but as soon as they hear Jama's name they are happy. They must think this city adventure is going to get better.

I wonder about how Baba will cross the streets, get off at the right stop, and find Jama's home.

"Are you sure you will find your way to Jama's and back to us?"

"I'll always find you," he says. His lips crinkle a faint smile. He takes out Jama's address.

"This paper is so crumpled it will be hard to read, Baba. Let me write it down again," I say. I tear the page on which I have copied the address, hand it to Baba, and slip the crumpled paper in my notebook.

seven

It is hard to have a footpath as your home with nothing to do but wait. I want to walk around, but when I ask Aai, she grabs my wrist and says, "No. Stay right here by me."

So we all sit like pebbles on the footpath and watch people. A girl a little older than me sells combs, plastic toys, and decks of cards, and another one with long braids sells magazines. These two girls are friends, because they smile at each other when they find a customer. Sita and Naren are playing with the marble, and Aai is watching the street like me.

Maybe I can sell magazines. That way I can read them, too. If I make some money I can stack up some boards and make a stall. I can sell some books, too. And after that I can have a store—a small one with more books and later on a bigger one with magazines and books in many different languages. There are so many people in this city that a store like that will do well, and I will make sure to keep books for young children. Naren and Sita love stories, so once they learn to read they will enjoy the books. They can even help me run the business. Maybe I will name the store Three Readers.

"Will you tell us a story?" Naren asks me, pulling my hand.

I already miss my *nimba* branch by the pond, where no one could interrupt me. It was the best spot for what Aai calls "building air palaces."

"Tell us a new story, not the marble one," Sita says.

"Why not?" Naren asks.

"Because we're not at Jama's house."

"So?"

"I haven't even said yes, and you two are already fighting," I tell them.

"We won't," Naren says.

"Promise! Tell us a Mumbai story," Sita begs.

Aai's lips are pressed together tightly as she scans the crowded street. I don't think she has heard a word.

It will take a long time for Baba to return, so if I tell a story, the twins will not bother Aai. "Here is a Mumbai story," I begin. "Once there was a poor girl who came to the big city of Mumbai with her family. One day she saw a thousand-rupee bill fall from a rich man's wallet. She picked it up and returned it. The man looked at the girl's tattered clothes and bare feet. 'Don't you think you need money more than I do? Why didn't you keep it?' he asked.

"'Because that would be wrong,' the girl replied. Her dark eyes shone brightly.

"'You are an honest child and I would like to help you,' the man said. 'What would make you the happiest?'

"The girl closed her eyes and thought. Ever since she was little she wanted to open a bookstore, but she was afraid to tell the rich man. He would laugh at her for being so foolish. Maybe she should ask for food, clothes, or a place to live.

"'Remember, you must ask for something truly special. If you ask for something you want or need, I will know.'"

"I'd ask for—" Naren says.

"You were not supposed to talk in the middle. You can't listen to the story anymore," Sita says.

She is so loud that a boy holding his baba's hand turns around. "If you bicker I will stop right now," I threaten them.

They shake their heads. "We won't."

I continue. "'I would like a bookstore,' the girl said."

Naren shoves his hands down under his legs as if he is stopping the urge to say something.

"'A bookstore?' The man's eyebrow went up in surprise. 'Are you sure, totally sure?'

"The girl replied with her hand on her heart. 'Yes, I am.'

"The man helped the girl open up a bookstore. The girl read all the books she sold to make sure they were good stories. The people of Mumbai liked her little store so much that she was busy from morning until evening. Now she had money to buy fruits, vegetables, and even fish. She bought shoes for her family and three sets of clothes for each of them. And the best part was they had a place to live. It wasn't as big as a palace, but she had four rooms and it was on the top floor of a building. When the clouds were low in the sky she felt like she could reach out and pull one in.

"She hadn't forgotten the man who had helped her, though. When she gave him a pile of books to thank him, he said, 'It is time for you to have a bigger store.'

"The girl liked the idea very much. She used the money she had saved up to buy a bigger place. The wooden shelves didn't have a speck of dirt on them. Each of them was filled with books, and the place smelled of paper, ink, and colors. All day long she talked and helped the book buyers, and at night when she locked up she thought about the next day. She smiled. The bookstore made her so happy."

When I am done Sita is looking at me with her head crooked to one side, and Naren is staring.

"You didn't like the story?" I ask.

"I think that was not a girl but a boy," Sita says. "It was you."

"How do you know it was not Naren?"

"Because I'd have asked for a toy store."

"Yes, he would have," Sita agrees.

"Will Baba be back soon?" Naren asks, looking around.

"*Ho*," I say. I have to think of another distraction. "I'll show you a new game called solitaire that Card-Man taught me."

I show them how to set it up. "This is hard," Naren says.

Sita rolls her eyes. "And no fun."

She turns to Aai. "I'm hungry."

Aai keeps her eyes closed and stays quiet. Quickly, I gather up the cards that I have spread on our faded rug. "Let's all play together," I say, waving a card. I divide the cards three ways and then one after the other we throw a card down until someone has a matching card—then they get to keep the pile and start a new round. We play for a while but I keep glancing at the street.

"I'm done. I want food," Sita says after about twenty minutes.

The storm of hunger whirls in our stomachs and can't be stopped by games. "Let's wash up. Then we will eat something," Aai says. She doesn't do anything, though, she just sits there.

The noise of traffic and people escalated all through the morning but has faded a bit now. It is the hottest part of the day, and even though we are in the shade the heat is unbearable. I look around for a tree. There are none nearby. The shade of a tree is different from the shade of a building. The building can't fan you like a tree can.

I close my eyes. All I can think about is food and water. My stomach is in knots and my mouth is quarry-dust dry. I try to moisten my lips with my tongue, but it feels as stiff as shriveled-up buffalo skin. Only my neck is clammy and sticky with sweat.

I hope Baba gets back quickly. The sooner he returns with Jama the sooner we can leave the footpath. But in the meantime, we must drink water. I force myself to get up, take a pan, and go to a public faucet. The water doesn't come with force like it did this morning when I washed my face, but trickles slowly. I fill up the pan. When I return, Aai, Naren, Sita, and I thirstily gulp the water. I wish we had some to splash on our faces but there is none left.

Still, drinking the water makes me feel alive again.

The twins stand close to the curb, gawking at a group of men who get out from a shiny car. When Aai and I sit down by our luggage, her sigh is as deep as the pond. "I thought your baba would be back by now. Where is he?"

"Now what will we do?" I ask.

"Buy something to eat. But then almost all of our money will be gone." She opens a knot in her sari, takes out a crumpled five-rupee bill, hands it to me, and reties the knot. "Take this and get what you can. Bring the change back."

I take Naren and Sita with me.

"Don't cross the street," Aai says.

"We won't," I reply.

We turn left from the station and walk toward the handcart where Baba and I bought *pakoras* last night. Before we get to it, I see a man in a khaki uniform, black shoes, and bushy mustache. It is the same policeman who kicked me last night. My knees begin to shake.

Naren and Sita pull me forward. "The other way is better," I tell them.

"Why? There's food right there." Naren drops my hand. Before he runs and attracts attention, I grab him.

I hold his hand extra tight. If the policeman sees us he might pounce on us again. Luckily, he is busy talking to a nicely dressed man. Aai used to tell us a story about a jackal who flattered the king of the jungle, a lion. The policeman reminds me of that jackal and he won't leave that important man, a lion, to trouble us, little rabbits.

We walk the other way and stop at a wooden makeshift eatery. The sign says PAV-BHAJI. It is a type of food I have never had before, but it smells good and people are lined up. There is no way I could carry this food back to Aai, so we return and get her and the luggage. Without Baba I have to carry the heavy jute sack while Aai carries the cotton bag and the one with the bedding. It makes me angry at Baba for not being back soon. I hope he and Jama are not sitting down and talking and have forgotten about us.

A plate of *pav-bhaji* costs four rupees. It comes with two *pav*, bread buns. We split them so each of us has half a bun. I tear pieces of *pav*, scoop the spicy *bhaji*, vegetables, as fast as I can and stuff it in my mouth. I want to be done before the policeman comes. "Don't eat in a hurry," Aai says.

I slow down as I scan the street.

Aai puts her hand on my shoulder. "Baba will find us. He knows we can't be glued to the place where he left us."

She must think I'm looking for Baba and I let her think that. Aai's got enough problems without worrying about the jackal policeman lurking on the next street. More than five hours have gone by since Baba left. I wonder how much longer it will take for him to return with Jama.

"Did you see the two girls selling things this morning?" I ask Aai to get my mind away from Baba.

She nods.

"Those girls were not much older than I am. I can do that."

"You can, but first you need the money to buy the magazines or toys or whatever they were selling. No one will give you those for free, Gopal."

"Money, money, money," Sita mumbles. "Why can't we have a pile of it, just like this?" She snaps her fingers.

"I'll become a magician and turn that pile into money," Naren says, pointing at a heap of garbage near the sidewalk.

We ignore the twins. "I can ask those girls how they got started."

Before Aai can answer, Sita says, "No magician can make money out of garbage, right, Aai?"

"Well, you can't make it by snapping your fingers," Naren says.

"I sure can." Then she sticks her tongue out and moves her head back and forth like a puppet.

Naren whines, "Sita can't, Aai, and she keeps saying she can."

I hate when the twins hijack our conversation. I raise my hand as if to slap them. "Naren, stop whining! Sita, shut up!"

They look at me with their eyes wide-open. Sita's tongue still dangles out of her mouth. I have never been this sharp with them. I give Aai a sideways glance. I think she is going to be mad at me, but instead she ignores all of us.

Once we are done eating we pick up our luggage and move away from the stall. Down the street there are fewer people, and one of the shops is closed. Aai takes out the frayed rug and spreads it on the footpath in front of the shop, and we both sit down. I hand the deck of cards to the twins and they settle on the bedding sack.

I watch two girls a little older than I get out of a car on the curb in front of us. They are wearing sandals with heels and their nails are painted red. "Come in an hour," they say to the driver. They walk into the shop next to the one where we are sitting. I get up and stroll past the store. The shop windows are full of fancy sandals—a pair of red with beads and shiny stones, a brown one with heels so high that you can trip over them, a gray pair with tassels. The girls must have gone to buy sandals even though they own nice ones. I guess when you have money you can buy more than you need. Someday, maybe I can buy a nice pair of dark brown sandals.

I see Aai twisting her sari and I come back and sit down by her. The twins are playing with cards and I silently thank the Card-Man for giving them to me. I take out my notebook, open up to a new page, and hold the pencil in my hand. Nothing comes to my mind. So I flip the pages without reading anything. I don't know how long we sit there, but it must be an hour because the girls come out each carrying a large bag. One of them pulls out her phone. "We are here," she says in Hindi. A few minutes later their car comes by and they get in.

After a while Aai motions me to follow her. She walks a few steps away to the edge of the footpath and scans the street. I join her. "I wonder how long it takes to go to Dadar and find Jama's home," she says.

"And come back here."

For a few seconds we both are silent. The sun is in the west and it will set soon. If Baba does not make it back tonight we must find a place to sleep. Maybe we can spend the night right here. "I'll be back," I tell Aai, and walk over to *pav-bhaji* stall. "Do you think we can sleep here tonight?" I ask the vendor.

"This place gets full at night. The people who usually

sleep here might kick you out. Maybe you should look for a place farther away from the station."

I thank him and return. "Aai, we have to find a place farther away from here, just in case we have to spend the night again," I whisper. "Should I look around before it gets dark?"

Aai nods, but from her face I can tell she doesn't want me to. "Don't go far, and come back soon," she says.

I stroll down the street away from the station. There doesn't seem to be enough space for all of us to sleep. Some of the stores' steps might work once they are locked up, but if someone is already sleeping there, they will throw us out.

Maybe I can find something on a side street. I peek down one of them.

One of the streets behind the station has a small hill at the end covered with rubbish. On the other side of it is a bridge and some people are standing under it. I squint, but it is hard to see with the sun in my eyes. I climb down the path people have worn into the hill.

Under the bridge, the dried-out creek bed is strewn with plastic bags, empty cigarette boxes, newspapers, and chunks of broken bricks. The scrubby grass is brown and matted. Still, it is cooler under the bridge, and there are only two couples here.

The men are sitting and the women are cooking in one corner. "You live here?" I ask the men.

One of them looks up. He is bigger than Baba, with

hairy arms and large hands. "Yes. Why do you ask?"

"My baba has gone out and will return soon. My aai, brother, sister, and I need a place to rest. Can we stay here?"

He smiles. "You speak *pakka*, real village Marathi. I like that." Then he tells me they arrived last week and have been living under the bridge.

He hasn't answered my question. "Can I bring my family here?"

"*Hamare baap ka bridge thodi hai? Aaa jao,*" the other man says in Hindi.

Even though he makes fun of me by asking, "Does the bridge belong to our fathers?" I like him. The way he invites us, *Aaa jao,* "come on," feels good.

"Does anyone bother you here?" I want to make sure the policeman doesn't come here.

"Besides you, so far no one else has bothered us." The first man laughs.

I tell them Aai and the twins are waiting with our luggage near the station, and they both offer to come with me.

When Aai sees me with the two strangers her *bindi* wrinkles in worries. The men stand a few feet away to let me speak to Aai. "There is a place under the bridge where we can sleep. It is not crowded at all and it is out of the way, so the policeman won't bother us. There are two women there too."

"We don't know these men. At least on the street we

were surrounded by people, it was safer."

"No, it wasn't. Remember I got kicked?"

"Yes, but who knows where these men are from and why they are after us?"

"Aai, they are not after us. They came to help us with the luggage."

From the way she looks at the men I think they will turn around and leave, but one of them says, "*Namashkar bahin,* we are from the village outside of Pune. We're new to the city too."

Aai's face loses its tension when she hears the man talk like he is from our village. "*Namashkar,*" she greets them back. "*Chala,*" she says as she grabs Naren's and Sita's hands. The men pick up a jute sack each and I carry the cotton bag.

Once we get under the bridge Aai talks to the women while I arrange a few larger pieces of brick to make a stove. Naren and Sita gather dried twigs and brush nearby and come back with enough to start a fire. "What are you doing?" Aai asks.

I stuff the twigs between the bricks. "We made you a stove, Aai. You can cook the *dal* and rice that kind man gave us yesterday."

Aai shakes her head. "It won't work. Those ladies told me that these twigs burn up too quickly and that the fire doesn't last. All we will have is heavy smoke and scratchy throats."

"Then what are we supposed to do?" I ask. The *pav-bhaji* we shared earlier would have been enough for the day if I were a rabbit or a squirrel, but my stomach still has a hunger hole in it.

"The women said we could use their kerosene stove."

While Aai cooks, one of the men tells me, "We found a job in the factory, so we will be leaving tomorrow."

"Where is the factory? Do they have more jobs?" I ask, wanting to know.

The man is quiet for a moment. "They need more people, but they only want men who can lift heavy loads. You're too young, and I assume your baba is too old." He continues, "I heard there was rain in the south, which means it will arrive here in a day or two. This is a low area and the water collects very fast. After tonight it won't be safe to sleep here."

Aai overhears and says, "Tomorrow night we will be with my brother."

eight

By the time I wake up in the morning our neighbors are gone and have taken all their things.

Aai goes up to the station to look for Baba. I wait under the bridge with Naren and Sita. "What if Aai doesn't find Baba?" Sita asks.

"Then Baba will find her," Naren says.

Sita looks at me. "Do you think so, Gopal?"

I don't know what I think. All I know is I want them to be quiet. "How would you like to hear about a giant who lived in a cave?"

"No, no," Sita says. "That giant lived under a bridge. Just like this one."

"Why would he do that?"

"Because he is the one holding the bridge up. Don't you know?"

"You're right," I say. "But I have a problem with the story. The giant can't move because he's holding the bridge."

"It is a moving bridge," Naren says.

"Yes, moving bridge, moving water, moving world. Everything moving. Round and round."

The twins hold hands and spin.

And that is when we hear the roar. It is a low groan, like the growl of a baby giant's belly, except it comes from the sky. Naren and Sita stop and point upward. "Come rain come, come rain come." The second rumble is deeper, louder, and longer, like the growl of a baba giant's belly. Naren and Sita run to me. In the distance I see Aai, with flailing arms, coming down the slope.

"The rain! It will be here. Hurry, we must leave this place," she says as she grabs the cotton bag.

Another rumble. It feels closer. The wind picks up and Aai's sari flutters wildly.

Aai hands Naren and Sita the cloth bag. "Hold one strap each and start walking." She takes the heavy jute one with pots and pans, and I take the one with the bedding. Going uphill is harder with our things, but we manage— until the rain pours down. I'd never seen such a moving wall of water in our village. We are soaking wet by the time we get under the overhang of the station.

Even though it is warm I shiver in my wet clothes. Aai takes her faded sari from the bag, wrings it out, and opens it up. "As soon as my sari dries out you can wipe

70

yourselves with it," she says.

Aai's sari is so old that it is onionskin thin and will dry out in no time.

The rain falls and falls and falls. Soon there are puddles everywhere. Out of nowhere the sidewalk in front of the station is covered with people carrying mostly black umbrellas. There are fewer people and fewer vendors, and the footpaths look wide. The handful of vendors that remain there have moved closer to the stores so that the overhangs of the roofs above can protect them. The girls selling buttons and magazines are gone.

I can't believe it is the same crowded, hazy, burning-hot place of yesterday. A car drives by a little too fast and splashes the people on the footpaths. Naren and Sita laugh out loud. In front of us, a woman gets out of a taxi. She tries to open her umbrella, but it is stuck. The twins cover their mouths with their hands to muffle their giggles.

Aai passes around her dried-out sari and we wipe the rain from our skin. No one mentions Baba—not even Naren and Sita—but I know Aai and I are both deeply worried now. If Baba had found Jama they would have been back. That means Baba got lost and never found Jama's house, and now maybe he is out of money and can't take a bus or a train from wherever he is.

After about two hours, the rain stops and the forest of umbrellas vanishes. The rain-washed air is cleaner, but it doesn't carry the fragrant, earthy scent of our village. All the water can't make the footpaths, the blacktop roads, or the auto fumes smell clean. I tell Aai, "I want to circle the station and look for Baba."

"Can we come?" Naren asks.

"You both stay with me." Then Aai tells me, "Don't go down to the bridge. Just look from the top."

"Yes."

"On your way back get puffed rice. Don't spend too much." She hands me some money and an empty plastic bag from the Deepak Food Store.

I hurry toward the bridge. The place where we were sleeping is underwater, completely. What if the rain had come at night? Would we have vanished along with the plastic bags, cigarette cartons, and newspapers?

Again I hear a faint rumble, a warning of more rain on the way. Time to return. On my way back, I buy paper packages of puffed rice and roasted lentils.

Back at the station Aai unwraps the packages and folds up the bag. She empties the lentils and puffed rice into a pan, cuts one of the onions we brought from home into tiny pieces, adds the pieces to the mixture, and sprinkles red pepper on top. Flavored with onion and red pepper, it is delicious. I wish there were four times as much because the handful I eat only fills a little hole in my stomach.

The sun that was out for a few minutes is swallowed by clouds bringing the second slapping of rain. Water pounds and floods the street. Aai and I look at each other. If Baba doesn't return, where will we sleep tonight? We're careful not to spill out the thought and scare the twins.

Naren and Sita are sitting quietly watching the rain, people, umbrellas, cows, rickshaws, and puddles. In the beginning, their eyes were sparkling with curiosity. They laughed when someone splashed into a puddle or a car sprayed water on a pedestrian. But now their faces are drained. They watch.

Simply watch.

"Baba has been gone for a day," I whisper to Aai.

She squeezes my hand. "I hope he comes soon."

I am afraid. More than I have ever been.

The rain still pounds. Aai tells me to wait with the twins while she goes looking for Baba. We're sitting right in front of the station so why does she have to go look for him? Maybe she wants to see the water under the bridge. "Don't go far," I beg her.

"I won't," she promises.

A minute after she leaves, Sita asks, "When will Aai come back?"

"Soon," I reply.

A few minutes later, Naren asks, "Is it soon already?"

I don't answer.

My eyes are fixed in the direction Aai went and I am praying silently. I want her to be back just as much as Sita and Naren.

When Aai returns she is soaked. "The water is this deep on the next street," she says, holding her hand mid-calf.

I close my eyes, listening to the footsteps. Every time I hear someone nearby, I look up. *Please, Lord Ganesh, let it be Baba and Jama.* As fast as it came, the rain moves away and the sun returns. A few of the stores open up. But it is quieter.

"I almost didn't come," one of the vegetable sellers says to a customer. He is weighing cabbage. My mouth waters.

"I don't blame you. It is too early in the season to have such a storm. We're not prepared for it." The lady opens her purse and pays him.

"The monsoon strikes on its own whim."

"So it does," the lady says.

The shopkeepers and vendors talk about how these kinds of storms can bring flash floods and death. Their talks gather and crowd my mind. Naren and Sita are quiet and don't laugh, talk, or fight. They have not asked when Baba will be back. They know Aai and I don't have an answer.

I shiver, wondering if Baba is caught in the rain.

It is past eleven in the morning, but the streets are still quiet, and many stores have remained closed. I think it is because of the rain until I realize it is Sunday! If we had made it to Jama's house, he might have taken us around Mumbai this evening in one of the buses. Instead, for the last two days we have been sitting on a footpath. We only have a little money left and if Baba doesn't return tonight we will be in big trouble.

"Aai, we must find Jama quickly. I know which bus goes to Dadar and from there we can find his house."

"What if your Baba comes back?"

"If Baba doesn't find us here, I am sure he will come to Jama's."

Aai is quiet.

"It will be easy to travel today because it is a Sunday and the buses have plenty of room. And look at the sunshine! We better move before the rain returns. Besides, we can't sleep another night on the street."

"Jama probably will be home today," Aai mumbles.

"Yes. And if we get there by this afternoon we can look for Baba. Aai, do you have more money tucked away in your cotton bag?"

She sighs. "I wish I did. This is what I have." Aai takes out a couple of crumpled notes and some change.

Without money my plans are as good as a lump of soil without seeds. I chew my lip. If only we could earn enough for the fare. But how?

Just then I see a lady getting out of a taxi at the end of the street. "I'm going to carry that woman's luggage," I tell Aai, and hurry off before she can stop me. By the time the driver lugs the woman's bag from the taxi, I am there.

She glowers at me. "I don't have money for a beggar."

My first thought is to run away, but I think of the

money we need. "I'll carry your suitcase."

She measures me while paying the driver. "I'll give you five rupees." I know that is a lot less than I should get, but still, it is better than nothing. The driver helps me put the heavy bag on my head and I walk behind the lady all the way to the gate. Loud music starts playing and the lady fishes out a phone from her purse, but keeps on walking. She presses a green button and says, "Hello?"

She listens and then says, *"Accha,"* and presses the red button. It would be so wonderful if Baba had one of those phones and so did we. Then we would know where he is.

As I am about to enter the station, one of the porters stops me. "You can't go inside without a badge," he says, showing an oval brass badge on the sleeve of his maroon uniform with the number 581 engraved on it.

"But I am with the lady."

"Yes, but when you come out you'll need a ticket, son."

He's right. I hadn't thought about that.

"Hurry, I will miss the train!" the lady shouts.

"The boy can't go in. I'll carry your bag," the porter says to her.

The lady gives me a look as if I have failed her. She looks at the porter, then at the waiting train. "How much?"

"Twenty rupees."

"What? The boy was going to do it for five. That's what I'll give you."

"No," he says.

She looks at her watch. "*Accha*, let's go."

"You haven't paid the boy," the porter reminds her.

"I'm not going to." She marches off without glancing at me.

I stand there as dumb as a goat. I'm the biggest fool, because I carried the luggage more than halfway and I ended up with a big round zero. I trudge back. This city is tricky. I wonder what Birbal would do to survive here.

I am mad at myself. Why did I rush to carry the luggage? Aai is right when she says I need to think things through.

From the corner of my eye I see the porter that carried the bag for the lady. He is waving at someone. He seemed nice. Maybe he can help me find work. The porter waves again and I realize he is calling me. I run to him. "What?" I ask.

"Here." he holds out a twenty-rupee note.

"But you didn't take—"

"The woman's compartment was right in front of this gate," he says, pointing at the station. "You carried the bag most of the way, so you deserve it. But don't do it again, because if you don't have a badge, you're not allowed to carry luggage. If the police catch you, they will fine you."

The image of the policeman marches into my mind. I didn't know I could get in trouble trying to work.

I run back to Aai. Naren and Sita are playing cards quietly. "I think we might have enough money for one full and three half tickets," I whisper as I slip Aai the money. I don't feel like a stupid wandering goat anymore.

"Then we must leave," Aai says.

"Where are we going?" Sita asks.

"To Jama's home."

Sita pounds her fist on the ground. "No."

"Why not?" Aai asks.

"Because when Baba comes he won't be able to find us."

Aai takes her hand. "Sita, he has gone to Jama's house and that is where we are going. We will see him there."

"What if he doesn't find Jama and comes back here?"

My gaze settles on the Deepak Food Store. "I'll tell the man in that store that we're leaving. Baba knows him, so when he returns the storekeeper can tell him where we went. Is that a good idea, Sita?"

Sita nods. "Yes."

Naren and Sita gather the cards. I slide the deck back in the box, put it in the bag, and take out my notebook. Part of it got wet and the pages are curled up at that end. I smooth them out as much as I can. I take out the slip of paper with Jama's address and put it in my pocket. On the way to the bus we stop at Deepak Food and leave the word with the kind shop owner.

When we cross the street Naren and Sita cling to me

78

like the baby monkeys cling to their mothers in Matheran. I don't blame them. The people and traffic are a lot lighter today, but compared to the dirt lane of our village, this is as wild as the tourist-filled main street of Matheran. And there are no cars, buses, or motorcycles in Matheran.

At the bus stop there are three people in the line. They stare at the stuff we are carrying and probably the way we look, but no one says anything. My heart thumps loudly as we stand behind them. I hope this is the right thing to do. What if we get lost? What will we do? How will we eat?

By the time the bus comes there are several more people in line behind us. Aai pays the conductor and he gives us the tickets. Sita and Aai settle in the seat right behind the driver, and Naren and I sit in the seat across from them. The windows are behind us, but there is a wider space between our seats, so we can put the sacks down by our feet and still have room left for other passengers to walk past.

I look out the window one last time to see if Baba has returned. I don't see him. The bus moves down the road quickly. I hope we get to Jama's house soon and find Baba there.

nine

Two days ago five of us arrived from our village. Now there are only four of us riding the bus.

Every time I think of Baba, my eyes get blurry. Naren and Sita sit quietly across from each other, maybe because they are too timid to call to each other across the aisle. But I don't think so. I think they miss Baba too. Aai stares down and wipes her cheeks. It reminds me of the last evening in our home, when Baba brushed off Aai's tear with his finger.

The bus has left the station and rushes through the wide road. I've been watching the road, but I don't think I can remember the way back to the footpath where we spent two days. To me all the streets look the same, even though I notice different shops and different buildings. I try to read the names of the stores as we pass them by but it is difficult. My stomach wobbles and my head spins. I close my eyes to calm down.

I wonder what Jama's home looks like. I think of my friend Mohan's copy of *Star Homes* magazine. As we thumbed through the pages the first time, we fell silent like people did when they saw the sunset from the Matheran hills. It had pictures of beautiful houses and beautiful people. As we got more familiar with the pictures, we would point and say what we liked and which house we wanted to live in. Later, when the magazine got beat up, Mohan found a plastic bag to store it in. When he showed it to us, he didn't allow us to flip the pages. He did it himself and we had to point at things from a distance.

I see a few buildings that are so tall they look like bridges between the earth and the sky. It would be wonderful if Jama lived in one of those fancy houses, but I don't expect that. I just hope he lives in a nice mud hut like the one we had in the village. It smelled of red earth and stayed cool in the summer.

Naren and Sita have not said a word since we left. Are they silent because they are watching all the fancy buildings, people, and shops, or because they are afraid? I can't tell and I don't want to ask them. I don't want to bang pots and wake up the elephant, as Aai would say.

This travel seems easier than I thought. Did Baba have difficulty going to Jama's house? It's true that Baba can't read—maybe he got on the wrong bus or got off at the wrong stop?

It takes an hour to get to Dadar, the closet suburb to Mumbai. Many people get off here. I show the conductor Jama's address. "Is this place nearby?" I ask.

He shakes his head. "How do I know? Ask one of the locals."

We get off the bus with our luggage. "Where do we go?" Aai asks, looking around.

"You wait here and I will find out," I tell her. The open shops are full of customers, and I don't want to wait in a long line to ask shopkeepers for directions. I walk a couple of blocks before I find a man waiting by his motorcycle. I ask him and he says, "Not from here."

"Not from here" is the answer I get from two more people. Finally I see a corner shop open with the old shopkeeper sitting close to the door. I walk over to him and show him Jama's address. "Go right down this lane, take the first left, and then walk all the way to the end. You'll find him in the last shack on the right."

"Do you know him?" I ask.

"I know everyone who lives in my neighborhood," he says.

I thank him and return to where Aai, Naren, and Sita are waiting. We follow the shopkeeper's directions and take the first left. If the man is right we are almost at Jama's. But the lane goes on and on. I am carrying the sack with pots and pans, and it is heavy and uncomfortable. The jute is rubbing against my fingers and palms and they burn. I can't put the sack down because right in the middle of the lane there is sewage flowing through an open ditch and a rotting smell rising from it. It is difficult to hurry along while carrying a heavy, clumsy load.

The dank air is stuffed with smells, and it is not the scent of earth but of rotting food and filth. In the fading light, people slide past, children stare, and snippets of conversations, laughter, and cries spill out from the plastic-and-tarp-covered shacks. The walls are made of plastered brick and corrugated metal sheeting. The man at the shop said Jama lives at the end, but there is a bend in the street so I can't tell how far we have to walk.

I hope the shopkeeper is right, because I don't think I can carry the luggage for much longer. Finally we come to the end. The last shack on the right has light in it. I look at Aai and nod toward the shack. She hesitates for a moment and that is all it takes for Jama to poke his head out of the door.

For a second, Jama has a blank look on his face, but then he breaks out in a smile. "Radha!" He rushes toward her. "Radha? Is that you? And Gopal, Naren, and Sita?"

Aai's answer comes as tears. This is the first time since Baba went missing that she has smiled or cried freely. Jama takes the sack from her hand and puts his other arm around her. "Come in, come in. All of you."

I put my sack down and look around. A dented, narrow metal cupboard leans on the back wall. In the far corner is a table that has a tall box covered with fabric. I wonder what is under it. There are two chairs and a table in the room, and a sofa that has some springs coming out but otherwise is in good condition. I sit on it and sink deep. To get up, I will have to put my hands down and push myself up.

I wait for Aai to mention Baba, but it is Naren who asks, "Have you seen Baba, Jama?"

With teary eyes and a few sobs, Aai tells Jama what happened to us while he listens silently.

"Radha, don't worry. The day is almost over but tomorrow morning I will go to the police office and file a report. I'll also go to Thane and see if he has returned, and talk to the grocer and the people by the railway station," Jama says.

"What if Baba is lost forever?" Sita asks.

"This city is big but not endless. Don't worry, we will find him."

She nods.

We are all quiet. Our fear for Baba has stolen our voices.

After a while Jama speaks. "You all must be hungry. I made some spicy potatoes and cauliflower *bhaji* and bought some bread today, so we can have *pav-bhaji*."

We all eat together. The fresh bread is spongy and soft, and the *bhaji* is spicy and tingles my throat as it goes down. I take a sip of water. It tastes different than the water in our village or by the station, but it doesn't taste bad. It feels strange to have a full stomach.

Jama takes two mattresses from a pile on a wooden bench in one corner and spreads them on the floor. They are lumpy and soft. I help Aai spread sheets on them. She sleeps between the twins and I stretch out on the other side of Naren. Jama takes the sofa. He has to curl up on it, but he says he is perfectly comfortable.

I hope Baba is warm and dry like we are.

I wake up in the middle of night. Aai is crying.

"I'm sorry, Radha," Jama says. "Tomorrow I will talk to people around the station, ask the police, and file a missing person's report. I'll also ask the man at the Deepak Food Store to watch the station area and give him my work phone number so he can contact me."

"I—I don't know how, I mean, what happened? What if we don't find him? The twins, Gopal, me, what will we do? Without their baba my children—"

"I am sure we will find him."

After a long silence, Aai says, "I hope so." She has stopped crying, but her voice sounds hollow.

I can't go back to sleep, so I lie awake wondering what I can do to help, now that Baba is gone.

I must find work soon.

The morning comes early with pots banging, children screaming, and people shouting. A voice as irritating as a buffalo's grunt fills the air.

On the station's footpath, there were traffic noises and blaring horns that drowned out everything else, but here we're a little ways from the big street. So why can't I hear birds? I wonder if parrots, sparrows, and pigeons can live in the city. Maybe, like people, some of them can. I hope I am the right kind of person to live in the city.

A cursing war begins between two men and it is loud enough to wake up the entire neighborhood. One voice is needle-sharp, the other is well-deep.

"What is it?" Aai asks as she gets up.

"Nothing," Jama says. "Just a couple of regulars fighting about whose turn it is to get water first."

"What do you mean by 'regulars'?"

"People who fight with each other almost every day."

"But why do they do that?"

"Radha, the water only comes for two hours and sometimes it stops after an hour, so everyone is in a hurry to get it."

There is enough light coming through one window to see Aai's face tense up. "We'll need water too."

"Come, I'll show you where the tap is," Jama says. They carry a pail each to fill with water.

I hear the sound of fighting stop. As soon as Aai and Jama leave, I cover myself with my blanket so I can doze off again. It doesn't work.

Soon they come back with pails of water and set them on the side of the house that is used as the kitchen. "I can make tea while you get more water," I say to Jama.

He looks pleased with my offer and shows me how to use the kerosene stove. First, he pumps the piston for a few seconds and as soon as the fuel comes up from the tiny holes on the top, he strikes a match and lights the stove. I make tea for all of us while Jama and Aai get four more pails of water to fill the barrel.

"Let me show you where the latrine is," he says after we drink our tea.

In the village, you could walk over to a bushy area and relieve yourself. But here there are people all around, and just like at Thane Station I don't see any bathrooms. Jama gives me a tin can full of water and asks me to follow him. He carries a can, too.

We walk to the back of Jama's house and onto a dirt path that leads away from the huts. An airplane flies over my head, and I am so absorbed in looking at it that Jama pulls me back. "Don't want you to fall into the *nalla*," he says.

I don't see any stream of water. "What *nalla*?"

He points to the wide ribbon of scum that meanders down on one side of the road. "That is the *nalla*, and if you are not careful, you will end up covered with the sewage." It looks so thick and settled that I can't believe there is water underneath it. I cover my nose with my palm and follow him silently. The open sewer in the middle of all the lanes must flow into this.

After a while, I know I am close to the latrine because it stinks.

This was one thing I hadn't thought about when I thought of the city. I knew there would be a lot more people, long lines, noise, and traffic, but not the smell. I wonder: If you live here, do you get used to it?

I don't think I'll ever get this stench out of my head.

There is a line for two latrines that look like giant wooden boxes with doors, and only adults are standing there. When I see a row of children crouching down outside, I know what I have to do. The city steals any modesty out of you. In the village, you hide behind a bush, a shrub, a stump of dead wood, or even a clump of grass. But here, you're out in the open. I don't see any women or girls. There must be a women's bathroom somewhere else.

After his breakfast, Jama takes a bath just outside the kitchen with his shorts on. The soapy water flows off into the street. Once he is done he gets ready quickly. "Where will I take a bath?" Aai asks Jama.

"Oh!" He scans the room. He grabs my hand and says laughingly, "Gopal, come, be useful."

We hang a sheet on nails around the kitchen floor drain making a small bath area. "After you are all done with your baths take this curtain out," he tells me.

"I will." I am glad Jama has made a small place for bathing so I don't have to take one outside in the open with so many people watching me.

Jama is ready to leave. He walks out the door, stops, turns around, and says, "Radha, we will find him soon."

"*Ho,*" she whispers, and wipes her tears after he turns around.

I help Aai unpack the two sacks and put away my

books. She unwraps the cracked mirror and hangs it on a wall. Then she washes the twins' hair and dresses them in their second set of clothes. I take a bath in the tiny stall, but I don't mind. It is better than being at the station. After spending two days on the footpath, Jama's home feels like a palace. Except for the smell.

Jama is gone only for an hour before he returns. "May I take your umbrella and walk around the neighborhood?" I ask him.

"No, you may not." He opens up his cotton bag and starts to empty it out. "Gopal, I bought some secondhand clothes for all of you. Try them on and see which ones fit you. If there're things we can't use, I can return them right away and they will give me money back."

"Oh!" No wonder Jama wanted me to stay.

I find two half-pants and three T-shirts that fit me. Now I have five pairs of half-pants, three T-shirts, and two shirts altogether. I have never had this many clothes before. There is a raincoat with a hole in the left sleeve, but it comes to midcalf, so it fits perfectly too.

"You look good in that bright blue raincoat," Aai says.

I go to the cracked mirror to look, but all I can see is my face. Jama laughs. "Here is what you need." He inserts a key, turns it, and flicks open the door of his cupboard. Inside is a big mirror. The only time I've glanced at all of myself is in the lobby of a hotel in Matheran.

Naren has put on an orange shirt as bright as the sky

at sunset. His hands are lost in the sleeves and it comes to his knees. "It is too big for you," I say.

"No, it isn't."

"Naren, you'll have to wait until you lose two more teeth before you can wear it," Jama says.

"One of my teeth will fall out soon. Look, I can wiggle it."

"You don't need to show us," I tell him.

"There are too many clothes and I like them all," Sita declares.

"You can't have all of them," I tell her.

She rolls her eyes. "I know that."

I turn to Jama to thank him but before I do that he says, "I checked with the school here. It started two weeks ago and they are full, but you can start next term." He motions me to the couch. I sit on it and sink. "Remember, the schools here don't need you, you need them. You can't be *bindaas*, carefree, and go and come as you please. *Samazne?*"

"*Ho*, Jama." I understand and tell him so.

"Since you are new, you must take an exam so they can decide which class to put you in."

I am impressed by how quickly Jama has bought the clothes and found out about my school. Maybe once I take my exams I will find some work to help him and Aai.

"Can we also go to school?" Naren asks.

Jama puts his index finger to his mouth. "Wait until I'm done talking with Gopal."

I can't help but smile. To be first is like climbing up a coconut tree before anyone else, winning a running race, or finishing planting the field while the others are still working. I expect Sita and Naren to pout, but they stand and listen. Maybe they are happy with the new clothes or maybe they have become patient and are ready for school.

Jama continues, "Gopal, there are classes you should attend to prepare for the school entrance exam." He gives me a pencil. "Do you have a notebook?"

"The one you gave me."

"That is too small." He snaps his fingers. "No problem. Go to my friend Chachaji's Used Paper and Cardboard Shop. Walk to the end of our lane and turn left. He is at the first corner. Tell him you're my nephew and ask him to give you blank papers. He won't charge you."

The way Jama talks about him makes me like Chachaji without meeting him. He seems very generous. But he and I are strangers. How can I ask him for a favor? But I can't mention that to Jama. He has done so much to help me.

As I walk down Jama's street an idea skips into my brain—I can work to pay for my notebook. I feel better when I reach the shop at the end of the street. When I see the shopkeeper I realize he is the same man who told me where Jama's house was. I stand to the side while he attends to a customer. "Three kilos," he tells the person as he finishes weighing the stack of magazines. He puts his brass balances on the side, counts the money, and gives the money to the man.

"Your name is Gopal, right?" Chachaji says with a twinkle in his one clear eye. His other eye is clouded with cataract. I know that because my teacher Mr. Advale's eye was clouded like that before he got a cataract operation.

I'm surprised for a moment that he knows my name. Then I realize that Jama must have told him to expect me. "Yes. I'd like, I mean, do you have some blank paper?"

"Actually, you need a notebook. Let's see how we can manage that." He rummages around. "Ah—han. These notebooks just came in. They might have some blank papers."

He searches through the notebooks. If I want to tell him my idea, I have to do it now. "Chachaji, I'd like to help you in the shop in exchange for the papers." There, I have said it.

"*Accha?*" He gives me a one-eyed, piercing look, and a little storm brews in my stomach. Did I say anything wrong? Did I insult him?

I am not sure what the right answer is. But I have told him I am willing to work, so I nod.

"Can you keep accounts for me? Can you get rid of these pesky flies forever? Can you repair my roof?"

I can't do any of those things. My head drops. But his laughter rolls into my silence.

Chachaji puts his hand on my shoulder. "Gopal, don't be scared. I was teasing you. As you get your notebook ready you will be helping me."

Those words make me feel like someone has handed me a piece of rock sugar. I smile and bow.

He points at the corner filled with notebooks. "Go through them to separate the covers from the pages, and stack them up neatly. The blank papers are yours."

I climb up the three steps and sit on a low wooden stool. The shop has a different smell to it than Jama's house. It is not a foul odor, but it is stuffy and stale. In Jama's house, it is hard to breathe because of the stench. Here it is hard to breathe because it feels like there isn't enough air.

I pick up a notebook. I flip the pages, tearing out the blank ones and ripping off the front and back covers. Most of the notebooks are full. Some already have papers torn out of them. Before me, the previous owners have gone through these notebooks. But I do find a few blank pages here and there. I take those that are less than half full, too. They are perfectly useable. Sometimes a cover catches my eye and I linger on it. There's one of a boy with hair the color of red berries looking over a lake. It reminds me of me standing by the pond in my village. I go through all of them, making three piles: used paper, blank paper, and covers. When I am done, I take the stack of blank paper to Chachaji to make a notebook.

He says, "*Shabash*, wonderful work. Have you picked out the covers?"

"I'll pick them out right now," I tell him. I look through the pile of covers once more. There are many I like. The one with three puppies and the one with a river flowing through two steep mountains are beautiful. But I choose the one with the boy looking at the sunset on a lake. I can always color the boy's hair dusky black.

When I hand Chachaji the pile of papers and a front and back cover, he takes them from my hand, puts a rubber band around them, and puts them aside.

"When do you think I can have my notebook?"

He doesn't answer right away, but his face is soft and friendly. I wait.

"Come back in two hours." His one eye twinkles.

As I slowly walk home, an older boy waves at me from across the street. I don't know him so I don't stop. He zigzags through the traffic and catches up to me. *"Tumhi Marathi bolta ka?"* he asks.

"Ho," I reply in Marathi.

"Do you know Gangadas Korae?" he asks.

"Not from here." I answer like other people have answered us.

"Don't you live here?"

"I just moved here," I tell him.

"From where?"

He's asking me question after question. As he talks, I notice that he has sleek black hair. Each strand seems to have its own assigned place on his head. It is kind of unnatural. Who is he? I am not sure if I should tell him anything. "My name is Jatin," he says. "Gangadas is my uncle, and I've been looking for him for two days. If I don't

94

find him I will get *xhun se laafa*." He rubs his cheeks as if someone has slapped him hard.

"Why?"

"Because my uncle has promised me a job in his factory. I need money badly."

I'm impressed. "Your uncle has a factory?"

"Well, sort of. Um . . . a small one."

"Is it around here?"

"Yes, I'm surprised you don't know."

"I only came here yesterday. I'm sorry," I say, and start walking.

"Thanks, anyway!" His eyes narrow. "Your name?"

"Gopal."

On the way home I think about Jatin. He must be around fifteen or sixteen. His clothes were not bad, but he said he needed money. Maybe one of his siblings or parents is sick and he needs money for medication. He said he would get slapped if he didn't find his uncle. Maybe I will ask Jama if he knows Gangadas Korae. If I see Jatin again, I can help him find his uncle.

It is only ten in the morning, and the hissing of stoves escapes from every shack. The smell of spices wafts from the houses and spills out into the narrow street, temporarily masking the smell of open sewage. On the lane some women are washing plastic bags, some are collecting rags from a garbage pile, and a couple of men are pounding a sheet of metal. The kids are playing with balls made of rags. Men hurry along carrying lunch boxes and bags.

Everyone is on the move, doing something.

Aai is sitting in front of the stove. In the village we ate late in the afternoon. "Why are you cooking so early?"

"I made Jama's lunch before he left and am making a few more *rotis* for us."

I watch Aai while she flattens a ball of *bajra* dough into a round *roti* with her fingertips. Her face is down, but when she lifts it up, I see so much sadness on it that my eyes tear.

"Oh, Gopal, what will we do without your baba? I, I miss him so much!"

Something soft and sad settles in my throat. I want to tell Aai that he will return soon, but how can I? I know Mumbai is big, but I can't imagine Baba not being able to find us. When we were on the footpath, Aai worried about getting here. But now that we have found Jama, she must ache for Baba like I do.

I sit by her and take her flour-dusted hand in mine. "I miss him too. He would have been excited about school and . . ." As soon as those words come out, I realize I have given up on his return. I choke up.

Aai squeezes my hand.

Without saying it, we both have understood it.

When the last *bajra roti* is done, Aai asks if I got the notebook.

"It'll be ready soon. I didn't take it for free. I helped Chachaji."

She touches my cheek with her finger. "That way you

96

keep your *samman*, honor."

"Aai, if I can find some work I can help Jama."

"Don't you worry! I will do that."

She will have to wait until Naren and Sita are in school to find work. I think of all the money Jama will need to feed us and send us to school. I wonder if I could work in Jatin's uncle's factory until my regular school starts. I have practically a whole term to earn.

"I just met someone only a few years older than me named Jatin. His uncle has a factory and he is going to work in there." As I am talking to Aai, I think of Jatin's sleek hair. For some strange reason, it makes me uncomfortable.

Aai is watching me. "Is something bothering you? Was Jatin rude to you?"

I wash my hands to get rid of the flour. "No, actually he was friendly. But still . . . I didn't trust him. Maybe because he is a stranger."

"It is different here, isn't it? Seems like there are so many people, there isn't enough trust and kindness to go around."

I dry my hands with a napkin. "Maybe that's it."

Aai washes her hands. "But we have found some good people, like the porter and the storekeeper."

"Yes, without them we would still be on the footpath."

I notice something in a corner. A television! That was the big box I saw last night, but it was covered with a piece of cloth and I couldn't see it. I've never been this close to a television. The glass is smooth and dark like the face of a pond on a still night. I know that turning a knob will bring it to life. "Aai, do you think we can watch TV?" I ask.

"Jama said we could, but I am afraid to touch it. I don't want to break such an expensive thing. He has unplugged it because he says in a heavy storm water might seep through these walls. That can be dangerous. When he returns you can learn how to use it and watch it tomorrow."

I finger the knobs. All I have to do is plug it in and turn the knobs one way or the other, but I don't. Aai is right. The TV is expensive and I don't want to ruin it.

"Where are Naren and Sita?" I ask.

"They have found friends here and are out with them."

"Is it safe?" I think of all the traffic and strangers at the end of the street where Chachaji's shop is.

"They're right across the lane."

I go to the door and look out. Naren and Sita are walking home hand in hand.

"Everyone went home for lunch. I'm hungry too," Sita says. So we all eat rice, *roti*, and *dudhi bhaji*. Aai also has buttermilk for us, which is the best part of the meal.

When we're done eating, it is time for me to get my notebook. Outside, the sun is pelting the lane with light and heat. I look for a tree and shade, but there are none.

This is a place without trees, without birds, and without a pond.

I am sweating by the time I reach Chachaji's shop. He's fanning himself with a folded-up newspaper. There are no customers and his eyes are closed. "Chachaji?" I whisper.

Without opening his eyes he points to a notebook on the floor. All the pages I had torn off are rebound in a new notebook with the front and back covers I had selected.

I pick it up and flip the pages. Since the pages come from different notebooks, they have uneven widths and margins. Some pages are so white they hurt my eyes. Others are as soft as the rising moon, and a few are as dingy as if there is a film of dust on them. It doesn't matter. All I need are empty spaces to fill with words. And I do have a nice pencil.

"Do you like it?" Chachaji asks me. How long has he been watching me?

"I've never had this big a notebook!"

"Study hard," he says.

I bow to him. "I will."

Once more the clouds have started to gather. I hurry back, clutching my notebook. I don't want to drop it on the street and get it muddy. When I get home, the twins are taking a nap and so is Aai. I stare at the TV and wonder how by just flipping a switch you can see different people. Some of them live so far away that you have to cross oceans to get there.

Like stories it is magical. I am tempted to turn it on and bring the other world in.

Late that afternoon, the rain comes banging, clanging, and thrashing. It thunders, roars, and pelts the metal roof, as if challenging it to a fight. The roof of our home in the village was made of grass and palm fronds and it didn't allow the rain to make noise. The drops fell with a dull thud and ran down the sides. Besides, it never rained this hard in the village. I am glad Jama has unplugged the TV and we are safe.

I hoist Naren and Sita onto the mattresses piled on the wooden bench so if the water comes in they don't get wet. I hand them my deck of cards. Outside, the water has nowhere to go. It gushes down to meet the overflowing sewer. The stink of everything mixes together: chemicals from tanning hides, melting plastic, people and animal waste, and rotting plants. They all mask the heavenly scent of the rain-soaked earth. The entire street has turned into a filthy *nalla*.

My mind wanders back to the village. After the first few rains filled the pond, Mohan, Shiva, and I would go to the bank and have a jumping competition. We would jump from one of the *nimba* branches that loomed over the water. "One, two, three," the others would shout, and down we would go. I wonder if Naren and Sita will remember our village, pond, or the wandering goats.

Sita and Naren won't be able to splash in the newly

refilled pond. They will have memories of a stinking sewer in monsoon. This is not what I thought we were coming to. I miss the village, but if we had stayed there, we would have starved. Here, Jama has good job and has enough food, and milk for tea. I will take Naren and Sita back to the village someday, I promise myself.

"What are you thinking, Gopal?" Aai asks.

"Nothing." I turn my head to look at her.

"Your hands are curled into fists and now you're chewing your lip."

"Oh, Aai. I miss the pond, *gorus-chinch*, and even the muddy fields."

She sighs. "I know."

"Sita and Naren won't remember all that. Will they?"

"They'll make their own memories."

"Of what? Dead rats floating by?"

"They're not looking out the window. They'll remember being perched on a stack of mattresses and playing cards with each other, safe in the house from rain and wind, having warm tea, their Aai and big brother close by."

Aai's words bring a smile back to my lips.

As I watch all the water coming down, I remember how two years ago the rains fell on our farm and gave us bumper crops. That's how we ended up here.

"Baba, Baba," Naren suddenly sobs.

"Don't cry, Naren. Jama will bring Baba back. Right?"

Sita looks at Aai and me.

I lift Naren up and take him to Aai. Sita hops down and follows us.

"Baba will be back soon," I say as I put him on the sofa. It is a lie, but it is the best answer I have and that's the truth.

Aai holds Naren in her lap and Sita snuggles up to her.

I look in the covered pan sitting in the corner next to the stove. There is enough milk in it. "How about some tea?"

"I want Baba," Sita says.

Naren's sobs get louder.

I pace the room, not knowing what to do.

Finally, I light the stove, put the water on to boil, and make tea.

While we sip the tea the rain slows down. What if Jama doesn't come back? What will we do? I push the thought away. Jama has lived here for years and must know how to stay safe during monsoon.

The sound of the rain dies, but the smell doesn't. In the last day, I have gotten used to the strong odor, but this is horrendous, like a field covered with a thousand blooming onions.

The storm has moved away and the sun comes out, but outside the rainwater has mixed with open sewage, forming a dark stream. We stay inside. Naren and Sita play their cards and I open my notebook. I write my name on the first page. Chachaji has made sure that the first page is completely blank. Aai fixes a hole in the dress Jama bought for Sita yesterday. When she is done, Sita puts it on and I can't tell there was a hole.

"Aai, maybe you can fix clothes. You're good at it," I say.

"Or sew new ones," she says.

"Will you make a new dress for me?" Sita asks, twirling.

"You will need a sewing machine for it. That costs a lot," I tell Aai.

"Jama says you can get one on a monthly payment."

"I want a purple and pink dress," Sita says, climbing onto Aai's lap.

"I don't think we should borrow money or anything. We had to run away from our debt." The words come out faster and louder than I expected.

"We will see," Aai whispers. I don't know if she is talking to Sita or me.

If Aai has a machine she can stay home and make money. Maybe I can help her buy one.

I must find work.

It is late in the evening and Jama is not back. Even though I want to stay up, I am so tired that I fall asleep before he gets home.

ten

In the morning, I want to find out if Jama has any news about Baba, but if he did he would have told me. Instead, I tell Jama about Jatin and ask if he knows someone named Korae in the neighborhood. "Korae, Korae," he chants. "I can't think of anyone by that name. Did you say he has a factory? What kind?"

I should have asked Jatin about it yesterday. "I don't know."

"Because not many people have their own businesses here. Does Jatin live around here?"

"I don't think so."

"Anyway," he says, "you'd better concentrate on your studies and not worry about *faltu* things."

I want to tell him this is not a useless thing and ask him if I should find out from Jatin if there is any work in his uncle's factory, but Jama has made it as clear as sunshine that he wants me to study, so I'd better not ask him. "Yes," I say.

But I do want to work. I'll go look for Jatin and if I find him I can ask him about working in his uncle's factory until school begins. "I am going to Chachaji's shop. I'll be back soon," I tell Aai.

The morning is breezy and light. Maybe it won't rain today. Three boys my age walk to school carrying their book bags. It won't be long before I join them. I think of Mohan and Shiva. The three of us used to race to school, and would reach there out of breath and full of red dust. One time walking to school Mohan sprained his ankle; Shiva and I helped him get back home. We reached school so late that Mr. Advale was upset, but once he found out the reason he said he was proud of us and gave us both a new pencil. When Shiva's baba died, Mohan and I spent our evenings with him, sitting by the pond, talking.

I'm afraid to make new friends, because I am not as smart as the boys here must be. They speak many languages and have seen and heard a lot more than I have. They can speak Bambaiya Hindi, and probably even English, know how to turn a TV on, and must have read many books. But I can't have Mohan and Shiva here, so I must make new friends. Will these boys talk to me or shun me?

There are too many people in the city, so it is difficult to know whom to trust, but some of them have been generous. Maybe I need to show kindness. If Aai had not offered Card-Man *roti*, he wouldn't have bought us *chai*, given me the cards, and helped us with the luggage. Maybe we should have trusted Card-Man and shown him Jama's address. Then maybe he would have helped us find Jama in the first place, and we wouldn't have had to spend two nights by the station.

We wouldn't have lost Baba.

Maybe we should have never left the village. There we had Baba and now we haven't seen him for three days. I sigh. The smell of this place bothers me, but I have to keep breathing. I miss Baba, but I have to keep on living. There isn't much I can do.

Baba, Baba, Baba!

Each day for the past three days I have thought he will come today, but by the evening I skip my hope to the next day. With each passing moment, there is less and less chance that I will see him again. It hurts me and I know it rips Aai apart. Naren and Sita miss him. I don't know how long I can keep my hope afloat.

Before I know it, I am at the corner by Chachaji's shop. I'm too early, because it is closed like most other shops. I walk up and down the street. There's no sign of Jatin. I feel stupid. Why would he just wait around this neighborhood? He probably is working in his uncle's factory, and meanwhile I have nothing to do.

At the end of the block, there is a *pipul* tree with new

106

leaves sprouting on it and beyond it is a bridge. I am surprised to see the tree standing alone. It has survived the city moving all around it.

From the bridge, I see tall buildings. I think of the magazine that Mohan had, with pictures of fancy rooms filled with expensive furniture and beautiful people. The pictures must have been taken in a building like those. That world seems so close and yet so far.

I don't cross the bridge, but turn back to go home.

By noon, the day that started out cool and comfortable is turning hot and steamy, and I am restless. I am wasting my time when I could be making money. I wish Chachaji had a job for me, but his shop can barely support him. There is no way he can pay me. I take a nap, think about the village and the pond, and play cards. Finally, I read my books, but my mind is muddied like the rainwater flowing through the street. My eyes just skim over the words, nothing reaches my brain.

When I see kids returning from school, I grab my notebook and pencil and take a walk, hoping I can talk to some of them. They all move in clusters of three or four, chatting, joking, and laughing. But they don't notice me. They are absorbed in their chatter.

I pass Chachaji's shop again. "Come here, Gopal. I have something for you," he says.

"Yes?"

He points to the floor. "Do you have time to separate

and stack this stuff?"

I survey the store. The piles of magazines and newspapers have taken over practically every centimeter of the floor. I make my way through the store by picking up the piles and stacking them. Some of the magazines are fun to look at and I linger on one with the picture of Shahrukh Kahn on the cover. "I can't pay you," Chachaji admits. "But you can take a couple of magazines home."

After about half an hour I am finished and have chosen two of the magazines. *"Shabash!"* Chachaji says, looking around. He takes out a flashlight from a cupboard. "Here is your reward for good, fast work," he says. "It is a used one, but it has new batteries and works well."

"Don't you need it anymore?"

"Yesterday I bought one with a more powerful light. You will be fine with this one. Always carry it with you. If nothing else, it will keep you from stepping into you-know-what." He laughs as loudly as temple bells.

"Thank you, Chachaji," I say. The red flashlight is only a little thicker than a pencil and about sixteen centimeters long. I slip it in my pocket. Many tourists carry a flashlight in Matheran but I have never had one before, and I can't wait to show it to Aai.

Two more people show up with large bundles, and Chachaji gets busy with them. I walk to the end of the street to see if Jatin is there. The street is crowded and I don't see him.

I am about to turn away when I hear, "Gopal, Gopal."

It is Jatin! He's waving his hand furiously, as if he doesn't want to miss me.

"Did you find your uncle?" I ask.

"My uncle?" For a second, Jatin's face has no expression. Like his sleek hair, it looks unnatural. Has he forgotten our conversation? "*Accha, accha,* my uncle! I found him."

"Are you working in his factory?"

"*Ho.*"

"Do you, I mean, can you ask him if he can give me a job?"

He gives me a lingering look. His face breaks out in a big smile. "For sure!"

"Really?"

"*Pakka.* You can work for my uncle."

How can Jatin tell me that I can work for his uncle for sure? But maybe his uncle is looking for more workers. It doesn't matter as long as I have a job. From the corner of my eye, I see Chachaji waving at me. I wave back. He probably wants me to pick up the magazines I set aside, but this is not the time, when Jatin is ready to give me a job. "What do I have to do?"

Jatin rests his palm on my shoulder. "You will like the work. It is making picture frames and easy stuff like that."

That doesn't sound as hard as lifting heavy luggage or breaking stones at the quarry. "I'll ask my aai and let you know tomorrow."

"Haven't you heard *Kal kere so aaj kare, aaj kare so abb*? What needs to be done, must be done right away. Why wait a second longer?"

"If I don't tell Aai she will worry. Come with me and you can meet her."

"I want to, but not today," he says. "Here is the thing: I've got to see my uncle now, so it will be rude to meet your mother and not have time to talk to her. But I can take you to my uncle. We'll be back in no time."

I look in the direction of our home. "I'll run and tell Aai. I'll be right back."

"See that tea stand? I'll be there for five minutes. If you're not back, I will have to leave."

"Wait for me, please," I plead.

When I reach home, I'm out of breath. Aai is folding clothes. "The boy I met yesterday, Jatin—he's here. He can give me a job in his uncle's factory. I am going with him. I'll be back soon."

"We don't know him. You should wait until you talk to Jama tonight."

"Jatin is going to leave in two minutes. This is my chance, Aai. I have to go. Here, take this notebook and pencil."

"You can't go, Gopal. It looks like rain, and listen—"

"He is waiting. I'll tell him I can't go and be right back."

I grab the blue raincoat hanging from a nail by the front door and run out.

110

"*Sambhalun ja!*" Aai tells me to be careful.

Jatin is sipping tea and there is another full cup on a wooden table. He moves it toward me. "For you."

"I thought you were in a hurry."

He gives a shrill laugh. "One must always make time for *chai*. Have some."

As soon as I drink a few sips, Jatin gets up. "Let's go," he says.

I am lightheaded. Jatin, the cups, the stall all float around me. I wobble along with him. The footpath seems to rise up to meet me. "I . . . I can't go with you. My aai doesn't want me to," I say.

"Come now." He waves his hand. "Taxi!"

"But . . ."

He puts his arm around me. A taxi stops. Before I know it, I am in the backseat. I close my eyes.

Then darkness takes me.

eleven

When I wake up, a man with a crescent scar on his right cheek looms over me. I have never seen him before. He is small-boned with a large head and close-set eyes. Who is this man? Where am I? Where is my family?

The faint memory of Jatin, tea, and the taxi wash over me. I sit up. "Who are you?"

He stares down at me cross-eyed. "I am your boss."

"Is this the factory Jatin told me about? Are you his uncle?"

He laughs. His scar bunches up. "Did he tell you he was taking you to his uncle?"

"Yes. You know Jatin, the boy who brought me here?"

"That boy is something!" Scar-Man shakes his head in amusement. "I know him. I just didn't know

112

his name was Jatin this time."

I don't like the way he says, "His name was Jatin this time." Who *is* Jatin? What's his real name? Why am I here? I look around. The insides of the front and the back doors have latches and they are closed with iron locks on them. Fear digs in my heart.

This place doesn't look like a factory. It is just one rectangular room with a window on each long side. The wooden shutters are closed, and the room is lighted by a single fluorescent tube light. I'm on a floor made of rough stones that no one has washed for many monsoons and the paint on the wall is smeared with stains. Some of them are red. Is it betel-leaf juice or blood? The ceiling is made of wooden boards, so there must be a room upstairs. A wall clock with yellowed, faded, unreadable numbers ticks away as its brass pendulum moves back and forth, back and forth. I look away from it before I get dizzy.

The man sits down on a cushion on a bench that runs almost the length of the room. There is a TV across from the seat. The kitchen is in the far corner. A narrow bamboo ladder leans against one wall.

I pick up my blue raincoat and hold it close to my chest. It helps me steady myself. "Do you have work for me?"

"Sure do."

My throat aches and my lips are dry. I move my tongue over them and they have a parched, scaly feel, like the earth before monsoon. "I'm thirsty."

"Have some water," Scar-Man says. He shuffles to the kitchen, fills up a tumbler, and hands it to me.

I clutch the dented tumbler and gulp down the water. When I try to hand it back to Scar-Man, he snarls, "I'm not your servant. You're mine."

From the cracks between the shutters, I can tell it is dark outside and I know Aai must be waiting for me. "I want to go home now," I say.

"Where? Back on the street?"

"To my aai."

"Are you still a baby or what? Grow up. Your aai isn't here and you must earn your keep. You are staying here."

"Let me go." I push myself up. He whacks me on the cheek and I fall back down.

Scar-Man hits me again. "Stay there, you rat."

I cover my head with my raincoat, put my hands on top of it, and curl up into a ball. Baba never kicked or slapped us. He used to say, "Animals don't beat their own babies, and if we think we are better than animals then we must behave at least as well as animals." So I decide that a person who hits me doesn't deserve *man* behind his name. He doesn't even deserve *beast* behind his name. He is Scar. Just Scar. Nothing more.

"Up!" he shouts.

Slowly, I get up. My head feels empty like my stomach. I need food.

"Here is the thing, boy," Scar says. "Tomorrow, you'd

better be ready for work."

Where have I heard "here is the thing"? It is familiar, but I can't think anymore. My mind is a fog-enveloped mountain. As a wave of sickness moves in, I close my eyes and collapse on the floor.

Scar, his voice, and the room all disappear.

"Wake up, lazy boy," I hear.

I open my eyes. It is Scar standing nearby. His feet remind me of the policeman who kicked me the first night we slept on the station's footpath. Morning light filters through the half-closed shutters, and the room looks dirtier than it did last night. Spiderwebs wink in the far corner, and a couple of black ants scurry across the floor. Under Scar's wooden bench are boxes, a stack of newspapers, and several jute bags.

Scar claps. "Up."

I am still groggy, and struggle to get on my feet.

He grips my right arm and pulls me up. "Enough laziness. Time to work. The others have been at it for hours already." I am close enough to smell his stale breath.

He lets go of my arm but leaves behind a red welt. There's no one else around and there is no sound. "Where are they?"

"In the shop upstairs."

"What about my pay?"

"Pay? You will get food, a place to sleep. And what other workers get." He points me to the kitchen. "Drink

115

your tea and use the bathroom if you have to. Be quick."

I use the bathroom that is across from the kitchen corner next to the back door. It is small and stinks. I am still standing in the bathroom when what has happened to me becomes clear. Jatin tricked me. He drugged the tea. He sold me to Scar. Sold me. Now I belong to Scar. A wave of panic grips me. I burst open the bathroom door.

I need to get out, now. I need fresh air.

The opened bathroom door blocks Scar's view of me. The back door is not locked from inside today, so I push it, but it doesn't budge. I look through a crack and see a big brass padlock hanging on it from the outside.

"What are you doing?" Scar shouts.

"I'm coming," I say.

On the floor of the kitchen is the dented tumbler half full of a strange-looking liquid. I take a sip. I guess it is tea, but there's not enough milk or flavor to it, and it is cold.

I smell *dal* cooking on the stove. A metal rack hangs crooked on one wall. It holds five other tumblers like mine, one stainless-steel one, and several bowls and plates. There is a small metal shelf on the side with one wooden rolling pin, two serving spoons, a couple of pots, and one flat pan.

Ting, ting, ting . . . the clock chimes nine times.

Clap! "Hurry up. Let's go!" Scar hollers. He is sitting on the pillow on the bench wrapping beautiful beaded frames in newspapers.

I gulp the last of the tea, rinse my tumbler in the sink, and place it on the rack.

"Take your raincoat and go on up," he orders, pointing to the ladder. I grab my raincoat from the floor and climb up. He follows me. *Khas-khas, khas-khas,* the ladder groans. I'm afraid it will break under his weight.

At the top, I pause. Five faces stare back at me. They sit cross-legged on the wooden floor in front of their short, slanted desks. One by one, I take them in. The biggest kid has a tiny bump of a nose and fat fingers. The one sitting next to him has his eyes downcast, the dark fringes of his lashes a curtain around them. The third boy has a dimpled chin and looks as old as Naren and Sita. The fourth one, with curly hair, is rocking back and forth, and the fifth one has stooped shoulders and eyes the color of a gray city cloud.

Scar claps again. "Move."

Stunned, I almost fall off the ladder before I steady myself.

I climb the last two steps. Scar follows me. The boys start working again. They bend low over their desks and their fingers hold blunt wooden needles. They dip their needles in their trays, pick up a bead at a time, and stick each on the frame. Maybe this is the factory Jatin told me about.

The sharp, biting odor stings my eyes and burns my throat.

I cough.

Scar thumps my back. "Take care of him," he says, looking at the boy with the small nose and thick fingers.

"I will." Thick Fingers looks at me. "Over here, next to me." The boy with dark, fringy eyelashes scoots over without looking up. I settle between them under a window with vertical bars and tuck my raincoat behind me. Now I am part of their circle.

Khas, khas, khas, khas. Scar is already climbing down.

Thick Fingers hands me a plain picture frame. Then he slides a metal bead tray closer to me. "We'll share the work desk and beads so I can show you how to do this."

He brushes his hair back and holds my gaze. "This is what we do." He puts his frame on the desk and spreads a thin layer of glue on one side. His hair has fallen down onto his forehead again. "Your turn."

I copy him, but the layer of glue is too thick. He slaps my hand. "Don't be so wasteful. Use as little glue as possible."

My throat is on fire and my eyes water. I can't stop coughing. Thick Fingers snickers. "That's what happens when you use too much glue. It gets in your breath and burns as it goes down, so one more reason to use as little as you can. Get it?" Thick Fingers pinches me hard on the side. I muffle a cry. He points at the paper. "This is our design. No mistakes are allowed. Work. If you don't get four of these done before lunch, you'll have to work right through and there won't be any food for you. Understand?"

I nod.

My last meal was lunch yesterday and the mention of the word *food* makes my stomach churn.

I look at the design and start placing beads on the sticky side of the frame. It is a challenge to pick up the tiny beads with the blunt wooden needle. But the geometrical design with shiny red, green, and white beads is pretty. I like the way it changes the look of the dull wood.

Thick Fingers watches me for a few moments. "You're not bad," he says.

I stay quiet. Maybe if I do a good job he will be nice to me. I concentrate on my work.

When one side is done, I hold my breath, take a very small amount of glue, and put as thin a layer as I can on the opposite side of the frame. Then I start putting the beads on. Halfway through the design, the beads don't stick to the frame. Thick Fingers is watching me. "What did I do wrong?" I ask.

"You didn't put enough glue."

"I thought I was supposed to put a little. You said—"

"Shut up! You have to use the right amount. If you put on too much, you're wasting it. Too little, the beads won't stick, or worse, they fall off when Boss tries to wrap them. He will be mad."

How will Scar be able to tell that I did this frame? I look around. Every one of the workers has a different pattern, except for Thick Fingers and me.

I apply a little more glue and try again.

Thick Fingers is twice as fast as I am. As I work, the rocking boy with curly hair sitting across from me catches my eye. His eyes shimmer like the pond at sunrise. He is thin, and his knobby knees stick out from under his wooden desk. As he moves back and forth, back and forth, he picks up beads and glues them on. Then his gaze drops as if he is praying, but that's not what he is doing. He is working as fast as he can.

Another sharp pinch on the side makes me yelp. "This is not a show. Get to work," Thick Fingers says.

I finish four beaded frames before the clock strikes one o'clock. Scar claps from downstairs. It is loud. If I hadn't named him Scar, I would have named him Thunderclap.

Thick Fingers lifts his head. "Time for lunch."

When I stand up, I am dizzy and shaky. I extend my hand to hold on to something and Rocking Boy grabs it. "Thank you," I say.

He nods.

No one has talked to me except Thick Fingers. They haven't whispered a word to each other. Even in school, when we were supposed to be quiet, we talked—and sometimes got in trouble. Once the classes were over the *kal-bal, kal-bal* of tongues grew loud. Maybe Scar has forbidden talking and so the boys must be afraid of Scar overhearing them and beating them up.

One by one, everyone goes down the ladder and

heads straight to the sink. There's a pail of water and a scrap of soap. Everyone washes his hands, so I do as well. The glue still lingers on my fingertips, so I wash them again.

"Don't waste water," Thick Fingers says. Scar is ladling *dal* in a bowl and is turned away from us. I am thankful for that. I don't need more trouble from Scar.

We sit on the stone floor and Scar gives us a bowl of rice and *dal*. I wait for other food, but everyone else starts to eat. I guess there is no *roti* or *bhaji*. Scar's *dal* is like his tea, watery and flavorless. Still, I will eat it all up.

"How did the new one work out?" Scar asks Thick Fingers.

Thick Fingers glances at me. "Slow, but it won't be long before he gets in line."

"My name is Gopal," I say.

Scar fixes his stare on me. "So? You're working for me. I'll call you cockroach if I want. No names are allowed in this place, you understand?"

I don't get that at all. "Why are names not allowed?"

"Don't open your mouth unless I ask you a question." Scar moves closer to me. I do feel like a cockroach about to be squashed by his big, bare, ugly foot.

Rocking Boy, who sits across from me, taps his fingers on his knobby knee. When he has my attention, he shakes his head ever so subtly between Scar's spread-out legs. He is warning me of the danger.

After lunch, we wash our bowls, dry them, and put them back on the rack. Then we return upstairs. Before I settle under the window with vertical bars, I glimpse a *nimba* tree covered with raindrop-size green fruit. It is so close to the window that I might be able to stick out my hand between the bars and touch the leaves. I sigh as I sit down.

Everyone works silently. The wind picks up and the leaves murmur softly. The window is behind me so I can't look, but I know the clouds are floating by because the room turns bright and shadowy, bright and shadowy.

I can't believe only a few days ago I was in the village by the pond, yesterday I was with Aai, and now I am trapped in this place. If I had not gone out looking for Jatin I would have been safe. I could have never imagined something like this happening to us. First we lost Baba and now I am locked in here. I wish Jama hadn't asked us to move to Mumbai and Baba hadn't agreed to it. It would have been better to work in the moneyman's quarry than to be here alone. We would have been safe and together in the village.

Tears start to flood my eyes.

Baba might be home by now and looking for me. I imagine him crying just like he did the day we lost our land. I can't imagine what Aai must be feeling. Naren and Sita must be staring at the street waiting for me, and Jama must be blaming himself. Oh, I wish I hadn't been so anxious to find work. I wish I had listened to Aai and Jama!

From the corner of my eye I see the boy with gray eyes watching me. I lower my head more, wipe my cheeks, and concentrate on my work.

When Thick Fingers gets up to fill our bead tray I get a break, so I turn around and look at the tree outside. It reminds me of my favorite spot by the pond at home. When I sat there I dreamed of being a king and riding horses. If I was able to build air palaces there, I can build them now. In my imagination I can visit the pond and see the sunsets in Matheran and the hills that surround our village. Scar and Thick Fingers can't stop me from doing that—or from planning my escape.

twelve

From where I sit, I can't see the street, but I can hear the sound of traffic. I wonder how far away I am from Jama's house.

The sun is sliding in the west behind the tree and makes light and dark stripes on the floor with a moving leafy pattern over it. It reminds me of the leaf-filtered light by the pond. If I am still in Mumbai, the ocean is somewhere beyond the western edge of the land and my family is close by. My heart aches.

Scar comes up. His forehead looks larger because his hair is glued with perspiration to his scalp, exposing his bald temples. A pencil sticks out from behind one ear. He and Thick Fingers gently put all the frames we have made in a cardboard box before carrying them down. Now there're just the five of us and I whisper, "Who has been here the longest?"

No one answers.

"Can't we talk?" I ask.

Rocking Boy shakes his head covered with dark curls. "Talk and get in trouble," he whispers. His voice is husky because he hasn't spoken for a long time.

"Trouble? What do—"

"Shh . . . someone is on the steps."

A hush falls. Thick Fingers's head pops up. He flicks on the light. It is a naked bulb like the one in the Deepak Food Store. Thick Fingers sits right under the bulb so he has the most light. I am lucky I am sharing stuff with him because across from us there is hardly any light. Rocking Boy squints.

"If we rearrange how we're sitting all of us can have some light," I say.

Everyone looks up. Their mouths hang wide open, as if a fish has leaped out of the river and landed on the shore. Thick Fingers puts his bead picker down and stares at me, and I stare right back at him. Not a single finger moves. "All of you. Get back to work." Thick Fingers points at me. "You just wait. I'll show you."

Show me what? I don't want to ask and I don't want to be shown, especially by Thick Fingers. I apply glue. Then I pick up a bead and stick it, pick up a bead and stick it. It is more boring than memorizing the times tables. Compared to this, carrying luggage in Matheran was like going on a hike. There, I met new people and was free to move around. Some tourists were generous and gave me good tips or shared their food.

I have to somehow flee from this place. I have to. I have to.

When Scar claps, Thick Fingers says, "Time for dinner." We can all hear Scar's clap, so I don't know why Thick Fingers has to announce it. Rocking Boy is the first one to get on his feet, straighten up, and start climbing down. How come he is not stiff?

My legs have fallen asleep and I can hardly go down the ladder. "Move," Thick Fingers says when there are only two of us left. He follows me. "Hurry!" he shouts.

I stumble down the last two steps.

Thick Fingers washes his hands first, even though all of us came down before he did. He is the *chota*, small, boss, so he gets special treatment. When I sit down to eat, I can't fold my legs, so I draw my knees up. It is a strange way to sit down to eat but I have no choice. Thick Fingers whispers something to Scar. I don't know what, but they are looking at me.

Scar only gives me half the food he gives everyone else. "If you can't control your mouth, you get punished."

"But—"

"Don't argue. You're lucky I'm not starving you. Other bosses would," he says over his shoulder.

How many other bosses are there in this world, and how many children are working like this? They can't all be making frames. I think of the *chai* boy at Kalyan Station delivering tea. If we hadn't left the village I might be working for the moneyman who wanted me to split stones in his quarry. Sometimes big farms hire children to harvest cotton and other crops. I remember Mr. Advale telling us that he didn't like fireworks because sometimes children work in fireworks factories and get killed. Maybe other children are sewing things, picking rags, cleaning dishes. If they have a boss like Scar, their bosses might feed them little. My head starts to spin with all the thoughts that pour into my brain.

"Finish as fast as you can and get back to work," Scar barks.

My mouth drops open. We still have to work after dinner? Everyone else is concentrating on eating. Thick Fingers picks up a lump of rice and shoves it in his mouth and then picks up another lump. He must gulp it down without chewing, because he is done before the rest of us and he had the biggest serving. I have barely started mine.

I take a bite of rice and *dal*. The mixture tastes exactly like the one we had this morning. Then something grinds against my back tooth and I spit it out on my palm. It is a tiny stone.

Scar hits my back. "If you ever spit out food again you will not get meals for two days. Put that back in your mouth."

I slip the tiny stone back in my mouth and swallow it with the last spoonfuls of gravelly *dal*.

"I will leave soon. Close the shutters before you sleep," Scar says when we go back up. I let out a silent sigh because it will be easier to get away without him.

The door slams shut and keys jingle. Scar has locked the front door.

The clock strikes ten times. Thick Fingers whistles, and everyone finishes what they are doing. Then we move our wooden stools against the wall. Thick Fingers hands me a jute sack and I follow his example, laying the sack on the floor where I was sitting.

Thick Fingers picks up my blue raincoat. "Is this yours?"

"Yes," I reply.

"Let me see if it will fit me." Not only has Jatin tricked me and Scar imprisoned me, but now Thick Fingers wants to steal my raincoat. Thug.

He wiggles his body in. The sleeves are short and he can't button it. I don't want him to give it to someone else. "Too tight for me," he says, wrinkling his small nose. I hold my breath until he hands it back to me. I fold the raincoat into a small rectangle and use it as a pillow.

Thick Fingers closes the shutters. All the kids lie down with their heads next to the wall and feet in the middle. The Rocking Boy's feet touch mine.

If I want to escape, I will have to wait for everyone to fall asleep, especially Thick Fingers. But as much as I want to run away, I can't stay awake.

I wake up in the middle of the night. The rain pounds on the metal roof with all its might. The wind hisses like an injured snake. The thunder follows lightning immediately. The storm is right above our heads.

Where is Aai? I look around for her and touch someone's feet. I sit up. Oh. The workroom. Jatin, Scar, Thick Fingers, and being locked up was not a bad dream. It is real. Everyone lies still. The racket of the pounding rain doesn't seem to bother them.

Time to leave. The door is locked, but maybe I can find a way to wiggle out of a window. It will be dangerous to be out in the pouring rain because the streets might have flooded. But what choice do I have? Lightning flashes through the cracks in the shutters again. Thunder follows.

Once I am out of here and standing on the street I will worry about the rain.

I get up. The room is packed with five other boys, so there are twenty arms and legs to step around. I point the beam of my flashlight in the center and slowly get to the other side and switch off my flashlight. Suddenly, I realize I forgot my raincoat, but if I walk back I might wake up someone. It is better to get wet than get caught.

I turn around to climb down the ladder. My foot hangs in the air. When I switch the flashlight back on for a second, I see that the ladder is gone. There's no way I can jump down without a huge thud—and I might injure myself.

In the flash of lightning, I see one of the boys sitting up. "What are you doing?" he whispers. Even in the dark I can tell he is hunched over. It is the boy with gray eyes.

I panic. "I . . . I have to go to the bathroom."

"Now?"

"Yes."

"You can't. You have to wait until Boss returns in the morning. Get back here."

I walk slowly without turning my flashlight on. I don't think he has seen it, and for that I am thankful. No one has much here, and if Scar finds out I have a flashlight he might take it away.

My jute bed is scratchy, but what I feel on my skin is nothing compared to what I feel in my heart. It is as if someone has rubbed this rough sack on my heart over and over again and made it bleed. Tears roll down my cheeks as I think of Aai. What she must be going through! First, she lost Baba and now she's lost me. How quiet Naren and Sita were after Baba disappeared. They would sit on the footpath, staring at the road. Now they must be looking out the window, waiting for me. With Jama's help, I was supposed to go to school, work, and make sure Naren and Sita get an education.

Oh, why did I listen to Jatin? I was impatient and stupid to rely on a stranger.

The boy with fringy eyelashes next to me talks in his sleep. He stutters and speaks a different language. Maybe he comes from far away. But even though I don't understand what he is saying, I recognize his tone. It is sad and begging, as if he has done something wrong and is pleading for forgiveness. I reach out and pat him on the head. He quiets down. I wipe my tears with the back of my hand and turn over.

The wind gusts and the whole place shudders. I tremble with it.

If my impatience and stupidity have brought me here, then the only way out is to have patience and cunning. I have to understand how things work here and plan carefully before I try to run away. As long as I am alive, I have a chance to escape—to escape for Aai, Naren, Sita, Jama, and Baba—especially for Baba. Because if he is alive, he will be devastated when he finds out I have vanished. And if he is dead, then I have to take his place and take care of my family.

Yes, I have to, and I will flee. It is only a matter of a few days.

I fall asleep thinking about all I have to do.

thirteen

The day starts with a quick trip to the bathroom and work. Today, Thick Fingers gives me my own desk and tray of beads but makes me sit next to him so he can keep an eye on me. It also gives me a chance to watch him. His fingers are not as nimble as mine, so he is not as swift in picking up the beads with the blunt needle. But he is experienced and organized. He picks up a bead with his right hand, places it on the frame, and then presses it in with his left hand while he lifts up another bead. He works fast. I try to copy him, but I find it too hard to do things with my left hand.

Scar comes after we have been working for a while. *Tarrer, tarrer, tarrer*, the sound of the clock winding floats up. After a few minutes Scar claps us down for tea. As I sip the weak liquid I look around. The windows are closed and so are the front and back doors. I wonder if Scar keeps them open during the day when we are upstairs. I must come down and check. "Drink quickly unless you want *kanpatti*," he says.

Kanpatti sounds like some kind of punishment. Everyone gulps their tea as fast as he can before going back up again.

After an hour or so, a song bursts out. Scar must have turned on the TV downstairs. I can hear every word. I try to follow the story, but that slows me down. So I concentrate on my work again.

But it is hard to focus—I can't stop thinking about how I am going to escape. I decide that I need to go down and check out the doors and windows. Maybe one of the doors is open and I can bolt. As I stand up, I put my hands on my back and bend backward. It feels good after being hunched over the desk for many hours.

Thick Fingers points at me with his blunt needle. "What are you doing?"

"I have to pee."

"You can't just get up and wander out. You must ask for permission."

"*Accha*. May I go?"

His nostrils puff up. "Sit down."

I look around. Everyone has his head down. "But I have to go."

"Start working. Now!" If his needle were sharper he

would've stabbed me with it.

My first thought is to sit back down, but if I want to escape I must stand up to Thick Fingers. I think of the statue of Annasaheb Kotwal that I used to see in Matheran in the park across from the Richie Rich Resort. In 1942 he fought in India's freedom fight against Britain. When the British Army came to capture him, he hid in the surrounding hilly jungles of Matheran. He never surrendered and was killed. I used to read his name and the plaque under his statue every time I went to the main street in Matheran. If I have learned anything from his story, it is that I must not back down.

I don't move.

"Didn't you hear me?" Thick Fingers asks.

"I will sit down after I go to bathroom," I say. The other kids have stopped working. The boy with fringy lashes lift up his fear-filled eyes, the Rocking Boy puts his wooden needle down but keeps on rocking, the gray-eyed one smirks as if he is enjoying this.

The youngest one with a dimpled chin says, "*Yaar*, let him go."

"Don't wag your tongue! And don't call me *yaar*, I'm not your friend."

Dimpled Chin starts working again. He looks down and I can't see the dimple anymore.

I shuffle my feet as if I might wet my shorts.

"Go," Thick Fingers says. "But get back right away."

I cross the room as slowly as I can.

134

"Hurry up!"

I don't change my pace. I am not going to be bullied by Scar's *chamcha*, sidekick. I like how I have not allowed Thick Fingers to squash me.

"*Oai ladka*, are you still in the bathroom?" Scar shouts above the noise of TV.

"I am."

"Hurry up."

I come out of the bathroom. The back door is locked from the outside. Scar must keep it permanently locked. The wooden shutters are open, but the windows are fitted with metal grilles, so I can't climb out of there. I walk toward the ladder and glance at the front door. It is closed and locked. There is no hope of escape. Suddenly, my mouth tastes like it is filled with dust and my feet turn into mushy *hajra* porridge.

Scar is watching the TV and eating. I don't know what it is, but the smell of onions and garlic fill the air. My mouth begins to water. My eyes fix on Scar.

A large piece drops from his hand, hits the side of his wooden bench, and plops on the floor. His face twists when he sees me. "Look what you did! You made my *roti* slip. Don't stare at me," he says. "Pick up the piece and eat it or else I will have a bellyache from your evil eyes."

Before he changes his mind, I grab the onion-and-garlic-stuffed *roti*. I know people always share their food, even with strangers when they are traveling together, like

Aai shared with Card-Man. It is polite, and sharing the food makes it better. It gets blessed. I can't think Scar believes that, but maybe he feels that I hold some kind of evil power, and just by looking at his food I can make him drop it or make him sick. I smile at his superstition and turn to go.

"Stay and eat here. I don't have enough for everyone."

I think of Rocking Boy, who held out his hand to steady me, and Dimpled Chin, who tried to take my side with Thick Fingers. I wish I could share with them.

Scar clears his throat. He is watching me.

As I stuff the piece in my mouth and chew, the moist, sautéed pieces of onion fill my mouth. It reminds me of Aai's *bajra roti* stuffed with onion.

I climb the ladder slowly. By the time I am up, I am finished chewing. Thick Fingers takes in a big breath. "I smell onions. Did you steal food?" Even with his small nose he can smell just fine.

"No." I am afraid he will check my pockets and find my flashlight. "Boss gave me a piece of *roti*," I say as I sit down.

"Show me your hands."

I open my sweaty palms. He looks at my shorts. Before he asks me to empty the pockets, I say, "Onion breath," and blow on him. His nose crinkles at the pungent smell.

There is muffled laughter. Thick Fingers looks around, but everyone's head is bent.

"Enough! Start working," he barks.

I follow his order, but not before I glance at Dimpled Chin and Rocking Boy. They don't look up.

I went down with a hope of running away and all I got was a piece of *roti*. There is no way to escape from here. I wonder if anyone has ever tried to flee. Maybe someone did and that is why Scar keeps the door locked all the time. How did the other boys end up here? Where are their families? Do they get paid? I have questions, but who should I talk to? None of the boys is friendly, and they seem to mistrust each other.

Thick Fingers is the leader, *chota* boss, but I can't ask him anything. Dimpled Chin reminds me of Naren— maybe that is why I feel like I know him. Night Chatterer with fringy eyelashes never looks up. He is shy or scared, or maybe both. I notice how precisely he presses each bead, how his shirt is tucked in evenly, and his hair is perfectly combed, too. He must have a comb tucked in his pocket. I don't know anything about the gray-eyed boy, except he is a light sleeper. Rocking Boy is kind, and maybe he is the only one I can speak to.

It is difficult to work in the silence. Time walks by on its hands, slowly and painfully. Fumes from the glue sting my eyes. Relief comes only when the *nimba* leaves flutter and the light scent wafts through the room, temporarily masking the stink.

Scar pokes his head from halfway up the ladder and

motions for Thick Fingers to follow him.

After they leave, I whisper to Rocking Boy, "What's your name?" He gives me a blank look that is filled with sadness before he lowers his gaze.

I sigh. "You do have a name, don't you?"

Rocking Boy looks in the direction of the ladder. He nods.

"Tell me, or else I will call you Rocking Boy."

Dimpled Chin giggles.

I put a finger to my mouth.

He whispers, "I like the name Rocking Boy. Can I have it?"

"You already have a nice name. I have named you Dimpled Chin."

"Is it better than Rocking Boy?"

"It is for you. Because you are the only one with a dimple."

Rocking Boy has not answered my question. I give him an encouraging smile. He stays quiet. "Just call him Rocking Boy," Dimpled Chin says.

The boy with gray eyes leans over and slaps Dimpled Chin. "You have the biggest mouth on this side of the moon." He is missing two front teeth, exposing his yellow gums.

Since he is the last in line and closest to the ladder, I ask, "Is someone coming up?"

He stares at me.

"What's your name?" I whisper.

"No names," he hisses.

"Here we're *anamik*, without names," I say.

"You are so good at giving names. Why don't you give me one?"

I think about it. He has stooped shoulders, gray eyes that are filled with anger, missing teeth, and yellow gums. "How about if I call you Gray Cloud? GC for short?"

"Just never talk to me."

"Sure. You've made a mistake in your pattern, but I will stay quiet."

He picks up his frame. "Where?"

The others snicker, including Night Chatterer. GC is mad. I can tell because the gray of his eyes gets darker. "I will tell Leader and he will complain to Boss, and then you will be in trouble."

"Why do you call him Leader instead of his name? You want me to name him, too?" I ask.

"*Chote muh, badi baat mat ker.*"

"I may have a small mouth and talk big, but what about you? Why are you afraid to talk to Boss yourself?"

"You'll pay for this. Just wait and see."

Rocking Boy starts tapping on his desk. I ignore him and tell GC, "Why should I worry? I've nothing anyone can take."

"I've been in your place and one thing is *pakka*, you have something to pay with. Until it is gone you won't know you had it. And then it is too late." His lips tighten as if some painful memory has pulled a string.

It's not only what he says but the sadness of his voice that shocks me.

When Scar bangs the door shut and locks it, Thick Fingers thumps back up the ladder. He plops down between GC and me. GC lifts up his chin slightly and nods in my direction. He is subtle, but Thick Fingers turns toward me. I smile at him. Then I grin widely at GC to let him know I'm aware that he tried to pass Thick Fingers a message about me. Thick Fingers looks confused, and GC looks frustrated.

"*Tea se jyada nai kitali garam hai,*" GC finally says to Thick Fingers. What does "the new kettle is hotter than tea" mean? Is he saying that the new boy is behaving badly?

Rocking Boy sits across from Thick Fingers. He keeps his face down, but nothing has escaped him. He taps his right fingers on the side of his wooden table.

Maybe he is telling me, "Be careful" or "Danger."

I pick up a frame and coat one side with a layer of glue. As I stick the beads on the frame, I think of how to trick Thick Fingers. One thing about him is that, even though he is Scar's favorite, he is not the reddest chili—the smartest one—of the bunch. He is like Naren when he plays cards and gets aces, kings, and queens, or low cards. He can't hide his joy or frustration. It is to my advantage that I can see right through Thick Fingers.

It is past noon and Scar has not returned. When the

clock strikes once, Thick Fingers says, "Time to eat."

I throw my head back and rotate it to get the kinks out. When I try to get up, Thick Fingers pushes me back down. "You stay here. You don't get food today."

"Why?"

"You know why."

"I don't." Rocking Boy is standing on the ladder, so his head peeks above the floor, like a little animal looking out of a hole. His concerned look reminds me of Aai. Night Chatterer is frozen with terror. Dimpled Chin looks from Thick Fingers to GC to me. I gulp down my fear. "What have I done?"

Thick Fingers glances at GC, who stands with his hands folded against his chest. "When Boss is not here, I rule, and I can do as I please."

"So you can punish me if you don't like the way I smile or the way I look?"

GC smirks. "Or the way you talk and the way you walk."

I want to tell him to stay out of it, but I don't. If he can convince Thick Fingers to starve me without saying a word, he is more dangerous than I thought. I have already done and said enough to hurt myself.

"Are you stuck on the ladder? Move!" Thick Fingers shouts at Rocking Boy.

Thick Fingers is the last one to leave. When he turns around to go down the ladder, he says, "Don't waste time. Keep on working."

This place is bad even without Thick Fingers and GC pushing me to the ground and kicking me. I must somehow break them up. It won't help me get out of here, but at least I won't miss meals and be so weak that I can't escape when I get a chance.

By three in the afternoon, my bottom hurts. My stomach rumbles often and pain fills my neck, shoulders, and arms. I need to get up and walk. There is no way I am going to be stupid enough to ask for permission or argue with Thick Fingers to let me go to the bathroom. I did that before and had to pay for it.

Before long I must find a way to get up. What would Birbal do if he were in my place? But he was too smart to end up here. I go through some of Birbal's stories. When I remember the one I told Naren and Sita a few days ago, I realize that Birbal was asked to go to heaven. He had to die first. Die! But he fooled everyone. I must somehow trick these kids.

A breeze picks up and I hear a muffled sound, *kreech, kreech, kreech, kreech*. One of the overgrown *nimba* branches must be rubbing against the roof or the wall.

No one notices. It is there again as the wind blows from the west. *Kreech, kreech, kreech, kreech*. GC looks around. "What was that?" he asks.

Kreech, kreech, kreech, kreech. This time it is louder. Rocking Boy stops rocking, because he has heard the sound, too.

"Listen," GC says to Thick Fingers.

142

Thick Fingers looks around. "I don't hear anything." Not only is he slow to think, I guess he is hard of hearing, too.

"The noise."

Suddenly, an idea blazes across my brain. If this works out right, I might even get some food. "Like there is a big rat around here," I add.

Thick Fingers's eyes are ready to pop out of his face. I bend over my bead tray and pick up a yellow bead. Only our hands move. There is not a sound in the room.

"I don't know. I thought I heard some screechy-scratchy noises," GC says.

Come on, wind, I pray.

Kreech, kreech, kreech, kreech.

Night Chatterer lifts up his fringy lashes and stares at the far corner. Dimpled Chin jumps up. His chin quivers with fear. "I don't want a rat to bite me."

Thick Fingers points his stubby finger to the floor. "Come, sit by me. There is no—"

Kreech, kreech, kreech, kreech.

Silence.

Kreech, kreech, kreech, kreech.

"Let me see where the noise is coming from," GC says.

"Be careful. My uncle got bitten by one and had to get shots," I say.

GC's face turns gray, the same color as his eyes.
Kreech, kreech, kreech, kreech.

Now everyone except me is up. "We'd better go down," our brave leader, Thick Fingers, says.

GC is already climbing down the ladder when I stand up. It feels good to straighten up, move my legs, go down, and use the bathroom.

"What should we do?" Thick Fingers asks GC.

"I don't know. You're in charge. You should go up and check it out."

Now Thick Fingers is not happy with GC. "Yes, I am in charge, and I am asking you to go," he says.

GC is furious. *Meri billi mujko meow?*

GC saying, "My own cat going against me?" to Thick Fingers makes me happy. I try to hide the smile sprouting at the corners of my mouth. GC catches me. "Send the new boy."

Thick Fingers follows GC's suggestion and orders me, "Go up and check it out."

I don't mind doing that, but I am going to get something out of it first. "I'll go only if you promise some food and—"

"I don't have to give you anything."

"Then I won't do it."

After a few minutes, I say, "I guess Boss will wonder why we have done so few frames. He won't be pleased."

"You want food and what else?" Thick Fingers asks me.

"Promise not to complain to Boss about any of us. If you do, I will tell him you are afraid of a rat."

"*Accha.* Go now."

I take two steps up, turn my face, and point to GC. "I need help. Come with me."

Panic fills GC's eyes. "I can't."

"You go," Thick Fingers says to Rocking Boy.

Rocking Boy hesitates.

I extend my hand. "Don't worry. Come with me."

He follows me.

Once we get upstairs, I put my finger on my lips. I whisper, "There's no rat. It is just the tree branch rubbing against the building or the roof."

"How do you know?"

I take him to the window. "Wait until there is wind and you will hear it." A breeze blows and the sound is there again. Rocking Boy puts his hand on his mouth to stifle a chuckle. "Will you tell on me?" I ask, just to be sure.

He looks at me unblinking. "Never."

From his deep, steady gaze I know he will keep his promise. I wonder if GC and Thick Fingers mocked and teased Rocking Boy. He has a frail body, soft features, and quiet eyes that make him look like an easy target. Maybe that is why he looks nervous.

"But how are we going to explain to them about the sound?" he asks.

I like the way he counts us together. Now Thick Fingers and GC are on one side and Rocking Boy and I are on the other.

"What does *Tea se jyada nai kitali garam hai* mean?" I ask him.

"It means you think you are smarter than you really are." He smirks and shakes his head. "But you really are clever."

Rocking Boy and I move frames around so it sounds like we are doing something. After a few minutes, we come down. "We looked everywhere but didn't see a thing. I think it is just the branches rubbing against the building. It is safe to come up. But I need some food first," I tell Thick Fingers.

"You are telling the truth, right?" GC asks.

"Why wouldn't we? We don't want to be bitten by a rat any more than you do." I turn to Thick Fingers. "I'm hungry."

"We ate your share."

"All of you?"

"Only I did, but let me see if there is any food in here." Thick Fingers finds a piece of stale *roti* on a plate. It is dry and brittle. Yet food is food. Better to have some than not.

They wait while I eat the *roti* and drink water from my tumbler. I'm the first one to go back up. GC and Thick Fingers are the last ones to come up.

GC stands by the window and looks out to make sure I told the truth. When the wind gusts and there is a *kreech, kreech, kreech, kreech* sound again, only then he settles down.

When Scar returns, he claps us down. I am a little afraid that Thick Fingers will complain about me even though he promised not to. But he keeps his word.

Today Scar didn't have time to cook watery *dal* and rice, so each of us gets two pieces of bread and lemon pickles. I like it better because the pickles are tangy and make the plain bread taste much better than it is. When I finish eating, I find myself licking my fingers. Dimpled Chin does the same. When our glances meet, he grins. Scar is watching us, but I don't care, because a thousand of his mean looks are worth one smile from Dimpled Chin.

"Stay down, you filthy pig." Scar points to Dimpled Chin as we are ready to go back up. As I climb up the ladder I shudder at the thought of Scar hitting Dimpled Chin simply because the little boy was happy for a split second and gave me a smile.

When I hear Dimpled Chin's yelp, I flinch and a bead flies off. Rocking Boy picks up the bead and presses it into my palm. I wait for Dimpled Chin. When he comes up his cheeks are wet and he stares at the floor. The tops of his ears are bright red.

I hate Scar more than I did when he hit me. Dimpled Chin is so young. It is like Scar hitting Naren or Sita. Even Thick Fingers is upset about it because he keeps throwing pitiful glances at Dimpled Chin. I wish Thick Fingers had complained about me. Then Scar would have been mad at me and would have left Dimpled Chin alone. Maybe Scar hit Dimpled Chin to make us all fear him more.

And if he did, he was successful. The terror fills up the space between us.

After Scar leaves Thick Fingers tells me, "You bring trouble to others. Do your work and never look and never ever smile at anyone else."

"But it was not my fault if Boss beat—"

"Yes, it was." He points to Dimpled Chin. "He got punished because Boss thought you are his friend. It is fine if you want to create problems for yourself, but don't drag others with you."

"So you don't care if Boss hits me and starves me?"

"No. Why should I?"

"Why do you care about him?" I ask, pointing at Dimpled Chin.

"I, I am not . . ." Thick Fingers fumbles. He looks puzzled and a little scared. Others have stopped working and are waiting to hear him. "I don't have to give you a reason. Do as I tell you."

I don't argue anymore.

We work for a couple more hours and all that time I wonder why Thick Fingers is so protective of Dimpled Chin. Maybe they have worked together for a long time and Thick Fingers cares for Dimpled Chin, or he reminds Thick Fingers of his own brother. Or maybe because Dimpled Chin is the youngest and it is hard to see him get punished.

Whatever the reason, it doesn't matter. It has not been

as easy to run away as I had thought when I first came here, so it is better if I keep to myself. The only way I can escape during the day is if Scar asks me to help him pack the frames. Then when he takes the boxes out, but before he locks the door, I can run away. For that to happen Scar has to trust me, and I must not smile at Dimpled Chin or be friendly toward anyone. Then maybe Scar will trust me. It will be hard to do because I like Dimpled Chin and I hate Scar, but I have to imagine Scar is nice like my teacher Mr. Advale.

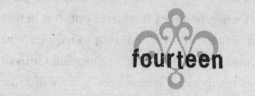

fourteen

I have been here for a week and Scar has not asked me to help him. Last night was hot, and as tired as I was, I woke up several times because of the mosquitoes. In the morning my legs and arms are covered with red, puffy welts, and it doesn't help that the day is muggy.

When you are trapped, each new day is the same as before. But today is different—it is a bath day. It brings a little variety. Scar hands me a pair of shorts but no shirt. Which means when I wash my shirt and hang it on a line to dry, I have to go shirtless. In this weather, that is fine. I will be gone before winter comes.

Three of us have to take a bath together to save water—Dimpled Chin, Rocking Boy, and me. GC is supposed to take a bath with Thick Fingers and Night Chatterer, but he refuses to do so. For some reason, Scar lets him take one alone.

There is one bucket of water among the three of us. Dimpled Chin takes his bath in his underwear. He uses half a tumbler of water to wet himself. The he rubs the sliver of soap on his body and rinses with just two tumblers full of water. While he wipes his body with a piece of towel Rocking Boy cleans up. Between the two of them they have used only half the water.

When it is my turn, I close my eyes and dip my fingers in the bucket. The water is at room temperature and feels good on this hot day. I don't touch the edge of the pail, so my fingers are surrounded only by water.

With my eyes closed, the bucket becomes a pond. I can imagine the water stretched out like a bolt of indigo fabric. I hear the soft ripples. I can even taste the fresh water. I smile. Memories make time walk backward.

Almost.

"You're taking too long. Boss will be mad." Rocking Boy brings me back to the present.

Before I can answer him a loud *clap*, followed by "Hurry up, you lazy dogs" from Scar rattles me. The other two are dressed and waiting for me. "Keep some water to rinse our clothes," Rocking Boy whispers. I quickly get ready. We soak and wring our clothes, hang them on the line in the bathroom, and are back up in five minutes.

It feels good to take a bath, but the thought that I won't be able to take another one for a week makes me sad. Maybe I won't have to wait that long. Everyone is clean and fresh. Night Chatterer looks the best with his combed hair. Even his lashes curve up like he has combed them.

Fresh and clean, we glue beads; morning, afternoon, and evening. Over and over until we are tired and dirty again.

For the last few days there has been no rain, no break in work, and no chance to escape. Scar locks up the doors not only when he leaves but even when he is here. In the beginning I thought I could escape, but now I am not sure. How can I plan something that seems impossible?

I was so eager to make money, and now I am trapped. I can only blame my foolishness. Aai must be heartbroken. I wonder if Naren has stopped talking like he does when he is upset or angry? And Sita? Just thinking about them brings tears to my eyes. Jama must be spending so much time looking for me. If Baba is back he must be miserable.

The mosquitoes are just as bad as before. I suppose there are enough puddles left over from the earlier rain for them to breed in and there is enough blood for them to feed on.

One thing about a dry spell is we can keep the window open during the day. Thick Fingers has moved me away from him, which is good, because now every time I look up to give my neck and back a rest, I see a sliver of sky and a branch of the *nimba* tree. Today I notice the fingertip-long fruits have turned yellow. Oh, how I wish I could pick a handful of them, pop them in my mouth, and let the bittersweet juice coat my tongue.

Today Scar gives us new patterns. "Here is the thing, boys. You must all do export-quality work on these frames. It is a large order and we have to finish in time for their holiday season, so get going. I won't allow a single mistake." He doesn't wait for us to start work before leaving.

"What is export-quality?" I ask.

"I thought you were the smart one. Don't you know what it means?" GC laughs, making his shoulders hunch even more.

Thick Fingers puts his stubby hand up. "Don't bicker. Do your work. Export quality means you have to do your best work because these things will be sold in faraway countries."

Ever since I checked for the rat and Dimpled Chin got punished, Thick Fingers has lost a few thorns and has mellowed.

"Which countries?" Dimpled Chin asks.

"I don't know their names, but it doesn't matter to me and shouldn't matter to you. All we have to do is work on the order," Thick Fingers replies.

I fill my bead tray, apply glue to a frame, and re-create the pattern on the frame as fast as I can. My palm is so sweaty that I can't keep a firm grip on the blunt needle that I use to pick up beads. It keeps sliding away. I wipe my hands on my shorts often, but that slows me down. The only good part is that everyone else is doing the same thing.

How far will these frames travel? Will they cross the oceans on a boat or fly on a plane? Will they sit in one of those fancy rooms like the one in Mohan's *Star Homes* magazine? Who are the lucky people who will buy them? Maybe one will end up in a young girl's room. She will never know a young boy like her made the frame with his sweat and tears while his heart ached for his family. Tears roll down my cheeks. I move my arm to wipe them on my sleeve before realizing I am not wearing a shirt.

"Tomorrow we get a haircut," Thick Fingers tells us as we put away our desks and beads for the night.

"Does Boss cut our hair?" I ask.

"*Mamu*," GC says. "You think Boss will touch your lice-filled hair?"

"I don't have lice and I—"

Thick Fingers puts his hand up. "We have to get up at five, so go to bed."

I wonder if we have to start work an hour early so we can take time for a haircut. I still don't know who will cut our hair. What if Scar takes us out? If he does I will make sure I run away. But as I think about it I realize he won't do that. He wouldn't want to spend money on us, take us out, and let others find out we are working for him.

Does that mean Thick Fingers will cut our hair? Or

GC? It would be so easy for one of them to poke me with the tip of the scissors and call it an accident. Maybe I should have been more careful and not made them my enemies. I am soaked in sweat and worried to my bones.

When we begin our work it is pitch-dark outside. I want to find out who is going to cut our hair. Who can I ask? They all must have gotten haircuts before and are not curious about it. Like Aai used to say, without good work there is no *bakshish*, tip. So it is better for me to do my work well and please Scar. If he is happy it won't matter who cuts my hair. Whoever it is will be careful. That will be my *bakshish*.

After tea Scar sends us all up except Night Chatterer and Thick Fingers. Soon Scar calls GC down. When Thick Fingers returns his hair is as short as a pencil point and he has taken a bath. He sends Rocking Boy down, which means GC must be taking a bath. I am the last one to go down after Dimpled Chin. Night Chatterer cuts my hair right outside the bathroom while Dimpled Chin is taking a bath. The pair of scissors is not big but looks sharp. Scar stands close by and watches us, tapping his foot nervously.

Night Chatterer combs my hair and snips away, combs and snips away. I wish I had a mirror to see how I look. When I am about done Dimpled Chin comes out of the bathroom. "Wash your hair and be out in five minutes," Scar says to me.

"Yes, Boss."

There is less than half a bucket of water left. I wash my hair and my body as quickly as I can. When I open the bathroom door Night Chatterer is ready to go in. I wonder if he gave himself a haircut or did Scar?

Why has Scar asked Night Chatterer to do this job? Maybe he has done this work before, or his father was a barber and he has learned it from him, or he is the only one Scar trusts with a pair of scissors.

In the heat, short hair seems to help. I don't perspire as much and I don't need to comb my hair. I wish we could keep our hair this short all the time but it is not going to happen, because when I came here everyone's hair was so much longer than this. I think Scar will let many months go by before he will allow haircuts again, and somehow I will be out of here. I have to be.

Around one, Scar gives us each a banana with *roti*. He must be feeling generous today because of the huge order. I wait for *bhaji* or *dal*, but there isn't any. When Scar gives something extra, he takes something back, so there is always a price to pay. The bananas are mottled black and soft. I take a bite of *roti*, a bite of banana, and a sip of water to make them all come out even like the way I used to when I was young.

My eyes droop after lunch. The heavy air makes me drowsy, and I have to fight it. Scar brings us water later that afternoon, which he hasn't done before. At least he makes sure we are not thirsty.

I take my tumbler and begin drinking. He quickly snatches it away. "I don't have a well here! Sip slowly so you can stay awake and keep on working."

Except for insults, Scar never gives anything for free. I must remember that.

We sip and work, sip and work. "You've become a rocking boy too," Dimpled Chin whispers to me. Without realizing it, I have started rocking back and forth, back and forth. When I get up I am not as stiff as I used to be. Maybe rocking helps a person stay limber and that is why Rocking Boy is always the first one to get on his feet. He has learned to cope with sitting cross-legged all day, every day.

"I have to deliver these frames and I won't be back again," Scar says around five. "There's some food for you, but don't eat before eight and keep on working. If one of you falls behind in work, all of you will be punished. Remember, no frames, no food."

As perspiration trickles down my shirtless back, it is hard to keep on beading, and there are still two more hours before we eat. The time would go faster if we could talk or share stories. I think of all the *kahanis* Aai told me. When Naren and Sita fought, or if one of them was sick, I made up stories. On the *nimba* branch by the pond, I pretended to be Shahanshah Akbar or Birbal or a warrior. It was fun. *Kahanis* are like the sky. There is no end to them. You can always retell the old one, make a new one up, or twist the old one to make it funnier, scarier, or sweeter. Aai used to say, "*Kahanis* are your best friends because they never leave you."

"How about if we tell *kahanis*?" I ask.

"*Tea se jyada nai kitali garam hai,*" GC says. I ignore his taunting, that I think I am smarter than I really am, but he keeps on pounding. "Just like you, stories are dreamed up, phony, and *faltu,* useless."

"Remember when you thought that a rat made a *kreech, kreech, kreech, kreech* sound? You ran down like a scared goat. Stories are like that. They may not be real but what we feel is real."

"I want a *kahani,*" Dimpled Chin says as he leans toward me. The fading sunlight shines on him. "Please." When he says the English word, his face swells up with pride. Even his dimple seems to deepen with satisfaction.

I wait for Thick Fingers to give me permission to tell a story or speak up against it, but he keeps on gluing beads and doesn't look up. That must mean at least he doesn't mind if I tell a *kahani.*

So many stories fly through my brain, *kahanis* about giants, ghosts, and angels. I let them go. I pick the one I know best, the one that means the most to me. "Here is a *kahani* about a boy and a trickster," I begin, applying glue to a new frame. "Once there was a boy who lived in a valley surrounded by hills. He helped his parents in their field and he roamed with his friends in their village."

"What a boring, no-name boy story!" GC interrupts.

I go on. "The boy thought he would always live there. One year the rains were good and every farmer in the village was happy. Their onion crop grew and grew. When the field was covered with yellowish leaves, it was time for the harvest. The boy helped lift the plump onions from the ground and dreamed of all the money they would get and the things they could buy with the money. The boy's baba promised him new sandals, a book, and maybe new clothes. Even though the boy's hands and arms were covered with red soil, he imagined himself holding a book and reading it to his younger brother and sister."

"What book did he get?" Dimpled Chin asks. He has put his bead picker down.

"You don't know how to read, so what difference does it make?" GC sneers.

Dimpled Chin looks at me. "But you know how. Right?"

"Yes," I say.

"Keep working!" Thick Fingers shouts at Dimpled Chin.

I continue. "The boy and his parents filled the jute sacks with dried onions. When the boy and his baba went to sell the onions, they didn't get much money, because everyone had a big crop and there were too many onions at the market. The price of onions fell, and with that, all of the boy's dreams shattered." As I say the last sentence, something soft and sad rises in my throat and I wait for a second to let it pass.

"Then what happened?" Dimpled Chin asks as he beads a red flower.

I tell the rest of the *kahani* about the boy and his family moving to the city, his baba getting lost, and him getting tricked by a stranger. I finish with, "And that is how the boy came to work in the bead place."

When I am done, the circle is quiet.

"It is your very own *kahani, na*?" Rocking Boy whispers.

"Yes, it is. Will you tell us yours?"

"I don't remember much." His voice sounds distant and cold as if the ghost of the Rocking Boy I know uttered those words. "But I do—"

"No more stories," Thick Fingers says. "We have slowed down and that will not do. I don't want to starve."

"Yes, especially for some dumb stories," GC says.

"It is almost eight. Let's eat," Thick Fingers says.

"In peace," GC snorts.

We eat leftover *rotis* without banana or pickles in silence. Then we work and go to bed. When I used to share stories with Naren and Sita or Mohan and Shiva, they listened with such delight! Sometimes Naren used to annoy me with his constant questioning, but he loved my stories and after I told them I felt happy. Tonight, after I shared my story with these boys, there is a tiny hole in my chest where the story used to stay. It hurts. Except for Dimpled Chin none of them deserves my stories and I will never tell them one again.

Instead of wasting my time with these boys, if I work faster and make better frames than the rest of them, Scar might make me the leader. He might ask me to help him pack the frames and then someday, when I get a chance, I can bolt.

fifteen

During the next few days I put all my energy into my work and try to ignore the mosquito bites, Thick Fingers's barks, GC's taunts, Rocking Boy's warnings, Night Chatterer's shyness, Scar's gravelly *dal*, and even Dimpled Chin's smile. I don't have time for anything or anyone.

Slowly, I have worked up a plan that allows me to work faster. Instead of finishing one flower with several colors and then going on to the next thing, I pick up the main bead color in the design and glue it first, then the second color, and then the third. The price I pay for working so speedily is that, when I get done, my neck is boulder-stiff.

One day when Thick Fingers gather up the frames to take downstairs, I am excited because I have two more than anyone else. His eyes narrow. "How did you do so many?" he demands.

I shrug my shoulders. "This was a simple design."

"Doesn't look easy to me," GC says.

Rocking Boy stops rocking and looks at my pile. His lips flutter as he counts the frames I have made and then starts to tap on the side of his desk. Night Chatterer's eyes are wide with surprise or fear—I can't tell.

Scar claps, Thick Fingers hurries down, and I wait anxiously. So far Scar has not noticed how well I have done my work, but maybe today he will be happy since I have finished two more frames. I hear Scar's and Thick Fingers's voices, but I don't know what they are saying.

When Thick Fingers comes up there is a beaming smile on his face and I wonder what he talked to Scar about. He looks at GC and winks. I am so anxious that I perspire more than usual. I have to calm down and wait for Scar to call me. He doesn't— not before lunch, when he calls all of us.

When we go down I am sure Scar will give me more food or ask me how I did extra work, but he doesn't even notice me. Instead he gives Thick Fingers and GC twice the serving he gives the rest of us.

It puzzles me. All afternoon while I work I try to figure out what happened. Scar must know that it was my design, so why wasn't he pleased with me? It must be that Thick Fingers lied, split the credit for my work between GC and himself, and fooled Scar and me. If I tell Scar that

I made those frames, would he believe me?

"What did Boss say when he saw the frames I made?" I ask Thick Fingers that night as we put in the last two hours of work.

He lifts up his eyebrow. "Nothing."

"That can't be true. He must have—"

"Are you calling me a liar? Do you know what happens when you do that?"

"He wants your place and to become the leader. Don't let him," GC says to Thick Fingers.

"I don't want any such thing. I want the credit for the work I did."

"You think that you can stomp your way up by making us look lazy and slow? Stop your demands. Or else I will twist your fingers so bad that you won't be able to work at all," Thick Fingers says.

Dimpled Chin puts his hands on his ears. "Don't fight, please, don't fight."

"Shut up, you little bug!" GC shouts.

Thick Fingers looks at Dimpled Chin. "Nothing is going to happen. Don't cry and whine like you did when you were a baby."

"How do you know what he did when he was a baby?" I ask.

Thick Fingers looks at GC, at me, and then at Dimpled Chin. "I meant all the babies cry. Don't they? And stop bothering me. All of you."

That week when we take a bath Rocking Boy whispers to me, "Please don't work fast, because Boss will expect it all the time, and from all of us. If we can't do it he will beat us up. *Sacch na?*"

"*Sacch*, true," I whisper back.

Dimpled Chin is with us in the bathroom. He shrinks in a corner. "I don't want *kanpatti.*"

I realize how foolish I have been. "But if I slow down now won't Boss be mad at me?"

Rocking Boy stops wiping himself and shakes his head. "No. You never got the credit, so you will never get the blame. *Sacch na?*"

"Yes, yes," Dimpled Chin says in a normal voice as he rinses his shirt. I cover his mouth so Scar doesn't hear.

"Let's get out before Boss yells at us," I say.

I take Rocking Boy's advice and slow down. It gives me a chance to glance at the tree, clouds, sky, and give my neck a break.

When Thick Fingers takes the next batch of frames down he looks at me quizzically. "You did the same number as we did. What happened?"

I shrug my shoulders and don't answer. Scar is downstairs so Thick Fingers can't ask me too many questions.

Soon after Thick Fingers goes down, Scar's raised voice floats up. "No excuses. Work like you did before and get the extra work done."

I hide my smile by bending down on my desk because I know GC is watching me. When Thick Fingers returns his face is grim. I avoid meeting his gaze.

At lunch Scar is in a sour mood because he yells at us to eat as fast as we can and get back up. He gives us all the same amount of food. I look at Rocking Boy triumphantly, but his face is expressionless as if he has no idea what is going on. Maybe that is how he survives—by looking clueless and keeping his mouth shut.

All day I dread the time when Scar leaves because GC and Thick Fingers will be so mad at me. They surprise me by not saying a word, which scares me more because it means they will wait like a patient tiger and strike when the time is right.

After being anxious about GC and Thick Fingers for a few days I stop worrying. On the next bath day Rocking Boy tells me that GC and Thick Fingers always stay together. They never bother Night Chatterer because he cuts their hair and they know how easy it is to "accidentally" hurt them.

"What about you?" I ask.

Rocking Boy dumps a tumbler of water over his head. "I was their favorite *bakra*, goat, until—"

"Until I came."

"No. They stopped before you arrived. One day when

166

they needed glue I mixed it wrong, and so their beads kept coming off. Boss got angry with them and beat them up. From that day on they have stopped bothering me." He looks at Dimpled Chin and adds, *"Sacch na?"*

"Sacch." Dimpled Chin stops wiping his back. "Leader is not mean to me," he adds proudly.

I scrub my toes with a sliver of soap. "Even before I came?"

"Never ever."

"He came a few months ago, but Leader has been nice to him. Maybe because he is so young," Rocking Boy says. He is almost ready and I must hurry up before Scar screams.

"Maybe," I reply, and get ready.

As I work our conversation goes on and on in my head like a merry-go-round at a fair. It seems strange that Thick Fingers treats Dimpled Chin so differently. But I know he does. I have seen it too. I just don't know why.

Like Rocking Boy, I have gotten GC and Thick Fingers in trouble and it seems that just like they left Rocking Boy alone after he made up a bad batch of glue, they have stopped bothering me when I stopped making extra frames and made them look bad. They may stay quiet if I don't do anything else, but if I try to get on Scar's good side they won't tolerate it. I know they won't, because I would be threatening Thick Fingers's position.

Somehow I have to divide GC and Thick Fingers.

Like Aai used to say, it is easy to ride a horse but

impossible to carry one. I know it is true. It is easy to ride this thought of splitting them but I don't know how is it possible.

The rest of the day goes just like other days, but tonight as I lie on the sack I realize it is a full-moon night like the last night at the village. That means I have been here for almost one moon month. How many more moon cycles will I have to endure before I am free?

It would be easier to escape on a night when the moon is bright. Then the silvery light could help. But there is not much moonlight in the city, so maybe it doesn't make any difference if the moon is round, half round, a sliver, or completely invisible. The only important thing is to be out of here.

My fingers hurt, my back is stiff, my knees ache. I need to sleep but the thought of escape doesn't leave me alone.

sixteen

One night I have a brilliant idea. If somehow I can get a piece of paper and pencil, write a note and float it out the window, then someone might read it and rescue me.

I know Scar has a pencil because sometimes he sticks it behind his ear and sometimes he writes down something in his notebook. It will be easy to get a piece of newspaper with white space to write on, but how can I ever steal his pencil? I will just have to be patient and look out for it. If Scar forgets to take it, I must grab it.

Usually, Scar leaves at eight in the evening, but today he pokes his head up around five. "I heard on the TV that a storm is moving up, so I am going to leave now. Make sure you close the shutters before you go to bed. If a single frame gets wet, I'll turn you into *murga*."

I don't know how he can turn us into chickens, but from the faces of other workers, I don't want to find out.

It would be nice to get some rain, because the heat has been building up and up like a roaring fire that someone has kept feeding with dried brush.

In the evening, the dark clouds tumble in from the west. The sky is menacing and reminds me of the day Aai, Naren, Sita, and I ran from under the bridge. It isn't just the curls of thick clouds that scare me. It is the wind. All six of us glance at the window often, and then the sky turns inky dark, and a whip of lightning strikes the sky. The thunder follows with a boom, and it sounds like both our shack and the sky above have crashed.

Thick Fingers closes the shutters and turns on the naked bulb.

Dimpled Chin covers his ears and huddles in a corner. Thick Fingers scoots closer to Dimpled Chin, hugs his knees, and rests his head on them. He can't stop shaking. Night Chatterer's lips are fluttering and his eyes are shut tight. Maybe he is praying. Even GC's gray eyes dart with concern. Only Rocking Boy is rocking and working, rocking and working. Then I realize my nails have dug into my palms.

We can't see out the window, but we can hear the water's force as it drowns the world. Thick Fingers lifts up his head. "Let's go eat early." He has to talk loudly, so his voice doesn't get buried under the storm's noise.

Today, Dimpled Chin is the first one on his feet.

"Where's the ladder?" he yells.

Scar must have put it away. I wonder if he forgot that we hadn't eaten yet and needed to come down. Maybe he didn't care if we ate or not.

Thick Fingers looks down the hole. "What do we do now?"

We are all silent, trying to come up with an answer.

"If two of you hold one end of a jute bag, I can slide down," I say. I twist a sack to form a rope. Thick Fingers and GC hold one end. I slide down and then jump the last few feet to the floor below. The first thing I do is check if Scar has left his pencil, but there is nothing on his wooden bench or underneath it.

"What're you doing? Bring the ladder!" GC shouts.

The ladder looks rickety, but when I try to pick it up it doesn't budge. It is too long, clumsy, and heavy for me to move it alone. "We need two people," I say.

Rocking Boy peeks his head through the opening. "I'll help." A few curls spill over his forehead. He slides down the same way I did. The two of us manage to move the ladder, and the rest of them climb down.

Everyone is talking, but Night Chatterer is silent. All this time I have not heard him say a word except in his sleep. He reminds me of Naren. Shutting up has been Naren's way of dealing with fear ever since he began talking, which was late, when he was about three years old.

My eyes rest on the TV, and suddenly panic grips me.

171

Scar has not unplugged it. I remember Aai telling me that Jama doesn't like to keep the TV plugged in during monsoon, because the roof and walls of the shacks are leaky. It can cause sparks and maybe even fire. It is only a matter of pulling the plug out of the socket, but I know telling Thick Fingers is useless. He will only ask me to do it, so I creep close to it and look around the TV. The floor and the ceiling are dry, but what about outside? What if something that is connected to the TV is soggy? Will pulling the plug give me an electrical shock? Wood doesn't conduct electricity, so I grab the wooden rolling pin from the kitchen and get one end between the two prongs of plug and pull on it. It doesn't move.

"What are you doing?" Thick Fingers asks.

"Trying to pull this plug out."

Before I can try again he is next to me, reaching to stop me. "Don't!" I shout. He stumbles back, knocks me down, and lands on my lap.

He manages to crawl away and I get up.

"Stand away from me," I say. My voice is commanding, and Thick Fingers doesn't argue. I take a deep breath and explain to him the wire might be live. I stick the wooden pin between the prongs again and move it back and forth, loosening the plug. Then I give it a big pull. It comes out.

"Now we don't have to worry about sparks or shocks," I say.

There is a loud crack and a big thud, as if a tree branch

has fallen down. The rain intensifies.

"Thank you, Gopal. Can we eat now?" Dimpled Chin asks me.

I don't answer him. Night Chatterer lifts up his fringy lashes and looks at Dimpled Chin, then at me, and back to Dimpled Chin. Rocking Boy gives me a quick smile. GC rolls his eyes at Thick Fingers. Not only has Dimpled Chin said my name, but he has also asked me if we can eat, instead of asking Thick Fingers.

After a long, awkward silence, Thick Fingers shrugs and turns away. I let out a deep sigh.

Dimpled Chin must have remembered my name when I first mentioned it. He must have been afraid to say it before. He is a smart one, but he shouldn't have insulted Thick Fingers by asking my permission to eat. Now GC will turn and twist things around, make Thick Fingers mad, and get Dimpled Chin and me in trouble.

Scar has left half a loaf of bread for supper. There is a small pan with milk in it that he must have forgotten about. "What if I make some tea for everyone?" I ask Thick Fingers.

"Boss won't be happy."

"The milk will spoil by the morning, so why not use it up?"

"Yes! Why not use it up?" GC mimics me. "Are you ready to take a thrashing and kicking from Boss?"

"We drink, we take the blame, *na*?" Rocking Boy says.

"Are you challenging me?" GC asks.

"I'm just saying that Gopal alone doesn't have to—"

"Why are you speaking against me? Have you forgotten the beating you got? Are you ready for some more?" GC's gray eyes flicker with rage.

Rocking Boy presses his lips tight together as if he is trying to contain his anger.

I don't care if we have tea or not. "Forget it. It is not worth the fight or beating."

Rocking Boy turns to Thick Fingers. "I'm sorry that Gopal found a way for all of us to come down and to unplug the TV. That day when everyone was worried about a rat he checked it out. Next time we're in trouble he won't help you, and I won't either."

Thick Fingers is quiet. GC shoves Rocking Boy against the wall. "You think we need your friend? We were fine before he came, and you behaved better too."

Rocking Boy tries to push back, but GC is bigger. GC takes hold of Rocking Boy's shirt collar, twists it, and pulls on it. If we don't do something quick, GC will choke Rocking Boy.

I throw my arms around GC's neck and pull him off Rocking Boy.

He lets go of the collar, turns around, and slaps me hard across the face and is ready to deliver the next blow when Thick Fingers steps between us.

"No fights. You touch anyone again, I will complain to Boss," Thick Fingers warns GC.

"You won't."

"I can't allow you to attack anyone. You know what will happen if Boss finds out. He will beat me to a pulp. So keep your hands away from others. Understand?" Thick Fingers shakes with anger.

"Traitor!" GC yells.

"I'm not and you know it." Thick Fingers turns to me. "Make the tea. I'm the leader and I say so."

I am not the only one surprised by what Thick Fingers does and says. GC's eyes are on fire. His anger smolders and now there is sourness between the two of them. Thick Fingers is simple, but GC is not. He will find a way to get back at me. I will have to be ready for him.

When the tea is made, we dunk our bread to moisten it, except GC. He eats his dry.

"Wa-wa-water!" Night Chatterer screams in a high-pitched voice, pointing at the back door. This is the first time he has talked. I stare at him and then at the water seeping from under the door. It is creeping into the room slowly, but if the rain continues like this, it could cover the entire floor.

"We should take the boxes of frames up," I say.

"Just because you want to?" GC says, and then turns to Thick Fingers. "Why do you let this know-it-all elbow you around?"

I'm surprised GC is ready to fight again. I guess he

knows that as long as he doesn't touch us he is fine.

Thick Fingers eyes are on the water. He looks confused. "I don't know. No! Yes!"

Is he talking to GC or me?

Night Chatterer is standing on his tiptoes as if that will help him avoid the water. Only half of his shirt is tucked in and he scratches his head. He opens his mouth and I see his perfectly even teeth, as if he has glued each one in its place. Finally he utters, "If-if the frames are ruined, Bo-boss will beat us up."

It is clear that he is terrified of Scar's punishment because I haven't seen such dread and fear on his face before. No wonder he stays absolutely silent. He doesn't want to get in any trouble and risk Scar's wrath.

I want to kick Thick Fingers and the others into action, but the friction between us is as brittle as a dry twig. I watch with everyone else as more water seeps in.

"Time to take the boxes up," GC says.

"It was Gopal's idea." Rocking Boy is again full of courage.

GC's face twists in disgust. "So?"

"So don't be the boss of us," Dimpled Chin cries.

GC grabs Dimpled Chin's hand. "Do you want your ears, nose, and arms twisted?"

Thick Fingers swiftly pulls GC away. "No touching."

Wah! Thick Fingers had warned GC before not to touch anyone, but I didn't realize Thick Fingers would move so quickly. He didn't do that when GC grabbed

Rocking Boy, so why is he so protective of Dimpled Chin? Maybe he knows that if he doesn't stop this right away we might end up with a big fight. And if anyone gets hurt, Boss will punish Thick Fingers.

While Dimpled Chin and GC sulk in opposite corners, Thick Fingers, Rocking Boy, Night Chatterer, and I move the boxes close to the ladder. There are four filled with beaded frames and six filled with plain frames. They're heavy. "How are we going to take them up?" Thick Fingers wonders.

When Baba worked in the quarry, he used to tell us that when the load was extra heavy, they stood in line and passed the stuff so each one had to carry it for just a short time. "If we stand on the ladder and pass the boxes up, we can do it. Each one of us will only be holding the box for a few seconds."

"You always have good ideas," Thick Fingers compliments me.

"Let's see how well this idea works," GC barks.

Thick Fingers is the biggest, so he stays at the bottom. I stand on the second step of the ladder. He lifts the box and hands it to me. I give it to Rocking Boy, who is two steps above me, and he passes it to Night Chatterer. Dimpled Chin is on the top floor, and when Night Chatterer puts the box down, Dimpled Chin slides them on one side. GC doesn't help.

Once we move the boxes, we go back up.

We work for about half an hour before *kadaak, kada-dad bhoom*. Thunder booms almost on top of a lightning strike, and with that, the yellow naked bulb blows out. It is ink dark in the room. Dimpled Chin screams. "We're all here. Together," Thick Fingers says.

No one says a word after that. I hope, once my eyes get adjusted, I'll be able to see, but it doesn't happen. It is not just our bulb that has gone out, but the whole area is without power, and there is no moonlight. Darkness drowns us.

I finger my flashlight and wonder if I should bring it out. Maybe I can trust Thick Fingers, but I'm not sure about GC. He might tell Scar about the flashlight, and then he'd take it away from me. It is not worth the risk. Let us all wait out the night in dark.

Someone starts crying. First softly, but then it turns into piercing, wailing sobs.

"Who is it?" Thick Fingers asks.

"Not me," Dimpled Chin says.

"I know it is not you. I want to know who is crying."

There is no reply except more sobs.

"What difference does it make? We don't know each other's names," I say.

"We know your name, Gopal," Dimpled Chin says.

"Who is crying like a *ladki*?" GC mutters, as if only girls are afraid of the dark. Naren has always been scared of the dark, but not Sita.

"It-it-it is me. Roshan. I-I-I can't breathe," Night

Chatterer—Roshan—whispers. His voice is shaky.

"If you don't stop, I am going to complain to Boss. He will give you such stiff punishment that you will forget you were ever afraid of the dark!" GC yells.

"No need to bully just because—" Thick Fingers's voice quivers.

"Are you afraid of it, too?" GC challenges.

This is worse than Naren and Sita bickering. At least I could yell and shut them up. I whip out my flashlight. As soon as I flick it on, there is light and quiet.

It is Dimpled Chin who breaks the silence. "Where did you get that?"

"A friend gave it to me."

"What's his name?"

"Chachaji," I say.

"Your uncle?"

"No."

"What is his real name?"

Jama never mentioned Chachaji's name. "I don't know."

"I bet you stole it," GC says.

I want to scream, "I didn't!" But that will only fuel his ire.

"See what I told you! He is quiet, which means he is guilty."

I point the beam at GC's face. His smile collapses.

"Gopal didn't steal the flashlight," Rocking Boy says.

Before I can say a word, GC threatens him. "*Aie* Gopal's *chamcha*, I'm going to fix you so well that your ribs will poke out even more than they do."

Thick Fingers is quiet. I guess he doesn't care as long as GC spews out verbal threats and doesn't touch anyone. I point the beam at Thick Fingers. He shields his eyes with his squat, square palm.

"We-we-we can't work, but that doesn't mean we have to ar-ar-argue and fight," Roshan says. He has stopped crying. No one responds.

There's no light, so we can't work. This is the perfect time to share stories, but how could I after what happened last time I told them my *kahani*?

I let the storm and the darkness continue outside and stretch inside.

seventeen

Night Chatterer cries and whines in his sleep. Clearly, he is afraid and upset. Only after he calms down do I drift to sleep, where past and present begin to blur.

Water has seeped into Jama's house. Naren and Sita bend to examine it, as if they have never seen water before. Aai puts our clothes on the shelf above the TV.

The water keeps on coming. In the beginning, Naren and Sita dip their toes in it and laugh. Aai hands them tea and a day-old *roti*. They have to eat standing up because the floor is wet.

While they're eating, Aai and I get busy. With small bowls, we scoop the water and dump it in the pail. When the pail is full, I open the window and Aai lifts the pail up and dumps it out. Then I quickly shut the window. Still, there is the same amount of water on the floor as before.

I don't know how many pails of water we dump out before Aai throws her hands up in the air. "This is not going to help."

"Look down. The water is past my ankles." Naren lifts up his left foot and wiggles it all around. Water splashes in front of him.

"Don't do that," Sita says. "I wish there were a hill we could climb." Her voice is pitched high with fear.

I want to tell her that there's nowhere to go, but she knows that. There are no trees or hills to climb.

Sita is done with her food, so I lift her up and put her on the stack of mattresses and pillows piled up on the wooden bench. I do the same with Naren. They dangle their feet, and Aai wipes them off with a rag.

"What if the rain comes up as high as these mattresses?" Sita asks.

I shake my head. "It won't."

"How do you know?"

"You know how much it has to rain for water to come so far?"

"A lot?"

"That's right. So play up there."

I hand them the cards Card-Man had given us, and both of them scoot toward the wall, fold their legs, and divide up the cards.

Aai and I fill the pail. When I open the window to dump water, I step back. Eerie quietness greets me and bright light floods the room. "The rain, Aai, it is gone."

She glances at the twins, who are busy playing, and then moves close to me. I make room for her at the window. Her eyes are moist with tears, but before I say a word, she puts a finger to her lips and whispers, "Let's not upset them."

She means Naren and Sita. No one is out in the street, which doesn't look like a street anymore. The water is still high, maybe up to my knees if I were to walk out. I watch as it swirls around our window and I see an aluminum pan bobbing in it.

"Should I get it, Aai?"

"No. It's too dangerous." We both stare at the perfectly nice pan we can't rescue.

The water has stopped coming in and we're safe for now.

A comb, a pencil, and a pair of underwear float by. I'm tempted to call Naren and Sita to watch, but then they would want to go treasure hunting, and the water is still too high. They could drown in it. The thought sends a shiver through my body.

"Are you cold?" Aai asks.

I wake up still shaking.

Aai's soft voice fades as the room comes into focus. The scratchy feel of jute on my back, the smell of glue, the bumpy new mosquito bites are what I have. I close my eyes to see if I can crawl back to my dream and touch Aai's face.

She is gone.

I want to be with her. But I haven't figured out how to get out of here. Even when things look impossible, there has to be a way. Will I find something? Or will I be like a goat that circles the yard looking for a small hole in the fence to escape but never finds it?

eighteen

I lie awake thinking about Jama's street, the bridge, and Chachaji's shop until I hear the clock strike six times. Thick Fingers opens the shutters. One of the *nimba* branches is broken and it brings tears to my eyes. On top of everything, it is a dull, gray day—a day without personality, so morning, afternoon, and evening look the same. We quickly use the bathroom, drink water, and start work.

Three hours later, Scar is still missing. It is hard to keep on working without any tea, but this place gives us no choice, because if we don't do the work, we won't get any lunch.

By the time I hear the jingling of keys I have finished four frames. The door slams open. As soon as Scar steps in, he screams, "I'm ruined! I'm ruined!"

Then there is a silence for a few seconds before he thumps up the ladder.

"What did you do with the boxes? Because if a single frame is damaged I am going to kill you." He pounds his fist on the wall and glares at all of us.

"We moved them up here," Thick Fingers replies.

Scar's face relaxes. He looks around. "Good job. How did you do it?" he asks, walking toward the boxes.

Thick Fingers glances at GC. GC stares back as if to dare him to say that GC didn't lift a finger. "Everyone helped," Thick Fingers says.

GC smirks. "It was my idea," he adds.

"You're a smart boy. You will go far." Scar thumps GC's back a little too hard because GC flinches.

Rocking Boy stops rocking and looks at Scar. "It wasn't—" he begins to say, but Scar doesn't hear him and climbs down the ladder.

Tarrer, tarrer, tarrer, finally Scar winds up the clock.

"Say a word and I will turn you to ashes," GC says. His words and steely gray stare deliver a threat right down to my bones.

I think Thick Fingers is worried about GC's temper and knows he can hurt one of us badly. Maybe that is why Thick Fingers doesn't speak up against GC.

Now Scar believes GC saved the boxes and maybe he will make him a leader. I can't let that happen. As scared as I am, I must tell Scar that it was my idea. If I do that he will trust me and ask me to help him pack the frames. That is one way to get a little more freedom. And the more freedom I have, the greater the chance I will have to escape.

I chew my lip, wondering if I really want to talk to Scar.

We wait for Scar to call us for tea. The clap never comes. I guess he figured as long as we are working fine without it, why bother?

At lunchtime, when GC is in the bathroom, I tell Scar, "I was the one who came up with the idea of moving the boxes."

He is sitting on the floor tying a string around a box. "And you want me to believe it, you stupid cockroach?"

I saved your frames and you call me a cockroach! I want to snap. "It is the truth. Ask any of them," I say, pointing to the rest of the group.

He stands up. "Here is the thing, boys. One of them is a liar. Who is it? If you don't know, stay quiet. But if you answer, make sure you don't make a mistake. If you do, you will pay a big price."

There is a smug smile on his face as if he is enjoying this game. He folds his hands over his chest, look around, and asks again, "Tell me, who should I believe?"

I wait. The four of them stare at their feet and don't speak up. It is as if they have lost their tongues. Scar goes to each one of them and asks again. Night Chatterer shakes his head. Thick Fingers does the same. Dimpled Chin looks up once but quickly drops his gaze back down. I guess he is afraid of his ears getting twisted again. Finally, Rocking Boy mumbles, "He is right."

"Have you sprouted warts on your tongue? Louder!" Scar yells.

Rocking Boy points at me. "He is telling the truth."

GC comes out of the bathroom.

"All of you go back except you two," Scar says pointing at Rocking Boy and me. "You will both stand at *murga*, chicken, for an hour as your punishment for lying."

"We told the truth," I say. GC is climbing up, so I don't see his expression. I am sure he is happy that Rocking Boy and I are punished.

Scar whips out a long, brown, rubber tube. "See this tube? She'll straighten you out."

Rocking Boy bends down, passes his arms between his legs, and grabs his ankles with his hands. It must be the way to become *murga*, so that is what I do too. My back is already sore from leaning over and working, but now it hurts even more. Scar raises the tube and it comes down on Rocking Boy's back, *satak*!

He flinches and his lips quiver, but Rocking Boy doesn't whimper.

Satak, it comes down again. I cry out in pain.

"Just checking how well it works." Scar puts the tube back on the wooden bench.

We have to stand like this for an hour. Time passes

slowly with my mind blank of thoughts and filled with pain. Slowly, the bowl of rice and *dal* I ate for lunch creeps back up to my throat. It tastes sour. I look sideways. Rocking Boy's eyes are closed and his face is scrunched up in pain. I am mad at Scar for punishing us, but madder at GC for being a lying rat.

My mind is no longer blank. It moves from one thought to another like a monkey moving from branch to branch.

Scar was quick to hand us punishment without finding out what really happened. GC has been with him longer and Scar must trust him a lot more than he trusts me. But his smug smile hid something. I think he knew I was telling the truth but he wanted to challenge the others. Did he want to see if anyone dared to take my side?

My plan didn't work and now that dishonest and shifty GC will be Scar's *chamcha*. GC will get me and the others in trouble, and Scar will kick, slap, beat, and starve us. GC and Scar will be two boulders squeezing us between them. We will be crushed to pieces.

The thought about being crushed sharpens my pain. If I stand too long like this my back will break. A fly lands on my face. I shake my head to shoo it.

"Why are you shaking your head?" Scar asks. I don't know why his face has an anxious look.

"Just getting rid of the fly."

"Oh!" He looks relieved. He goes back to wrapping the frames.

Scar turns the TV on. I lift my head to try to watch, too. It is no easy task when your whole body is doubled over, but I curve my upper back and neck up as far as I can.

It takes Scar a few seconds to realize what I am doing. "Don't stare like that."

Scar and I wait for the TV to come on, but nothing happens. Then I remember I unplugged it last night. When Scar sees the dangling plug, he is puzzled. He glances at me. "What? How did it come undone?"

I lower my head. Is Scar confused about how the TV came unplugged? Does he think my stare has something to do with it? When Scar gave me some stuffed onion and garlic bread, he had the same fearful look on his face. He didn't share his food with me out of generosity, but because he was afraid I had cursed his food and made it drop from his hand. Maybe he thinks my evil look has magically unplugged the cord. If he is that superstitious, I must make him think I have some kind of strange power.

I lift my face up to look at Scar again.

"What . . . why do you keep doing that?" he asks. His voice trembles.

I keep my gaze on him and move my lips as if I am whispering something. His face sags in fear. I don't blink and move my lips faster. "Are you casting spells on me?" he asks.

It is not a question I need to answer.

"Stop it! Go up, right now."

I straighten up. "Us?"

"No. Just you alone."

Inside I'm melting with fear, but I think of the story of Annasaheb Kotwal from Matheran to give me strength. "Can't do that." I fold my arms in front of my chest and flutter my lips.

"Go. Both of you. Now."

Rocking Boy's eyes are open, but I don't think he knows what has happened.

"It was my idea to save the frames by moving the boxes," I say.

Scar looks from me to the TV and back. He is still puzzled.

I smile as I turn to go up.

Our punishment lasted less than an hour, so when we go up I expect GC to smolder with anger. He gray eyes flicker with surprise, but he doesn't look mad.

Dimpled Chin's face is radiant with happiness. "I knew you'd be back soon."

Even though he didn't take my side, I forgive Dimpled Chin. He is so young, and Scar is so big and scary. Dimpled Chin must be terrified of Scar more than I am. I ruffle his hair as I sit down. Night Chatterer—I mean Roshan—doesn't look up. I wish he and Thick Fingers had said the truth like Rocking Boy did. Then Scar would have had no choice but to believe them. In this place I feel like I have one true friend, Rocking Boy. He

191

has already started working and rocking as if nothing has happened.

GC or Scar can never break Rocking Boy. Or maybe he is so crushed that there is nothing more they can do to hurt him.

The rest of the day, we all work in total silence, but tension has seeped in.

nineteen

It is hard to believe three more weeks have gone by since the big storm and I am still here. Every morning I wake up with a flame of hope that I will run away today. It burns all day and every evening when Scar locks the door, it dies. After we saved the frames, Scar doesn't move the ladder away at night anymore. I wish I had the power to click open the lock and escape.

No such luck.

Somehow I must make my luck with the help of the other boys, but GC is the one I can't trust. He will not let the others come together. And if I try, will he get me in trouble like he did before? He might. Still, I must take a chance because if I don't, I have nothing else.

At ten o'clock, we put away the beads. Roshan flattens out wrinkles from his bed. His jaw is clenched tight and he is smoothing the sack over and over with his palms to get rid of the smallest creases, but the jute is so itchy, I don't know how it can make any difference.

I thought Night Chatterer would be one of the last ones to reveal his name because he hardly speaks. It is strange; I knew his name before anyone else's. I guess he was so scared that night when GC asked who was crying that Roshan blurted out his name. If I want the group's help I must know their names and make them my friends.

"What's your name?" I ask Rocking Boy.

He clutches his sack close to his chest, darts a look at GC, and hesitates.

I put my hand on his shoulder. "I want to call you by your real name. That is who you really are."

He stares at his feet for a second. "My name is Sahil," he says as he looks up. "Someone told me it means leader."

"You? A leader?" GC snorts. "That's an *oulta*, upside-down, name for you."

"Leave him alone," Thick Fingers says.

Slowly Thick Fingers seems to be standing up against GC. "I like it better than Rocking Boy," I say.

"Sahil is a nice name," Dimpled Chin agrees. "I am Amar, but no one has called me Amar for a long time."

I glance at Thick Fingers. He is quiet as if nothing is happening around him. As long as he doesn't ask me to stop I must keep on going. "Amar means everlasting, forever."

"Really, Gopal? I never knew that Amar meant something. I want everyone to call me Amar." His voice drops to a whisper. "But Boss will be mad if he hears it."

"We never talk when Boss is around," I remind him.

"You're right. May I please tell Amar's story?"

"A made-up one or the real one?" GC asks.

If GC doesn't want to be part of the story circle he should stay quiet, but it is clear that he is listening.

Amar begins. "My baba said I was a naughty boy, and that is why he hit me so I would behave better. It only happened when he came home smelling bad and said bad words. He slept until the sun was way up in the sky."

"Where was your mother?" Sahil asks.

"My mother died when I was three. I had a stepmother who was busy with my younger brothers and sisters, and they always behaved well. That is what my stepmother told my father. Even when I was good, I was bad. I was always bad." His voice shrinks to a whisper.

"You were good," Thick Fingers says.

GC stops spreading his sack. "How do you know?"

"I, I mean, we don't know that for sure, but how can he be bad? I mean, don't you think he was too young to know what *bad* meant?"

GC waves his hand. "*Accha, accha.* I don't have time for this babbling explanation."

By now we are all ready to sleep.

"We haven't had a *kahani* for a long time." Amar turns to me and adds, "Gopal, can we have one tonight? It will make me happy."

I want to pick him up, give him a great big twirl like I used to give Naren, and say yes. GC folds his hands across the chest and stares at me. The tension between us is as sharp as a pointy pencil, and I don't want to say yes to Amar before asking Thick Fingers. Besides, GC might complain about it to Scar. I shake my head.

"Why not? I like the one you told us before. I want to hear it again. Please?"

I glance at Thick Fingers and he turns away.

Amar draws up his knees, hugs his legs, and rests his head on his knees. I can't see his face but with his slumped shoulder he looks so sad. I sit down next to him. Amar raises his head. His eyes are teary and his face is hopeful.

"Don't cry, Amar. I will tell a story," I say. I don't care if ten GCs go against me and complain to Scar.

"We can't have light. I don't want Boss to have a bigger electricity bill and find out we stayed up late. He will make us work more hours," Thick Fingers says. So we turn the naked bulb off and form a circle. The only person who hasn't joined the circle is GC. He is stretched out on his sack.

Before I begin the story, I take out the flashlight, turn it on, and set it in the middle. "Summer vacation was my favorite time because I got to spend the days in Matheran."

"Telling everyone he spent summers on a hill station to get away from the heat as if he were one of the Khans! Total liar," GC snorts.

I ignore him and continue. "Every morning, I would wake up at four, and by four thirty Aai and I would begin climbing the hill to Matheran. My friends Mohan and Shiva and their mothers also came, so it was fun. Matheran means "forest on the top," and the place was filled with trees, birds, monkeys, snakes, and other animals. It was a long hike, and it took us almost two hours to climb the mountain, but we got there before the morning train arrived, bringing people from Mumbai. The best part was that when we started out, stars twinkled in the sky and the moon shone like a plumeria blossom. But by the time we got to the top, the moon and stars had disappeared, and the sky was as pink as *gorus-chinch* as the sun peeked from behind the hills."

"O-o-oh, so beautiful." Roshan sighs.

"Shhhh, don't disturb him, *yaar*," Amar says.

"When the train arrived, we would carry the tourists' luggage to fancy hotels like the Richie Rich Resort and the Verandah in the Forest. After that, we hung out by the car-and-taxi parking lot because the train only came at certain times and brought tourists all at once, but the cars and taxis came all day long, and we were able to find work."

"With all the money you got paid, you must have been rich, Gopal. Are you hiding your money in a pocket like your flashlight?" GC jeers.

"No. Whatever I earned I gave to Aai and Baba because they needed it."

"You were a good son," Thick Fingers says.

I am so surprised by Thick Fingers's comment that I forget what I am saying.

"Ye-ye-yes," Roshan agrees.

"Are you listening?" I ask Sahil, throwing the beam at him and to gather my thoughts. He nods. "In the afternoon, Mohan, Shiva, and I would go to Lake Charlotte and have our lunch under a *nimba* tree on a hot afternoon. If the day was cool, we would walk out on one of the rock outcrops and sit in the sun. The manmade lake and the god-made hills belonged together, and we never got tired of either one of them. Many tourists traveled by horse, and one of the horse owners was from our village. He would let us ride his horses when there were no customers."

"What color were the horses?" Amar asks.

"They were green like parrots." GC laughs at his own joke. The rest of them are silent, as if a rude student has disturbed the teacher when he was talking about something interesting and important. I wish GC would just sit in his corner and keep his mouth shut. He enjoys interrupting us, especially me, and if he knows I am irritated he will keep on doing it. Like Aai used to say, "Why give a monkey a ladder?"

Her round face comes to mind and I want to give her a hug and take in the smell of her clean sari. I am glad the yellow naked bulb is off. In the light of the flashlight, no one can see my face. I wait for the sadness to pass away.

The rest of the group waits patiently. "One horse was cinnamon and the other was black. My favorite was Prince. His coat was shiny black with a tear-shaped white mark between his eyes, and I could feel he liked me, because when I got close to him, he moved his head forward as if to greet me."

"Why do you all listen to this nonsense and lies?" GC asks.

"We-we listen be-be-because the lies are better th-than the truth we have. If-if you have better lies, then we will li-li-listen to you. Un-un-until then, just be quiet." Roshan stutters like he did in his sleep. But his voice is sharp, as if it has been whittled down by anger. Even GC must feel it, because he doesn't argue.

"So you like the black horse and he liked you, *na*?" Sahil asks. He is enjoying the story. It makes me smile.

"The black horse was gentle and sunny most of the time, but when he was upset he turned dark and threatening. One day when I rode him, a loud noise startled him and he took off. It was a foggy day and I was certain that Prince would run off one of the cliffs and we would plunge into the valley. My heart pounded faster than his gallops."

Amar leans forward, resting his chin on his clasped hands. "Did he?"

"Then he wouldn't be telling us this tale," GC says.

"I tried to slow him down, and when he finally calmed down, I whispered in his ears that I still loved him even though he had scared me. After that day, he was always gentle with me. When I rode him, the breeze brushed my hair, the red dust sprayed about, and the hills surrounded me. It made me feel like I could do anything. I dreamed that someday I would have a horse just like him." I close my eyes and see Prince prancing in front of me, and I can hear his whinny.

"Do you still dream that?" I don't even know who asks, but it brings me back to our circle.

"I do. Someday I want to get a horse like Prince."

GC gets up and stands in the middle of the circle facing me. "How can you own a horse? You are sitting in this prison working away like a slave and dreaming like a prince. And you like a horse named Prince. Ha, ha, ha! Your dreams are nothing but dust under the horse's hooves."

"I never dreamed I would end up here, but I did. Who knows what tomorrow might bring?"

"Tomorrow is going to be same as today—full of glue, beads, and frames."

"Still, it is better to have dreams, because then someday they can come true. But if you don't have them, then you have nothing. So tell me. Is it better to have nothing or have something?" I ask.

"I don't know. I never had anything," GC mumbles.

"What do you mean? Tell us about your family."

GC thumps his foot. "I don't have a family and you don't either, Gopal. Stop talking about Aai and Baba.

You never had them or a village or friends. You've never even seen a horse. You tell all these stories to make yourself feel better and make us feel bad. Isn't that right?" GC picks up my flashlight. "Tell me these are all lies or else I will smash your flashlight against the wall."

I reach to snatch the flashlight from his hand, but GC is taller than I am and he stretches his hand above his head. The beam that was steady on the ceiling is shaky. Before I know it, someone grabs the flashlight and hands it to me. It must be Thick Fingers, because he is the only one as tall as GC and he doesn't want any trouble.

It is time to go to bed.

What GC said tonight makes me sad and mad, all mixed together like swirls of marble. It is sad that for GC this is home, and as bad as Scar is, GC wants only to please him. I am mad because GC tells me that I am making up stories and I don't have a family.

If it weren't for GC we would be a story circle.

twenty

Because GC and I fought, again there are no more stories. Every night, Amar wiggles his loose tooth and he has this pleading look in his eyes, and I can tell he wants to listen to *kahanis*, but there is nothing I can do. Except for GC, everyone enjoys the story circle. I think even Thick Fingers misses it, but he won't say so as long as GC is against it. I wish our leader had the courage to stand up to GC.

One day, Scar calls GC down to pack the frames. It is the first time Scar has asked for GC's help since I came here. Does this mean he is now in charge? Has GC told one of our secrets to Scar? I am not sure.

The elongated *nimba* fruits have turned yellow. Now that GC is gone, it is time to pick them. I get up, stick my hands through the bars, and pluck as many as I can reach.

"These are bittersweet. Who wants them?" I whisper.

All of them do, so I pass them on. With the bars on the window I can't reach too far, but still we each have a handful.

"Eat quickly," Thick Fingers whispers to Amar.

"I can't chew any faster, because they're bitter. They make my mouth slow down."

We all smile at his excuse.

"I know, Amar," I say, "but my aai says that *nimba* is good for you. It will keep us healthy."

"Your aai knows a lot of stuff. Can you tell us one of her stories again? Please?"

"GC doesn't like them."

"Who is GC?" Thick Fingers asks. He was not here when I had asked GC his name and he had refused to tell me.

"The one who went downstairs is Gray Cloud," Amar says. "Right?"

"Yes."

"Bu-bu-but except for GC we all like *kahanis*," Roshan says.

"Yes, but—" Thick Fingers starts to say.

"Let's take a vote," I suggest quickly.

Sahil has stopped rocking and working. "What is a vote?"

He listens intently as I answer. "It is when we ask everyone what they want to do. Then we do what most of us agree on. If GC is the leader he may not allow us, but if you don't shout your wares, you can't sell. We must at least try."

"Just because Boss asked GC to help him today doesn't mean he is the leader," Thick Fingers says.

I bite my lip. It was a mistake to say GC is the leader. "I am sorry," I quickly say to Thick Fingers.

"Let's vote tonight," Amar says. He smiles so broadly that I see another dimple on his right cheek. How could I not have noticed it before?

Thick Fingers gives him a stern look. "It is like ganging up on GC. I don't like it."

I remember how he and GC were so mean to me when I came. This is not the time to remind him of it, though. "Maybe GC will go along with it and we won't have to worry about taking votes," I say.

After our whispered talk, Amar can hardly sit still. He still fidgets when GC gets back. GC tells him to calm down, but every time my eyes meet Amar's, he smirks like he is going to a fair.

"Are we going to have a *kahani* tonight?" Amar asks when we spread open our sacks.

I wait for GC to oppose, but he ignores us.

"Roshan, can you tell us a story?" I ask.

"I-I-I don't have stories and I can never ma-make them up. If-if I could, I would tell you that I rode on an ele-ele-elephant every day." Roshan laughs, but his voice is empty and hollow, like a carved-out pumpkin.

"It doesn't matter. Tell us your story," Thick Fingers says.

Roshan takes a few deep breaths. It seems to help him because when he speaks he doesn't stutter much. "I have eight brothers and sisters and I stood third. My pa-pa-parents had little money, but we lived at the edge of a forest and it gave us many things we needed.

"B-b-by the time I was six, I would go to the forest with my sisters. W-we got fruits, firewood, and even medicine from there. M-m-my favorite job was to gather wild acacia fruit when it turned golden yellow and slightly sweet. It was a short walk or so from our home, but once I got there, I could eat as many as I wanted. When I was full, I filled my po-po-pockets to bring them home for my younger brothers and sisters."

This story reminds me of Mohan, Shiva, and me picking *bor* fruits.

"Wh-when it was hot, my sisters would cover their heads with scarves. If there was no shade, they would cover me with one too. Once we got to the acacias, the sh-sh-shade cooled us. Sometimes, I fell asleep under a tree."

"With a hundred fans above," Sahil whispers. His head full of curls seems to throw a halo around him.

GC laughs. "*Bakvas bandh kero!* Stop blabbering, Sahil and Roshan!"

"I'm n-n-not. I used to go with my sisters to gather the wild acacia pods." Roshan's voice is firm, as if he is not going to allow GC to snatch the memory from his heart.

"I don't like acacias. They are covered with thorns."

To argue with GC is to argue with one of the monkeys in Matheran. When you win, you realize you have turned into a monkey. I ask Roshan, "How did you end up here?"

He takes time before he answers. "I-I was about eight years old when they cut many tre-trees to built a road through the forest. Then shops, buildings, and houses replaced all the trees. They sold food in the market, but us fo-fo-forest people had no money. One day some people came to us with a me-me-megaphone and ann-ann-announced that they would find us jobs in the big city that would pay well. My-my baba asked them how much I would make and they said, 'Yo-yo-your son will make enough to feed your family and he will attend school and have a city ad-adventure.'"

"But you don't make any money, you don't go to school, and you are not having a city adventure," Thick Fingers says. "None of us are."

"Scar sends the mo-mo-money I earn to my family."

"That's a lie that doesn't cost Boss anything," GC says.

"Wh-what do you mean?"

"After all the expense for keeping you and feeding you, do you think there is any money left to send to your parents?"

I know GC is right. Scar had told me I'd make as much money as the other boys. Like the others, he hasn't paid me a single rupee.

Roshan sighs. "May-maybe Boss keeps all the money, but at that time the people who brought me to the city gave my baba some money and said they would send more later. Th-they took me and some other boys in a truck with them, and after a few days I ended up in a place where they made clo-clothes."

"You can sew?" Thick Fingers asks.

"We-we only stitched buttons, hun-hundreds of them. One day, the owner got the news that the police were going to raid the place and so he tran-tran-transferred us right away. There were five of us, but I don't know where everyone went. All I know is, I ended up here."

"You miss them, *na*?" Sahil asks.

"I don-don-don't. I never became their friend."

Amar scoots closer to Roshan. "But you are our friend, right?"

We all wait for Roshan to answer. "Yes, I am your friend." I am amazed he doesn't stutter at all.

"You're not my friend," GC says.

"But I am yours."

"Why?"

"It is b-b-better than having you as an enemy."

"So you are afraid of me then."

I know why GC challenges everything and everyone. It gives him a feeling of power. Which means he wants real power, and he might get us in trouble so he can please Scar. I want to throw the flashlight's beam on his face and ask him to shut up, but I have to control myself. "I am not scared of you. You are one of us." Roshan speaks slowly and clearly.

"How can I be? I am not part of your circle."

"You are. You listen to our *kahanis*," Sahil says.

"No I don't."

"You argue and challenge them, *na?*"

"When you tell stories I can't shut off my ears or walk out of here, can I?"

It is my chance to speak up. "Is it so bad to share stories? We live, work, and eat together, so why not share our *kahanis?*"

"I want to keep my stories to myself. I don't want someone telling them to Boss."

"I will never do that, *yaar*," Amar says.

"You are too young to know what is good for you. Stay out of it or you will get in trouble with Boss," GC says.

"If you complain against Amar or any of us to Boss, he might give you a little more tea or a spoonful of rice, but that is all. Tomorrow he might favor someone else, turn against you, and starve you," I say.

"We must stick together," Sahil says.

He doesn't ask if he is right by asking, *sacch na?* at the end.

Silence follows Sahil's words until Amar breaks it. "We are like a family. Will you tell us more about your brothers and sisters, Roshan?" Amar reminds me of Naren, innocent and trusting. It is nice that he asks Roshan to continue, because it takes away the tension.

"I don't re-re-remember much about my two sisters except what I told you. By the time I got a little older, th-th-they were already working on a farm and left before the sun came out. They didn't get back until after dark. My younger br-brother couldn't walk properly, so he stayed close to my aai, and the other two were too young for me to know."

"But you said there were eight of you. This only makes six," I say.

"You are so good at counting," Amar says. "If some-day I make a lot of money, I will give it to you to count."

"You won't make any money. Not now, not ever. None of us will," GC mumbles under his breath. I am glad Amar has not heard him.

"M-m-my two brothers di . . . di . . . died before they were one year old. I-I-I don't remember much about them," Roshan says.

"*Yaar*, how can you not rem—"

"St-sto-sto-stop calling me *yaar*, Amar, and st-st-stop bothering me!" Roshan shouts. "I am not yo-yo-your . . ." He breaks down crying.

"No more stories," GC declares. "Stories are rubbish and a waste of time. We were fine without them before. If you don't stop I'll tell Boss that Gopal has a flashlight and all of you stay up late every night sharing *kahanis*."

"If you tell our secret, we will . . ." Sahil can't come up with anything. Amar covers his face with his hands.

Quick, think of something to argue about, I urge myself.

"So no stories, right?" GC's voice swells with pride and triumph.

"No more bickering. Let's go to sleep," Thick Fingers says.

I pick up the flashlight and flick it off. The story circle is done. When we stretch out on our sacks and everyone is done shuffling their arms and legs, Roshan's soft cry goes on. The moonlight filters between the window bars and in its light I see Amar stroking Roshan's hair.

"My aai used to rub oil in my hair," Sahil whispers. "Except I didn't call her Aai."

This is the first time Sahil has talked about his mother. If I know what he called his mother I might be able to tell where he is from. "What did you call her?" I whisper back to him.

"*Maa*. I loved going with her to our shop because it smelled of hot chili and turmeric."

Not only is Sahil remembering his mother, but he is also telling me about their shop. It seems like his family was not poor like mine. "When was that?" As I wait for his answer my heart flutters like the wings of a swift ready to take off from a cliff.

"When I was younger than Amar." There is silence for a minute and then, "She had a long braid that was thick and dark. Darker than mine because I used to put the end of her braid on my head and say, 'Maa, look how black your hair is.'"

I touch his hand. "What about your baba?" I ask.

He shakes his head and turns away from me.

I should've listened patiently and not asked about his baba. When I close my eyes I imagine Sahil as a five-year-old boy tugging his maa's braid and putting it on top of his curls. How did Sahil get here? Where is his family? Sahil is breathing heavily. Now that he talked about his past, maybe he will dream about his home and his mother, and again he might share a little more of his story.

We must stick together. We are like a family. Sahil's and Amar's words swirl in my head. We stay together and we are connected, not only by our work and our imprisonment in this place, but also by our stories and our feelings. If we can comfort one another, we can be a family. But GC has threatened us in such a way that I wonder if we would ever be able to share stories again.

I turn on my left side, away from Sahil, and squeeze my eyes shut tight to imagine Aai's round face. It is hard to bring her into focus. Tears roll from my right eye, trickle down from the bridge of my nose, and mix with tears from my left eye.

It is difficult to muffle my sobs, but I don't want GC to hear. I shove the end of my jute sack in my mouth and let the raw, itchy fabric dull the sound. But I can't do anything for my heart that aches like it has been twisted into *murga* position. Forever.

Before I know it, I am walking to the pond behind Mohan and Shiva. It is the middle of monsoon and everything has turned parrot green. The scent of earth is strong. I try to touch my friends, but my hands are bound by something invisible. I try to speak to them and the words stick in my throat. My legs move, but they don't take me closer to them. Something is wrong. I can't touch what I want, say what I want, and move where I want. I have lost the will to act the way I want to.

Mohan and Shiva disappear, and in their places are Thick Fingers, Amar, Sahil, Roshan, and GC talking among themselves as if I am not there. Don't they care? I kick my arms and legs and gather all my energy, and force my voice to come out.

My scream wakes me up.

twenty-one

In the daylight I stare at the *nimba* trunk with a gash where the big branch broke off many weeks ago. It has left a hole in the tree. I have a same kind of wound in my heart since I got separated from my family.

Scar comes early and doesn't leave until after the clock strikes eight so he can supervise us. The export-quality work order must be very important. One muggy day, when he pokes his head in to see if we are doing a good job, he has to keep swatting at the mosquitoes that buzz around him. He spreads his arms wide, "We have another big order." Sweat beads form on his temples and balding head. A small pencil is stuck behind his ear. I imagine reaching out and grabbing it.

We all look at him blankly.

"How come there are more mosquitoes here than

downstairs?" he demands, as if we invited them to come and suck our blood.

The mosquitoes have been bad for so long that we have gotten used to it, but Scar only notices them now when we have an important and urgent order. "I think because at night they find their way up," I reply.

"It must slow you down. What can we do?"

None of us has an answer. So Scar answers his own question.

"I will bring a spray tomorrow."

Mr. Advale told us that some sprays are very dangerous and I don't want Scar to bring something that will hurt us, but I have to tell him in such a way that he won't do it. "You have to spray every few days to keep them away. It will cost too much."

He narrows his eyes. "You have a better idea, smart mouth?"

"If we put some fresh *nimba* branches in a pail and run a fan, it will drive the mosquitoes away."

Scar's eyes settle on the *nimba* tree. "That's a good idea, but here is the thing. The fan will cost money."

I am afraid he will order us to work extra, so I say, "A used one will be cheaper than the spray."

"Hmmm." He doesn't tell us what he is going to do. I hope he buys a fan.

The next day he brings in an old fan and a pail filled with *nimba* stems. The yellowed fan blades are covered with a layer of grime and one of the knobs is broken, but the *nimba* leaves are fresh. There are some ripe, fleshy fruit hanging on the branches, and my mouth waters. "Run the fan only when the mosquitoes are bad. Turn it off at night or else all my profit will be eaten up by electricity," Scar says.

It is nice to have a fan, even an old gurgling fan, while we work. It throws *nimba*-scented air around. When we turn it off the glue smell creeps back. I wish we could keep the fan and share stories so I can imagine I'm sitting on a tree branch on a breezy day.

At night I pick the *nimba* fruits. Everyone except GC eats a few. Amar, Thick Fingers, and Sahil like the ones that are yellow and fully ripe because they don't taste bitter. Roshan is the only one who loves half-ripened ones like I do.

Since Scar brought us the fan he expects us to work one extra hour a day. We split the hour. We get up half an hour early and go to bed half an hour late. The kink in my neck has become permanent. No matter how much I rotate my neck, I can't get rid of it.

Our days are like a worn-out path—dull and the same. Since GC threatened us we have not shared stories. The only new thing I notice is the pain I have in my elbows, knees, and shoulders. In the beginning I used to plan my escape, think about how I would fool Scar, but now I don't bother to do that.

All I know now is it is hard to fall asleep with an uneasy

mind and an aching body. And once I do fall asleep, it is hard to wake up.

Today the day starts with bright sunshine and Scar comes in humming. As soon as he turns the television on, the chant, *Ganpati bappa morya, pudcha varshi laukar ya*— "hail Lord Ganesha, return again soon next year"—floats up. It tells me that it must be the festival of the elephant-headed Lord Ganesha, which comes around the end of August.

I think how last year Aai, Naren, Sita, Baba, and I went to the village temple and listened to the priest's chants. We offered red hibiscus blossoms and a few grains of rice to Lord Ganesha, and the priest gave us sweets, coconut pieces, and rock candy. Maybe the rock candy Aai gave to the twins at Thane Station were pieces she had saved from the festival.

I tell myself a story about Lord Ganesha that Aai used to tell me. Once Ganesha and his brother, Kartikay, fought about who was the wiser of the two. They went to their parents, Lord Shiva and Goddess Parvati, to decide the matter. Their parents were sitting in their abode on top of the Mount Kailash in the Himalayas.

Lord Shiva and Goddess Parvati said that whoever could travel around the world and return first was wiser. Lord Kartikay flew off on his peacock to go around the world. But Ganesha circled his parents and bowed saying, "I am back."

Lord Shiva said, "Beloved son, you did not go around the world."

Ganesha replied: "No, but I went around both of you. My parents symbolize the entire universe for me."

Lord Shiva and Goddess Parvati declared that Ganesha was indeed the wiser one.

Aai told me that Lord Ganesha was the god of wisdom, intelligence, and worldly success. Maybe if I pray to him he will help me.

After several days the festival of Lord Ganesha ends, but I am still here.

twenty–two

The monsoon seems to have tapered off with soft rain, and in a few weeks the seasons will change. Nothing will change for me. I have been here for almost three months now, and each passing day glues me more firmly to this place.

Now I don't have to fight tears because even they have disappeared.

Today Scar brings in fresh-cut *nimba* stems and they fill the room with a pleasing scent. And there are more fruits to pop in our mouths tonight. As soon as I think that, I hate myself for not even planning to escape. I have become as lifeless and dull as a dried-up clump of soil.

For lunch, we have cabbage with *dal* and rice. I think of how Aai used to make fresh cabbage-and-onion salad seasoned with mustard seeds. It was delicious.

Sahil doesn't eat anything. "What's the matter? Are you on a hunger strike, or don't you like the food?" Scar snaps.

Sahil looks at the floor. "I don't feel good."

"You look fine to me," Scar says. "Don't think that by not eating you can fool me and be lazy."

Sahil doesn't look up.

"Well, don't waste your time staring at the floor waiting for an ant to cross it. If you don't want to eat, start working, you fat donkey."

Sahil goes to the ladder. I watch as he wobbles up on his skinny legs. "Fat donkey" is the wrong name for him.

"Hurry!" Scar shouts.

I want to smack him for not caring at all. Sahil has been here for such a long time. He must have made hundreds of frames for Scar, and when Sahil is sick, Scar doesn't show even a little kindness to him! I am so upset that I can hardly swallow the food. The cabbage tastes like dried-up onion leaves.

Once back upstairs, I keep an eye on Sahil, and in the afternoon his face turns red. "Looks like Sahil has a fever. He needs rest," I whisper to Thick Fingers.

He keeps on working and shakes his head. "I can't allow that."

"But look at him. Just look at him." I realize I am not whispering anymore.

By now all of us have stopped working. Thick Fingers glances at Sahil. "If Boss comes up, he will give us all a thrashing," he whispers.

"What if he gets worse? What if someone else becomes sick? What if we all do?"

Thick Fingers's mouth turns glum like he has eaten a handful of unripe *nimba* fruits.

"I will watch for Boss. Let Sahil rest," GC says, scooting closer to the ladder. It is so unlike GC to offer such help to Sahil. Maybe GC has changed in the last few weeks. I don't know how, though. Maybe he is disgusted with Scar because he has been so mean to Sahil or GC is worried about getting sick himself. The reason doesn't matter. Right now I am glad that he wants Sahil to recover and has offered to help.

"Close your eyes and take a break," Thick Fingers says to Sahil.

"I'll fall behind, *na*?"

"We can all divide up your work," I say.

"Sma-smart idea," Roshan agrees.

Sahil rests his head against the wall and closes his eyes. I wish he could lie down, but until Scar goes home it is dangerous to do that, because he could come up at any minute. We work so fast and furiously that we don't hear Scar coming up the stairs. "Why are you sitting so close to the ladder?" Scar asks GC as he pops his head up like a crocodile lifting his snout out of the water.

Before we know it, Roshan is on his feet blocking Scar's view of Sahil. It gives Sahil a chance to wake up and look busy. When Roshan sits back down, he knocks over his bead tray and the beads spill and roll in all directions. "You clumsy fool. Look what you did! Come here," Scar says.

When Roshan gets close, Scar gives him *xhun se laafa,* a solid slap, on his right cheek, and Roshan staggers backward. His lips tremble, his mouth clamps shut, and tears fill his eyes as he bends down to pick up the beads.

"I came up to check on the lazy boy. Is he working?" Scar asks.

"He is, he is," Thick Fingers replies.

"Good. You make sure he keeps up with his quota."

"Yes, Boss."

"I am going to leave early today. There is bread and pickle in the kitchen. The ladder will be here, but after dinner you cockroaches stay up, understand?" He points at Roshan. "That one must work an extra hour for being careless."

"Yes." Thick Fingers's voice is so low that Scar gives him a sharp look.

As soon as Scar locks up and leaves, I spread Sahil's sack on the floor and make a bed for him. "Sahil needs medicine to bring his fever down." I say it out loud.

Thick Fingers throws up his hands. "Where are we going to get medicine from?"

Sahil is lying down with his eyes closed. "We should at least put cool, wet napkins on his forehead," I mumble.

I go down and fill my water tumbler and add some salt to it, as I have seen Aai do when Naren was sick. When I come up and ask if we have a piece of cloth, Thick Fingers hands me his extra shirt. "If we use our towels they won't dry out by morning and Boss might get suspicious," he says. It is a long-sleeved plaid shirt and he must wear it in the winter. I soak one of the sleeves in water. Then I squeeze the excess water out and spread it on Sahil's forehead. After a few minutes, I do the same with the other sleeve. "Gopal, you will fall behind," Thick Fingers says.

"Let Gopal take care of Sahil, and the rest of us can stay up a little later," GC says. I stare at him with disbelief. It is wonderful. If GC is on our side, we don't have to worry. And then maybe, just maybe, we can plan our escape.

As soon as I think of escape I tell myself not to dream about it. GC is selfish, and right now he probably wants to help because he is afraid of catching the disease from Sahil. Once GC doesn't have that fear he will return to his old nasty self.

After half an hour of cool salt water on his forehead, Sahil's fever seems to have come down a bit, but it is not completely gone. "Do you think Boss has some medicine hidden around here?" I ask Thick Fingers.

"He keeps his stuff by his wooden bench. I remember him taking a pill for his headache the other day. Let's go down and look."

Thick Fingers and I check on, under, and around Scar's bench. We snoop in the kitchen and on the two

222

shelves that hold our tumblers and plates, but we don't find any medicine. I am so mad at Scar for not even getting Sahil a pill to bring his fever down. I punch Scar's bench with my fist. "I hate Scar. I hate him."

Thick Fingers brushes his hair back from his forehead. His eyes are wide with surprise. "Who is Scar?"

I hold my breath. This is the first time I have called Boss by that name aloud. I am the biggest *khajoor*! But Thick Fingers flashes a smile. "I like the name. It suits him well."

I breathe again. "I don't want GC to know Boss's nickname."

"Don't worry about GC. He is with us."

What does he mean by saying GC is with us? I'm not even sure if Thick Fingers is on our side. "I don't trust GC. He threatened me and stopped us from sharing our stories."

"Yes, but he never told Boss about your flashlight." He locks my gaze. "You don't know GC like I do. When I first came here, I was slow. Boss—I mean Scar—was furious. He wanted to send me to a fireworks factory. It is the most dangerous place because if you make a mistake, you can get burned. GC helped me with my work so Boss would keep me here. When Boss found out he beat GC up."

"You are so fast now. I can't believe you were ever slow."

"I was. GC saved me and paid with his front teeth.

223

Still, I won't say a word to him. What about Sahil?"

"Let's just hope his fever comes down without medicine," I say as we go back up the ladder.

Roshan has picked the fruits and leaves of the *nimba* and is feeding them to Sahil.

"Do I have to?" Sahil protests.

Roshan gives him an encouraging smile. "Yes—only a few more."

"Are you turning Sahil into a goat?" Thick Fingers asks.

"No, no let him eat *nimba*. That is what my aai gave us when we got sick," I say. We make our beds while Sahil is still chewing the tender leaves. His face is scrunched up with bitter taste.

Amar sighs. "I wish we could tell stories."

Sahil opens his eyes. "It will make me feel better and sweeten this horrible taste, *na*?"

We all look at GC. He shrugs his shoulders. "As long as we keep working."

"No," Thick Fingers says. "It will slow us down and tonight we have more work because we have to do Sahil's too."

"We can stay up a little extra," GC says.

"Will you please tell us a story, Gopal?" Amar asks.

I wink at Amar and he beams his dimpled smile.

So we don't turn off the naked yellow bulb and don't turn on my flashlight, but keep on gluing the beads during story circle to make sure our work gets done. I tell them a story about a bull named Giant, whose job is to turn the water wheel. Giant is lazy and he traps six calves to do his work. This is a story I have never heard or told before and I make it up as I go along.

"I think—"

"Don't say a word. I want to hear the story," Thick Fingers says to GC.

"*Suna*, tell us, Gopal."

"All day long, the Giant makes the calves move the wheel. If they stop to take a break, he hits them. He gives them just enough hay so they can keep working, but not so much that they become strong."

"Does he make them wo-work at night?" Roshan asks.

"No. He gives them enough rest so they can work the next day."

"Wh-why don't they just run away at night?"

"Because he ties them up in the shed."

"Poor calves," Amar sighs.

"One of the calves decides not to listen to Giant and doesn't move. This makes Giant very angry and he whips him. That night other calves take care of the hurt calf and they make a plan to escape. They must wait until the injured calf is strong enough to run."

"I hope they get away," Sahil mumbles.

"One day they all pretend they are sick. Foam covers their mouths and their breath is heavy and labored. Giant thinks they have come down with some mysterious curse.

225

That night he doesn't tie them, because he doesn't want to get close to them. It is the night they run away."

When the story is done, Amar asks, "Do the calves go back to their families or stay with each other?"

I haven't thought about that and I don't know what to say. "I guess you can decide."

"I think they go back to their families, but they always stay friends."

"That is a good ending to the story."

"What if one of them doesn't have a family?" GC asks.

"I suppose he can stay with a friend's family and become part of that family," I reply.

GC stares at the floor. As he picks up a purple bead and places it on the frame, he seems to shrink with sadness.

We are putting away our bead trays when Sahil babbles, "We had many goats and three camels. And my father had a shop." His eyes are closed as if he is dreaming about his childhood.

"What happened to those goats and camels?" I ask.

"I don't know." He covers his face with his hands. "One day when I was in school the earth began to shake and the building collapsed. I escaped and got caught in the sand. The sea of it whirled around, slapped my face, and stung my eyes."

Sahil is talking about an earthquake and a sandstorm. He must come from the desert area in Gujarat or Rajasthan, because that's where they have sand and camels. Each thing he tells us about his life before is as tiny as a bead, but when they all come together they can make a pattern.

"Were you good or were you like me?" Amar asks Sahil. "My stepmother said I was always bad."

"Your stepmother lied," Thick Fingers says. "I know her. She is a liar."

Amar looks up. "How do you know that?"

We all wait for Thick Fingers to answer. His eyebrows bunch up with a puzzled expression. He speaks after a few moments. "Amar, you don't know this, but we are from the same town. My mother and yours were sisters."

My hand flies to my mouth.

"My real mother?" Amar says.

The room turns still as if we have all forgotten to breathe. Even the wind has stopped to hear Thick Fingers.

"Yes."

Amar untangles his crossed legs and folds his knees to his chest and leans over. His eyes are wide, his mouth is open, and his face is flushed. "So, you and I, our mothers, I mean we two are like, like kind of cousins?"

Thick Fingers whispers. "Not kind of. We are."

"Are you, I mean, are we? For *pakka*?"

"Yes, *pakka*, sure. I used to play with you when you were as tall as this window. You couldn't say my name, Barish, so you used to call me Ish. Don't you remember?"

I feel goose bumps on my arms. Thick Fingers—I mean Barish—must have known Amar all his life. When Amar came here, Barish must have recognized him right away. How could Barish keep it a secret all this time?

Amar shakes his head.

"When your baba began to beat your mother I stopped coming to your house."

"No." Amar springs up. "Don't talk about my baba like that."

"It is the truth. Your baba got drunk once a week. Always on payday."

Amar punches Barish.

Barish grabs Amar's hand. "Don't hit me for telling the truth."

The next thing we hear is Amar's sobs, loud and uncontrollable. Sahil reaches out to Amar. "Come, sit down."

"I came here this spring. Why didn't you tell me then?" Amar asks Barish between his sobs.

"I was afraid Boss would find out."

"Then why did you tell me now? Why?"

"All the stories others have shared reminded me of how I used to carry you, feed you mashed rice and yogurt, count your baby teeth, and take naps with you. I tried to keep it a secret, but today I couldn't. I just had to tell."

"If Boss finds out, what will he do?" I ask.

Before Barish can reply, GC says, "Boss might send one of them away. He doesn't like relatives working together because they can gang up and create problems. Barish knows that, right?"

"Let's not talk about it," Barish says.

"It is not my rule, but I guess you know it as well as I do. No two blood-related people in one group."

Barish sighs. "I know." His voice shakes as if GC has dumped a bucket of icy water on his head.

"I just thought of this. You are Barish—as in 'rain.' No wonder you didn't want to share your name!" GC chuckles.

I am nervous. Will Barish get angry at GC for making fun of him?

Instead of getting mad, Barish laughs. "It is a funny name. The night I was born it rained so much that everyone called me Barish Boy and then the name stayed."

I smile. Even Amar giggles.

Now we can call one another with proper names except for GC. When will he share his name?

I hope GC doesn't rat on Barish and Amar and tell Boss that they are related. Barish must have known Amar was his cousin as soon as he saw him. He must have kept it a secret because he wanted Amar to stay here. Like GC says, Boss doesn't want relatives working together because they might gang up on him. Since Barish and Amar's secret is out, GC might bully Barish, which means he might bully us all.

No matter what, it is nice for Amar to know Barish is his cousin. It is so strange they have ended up together.

Maybe the same person brought them here. If that is true, it is possible that Jatin might bring Naren and Sita here. Worse yet, he might take them somewhere else. I shiver in the warm night, thinking about Naren and Sita separated from each other. They will not know how to cope, especially Naren.

I try to throw the thought out of my mind. Like the *gorus-chinch* pit I spat into the pond, I want it to be gone forever. I must think and solve the problem I have and not worry about the imagined one.

That night Barish stays up to take care of Sahil. When I wake up in the morning, Roshan is sitting by Sahil. When I ask him why didn't he wake me up, Roshan lifts up his eyes with long lashes and smiles at me. "There was no need."

Roshan and Barish must be tired. I am rested, so I can stay up tonight.

"I wish we could share stories while we work," Amar says. Scar has not come in yet and that is good, because we can talk while we work and it makes time go by faster. I don't want Scar to come too late, though, because then he will skip our tea.

"We can do that until Boss comes," GC says.

"And we can whisper after he comes, *yaar.*"

"No. If Boss finds out we waste our time by talking and laughing, he will tie our mouths shut."

Amar cringes with fear.

"Don't worry. He has never done that before," Barish assures Amar.

"Just because he hasn't done it before, don't be so *bindaas*. I had a boss before who did that to me with old, oily rags. Let me tell you. It is not fun to gag on a smelly cloth." GC's gray eyes fill with sadness.

Amar's mouth turns as round as an onion.

"I think—" Barish tries to say.

GC gestures with a sweep of his hand and cuts in, "None of you have suffered like I have, and you think this boss can't be so cruel, but he can be. Just wait until something goes wrong. He will slap, kick, starve, and whip us up. Just like he didn't show mercy to Sahil even though he is sick and has worked for him for a long time, he won't be easy on Amar because he is the youngest or forgive you because you are the leader. He has a boss to report to himself and if things don't work out, he will make sure that we get blamed and punished."

My fingers and toes curl with dread.

GC continues, "If we hadn't saved those boxes of frames during the big storm, what do you think would have happened?"

A bitter feeling goes through my veins as I think of how GC took credit for moving the boxes and Sahil and I suffered. "What did it matter? Sahil and I were punished anyway."

GC shakes his head. "I shouldn't have complained about you. I am sorry."

"You lied," Sahil says. "It was Gopal's idea and it didn't do him any good."

I don't glance at GC because I know his anger will show through his eyes. I wait for his words. They come slow and soft. "I thought Boss would be upset that someone new thought about how to save the boxes rather than me. I was scared I would be punished. I am really sorry." We have all stopped working to stare at GC, whose face crumples. He doesn't cry, though.

The key in the lock turns and the door bangs open. We all shut our mouths and concentrate on our work. *Tarrer, tarrer, tarrer*, Scar winds the clock. When he claps for us, I'm the last one to get down, right behind Sahil.

"Are you still pretending to be sick?" Scar yells at Sahil. "It costs me money to keep you fed, and you must earn it."

Can't he see Sahil's bloodshot eyes and feverish face? "If you give him medicine he will feel better," I blurt out.

"And who will pay for it, *tera baap*? This is not a charity clinic."

I have to convince Scar to give Sahil medicine. *Nimba* will help, but medicine will bring his fever down quickly. "All you have to do is give him a few pills and he will feel good soon." I take a step backward and brace myself for his reaction.

"Has he kept up with his work?"

"Yes," Barish says.

Scar's eyes narrow and his brows knit together.

"Good. I will get him medicine."

I am speechless.

"Thank you," Amar says in English.

Scar stares at Amar before asking Barish, "First the new boy wants me to buy medicine for the sick one, and then this young English-mouth is thanking me." He twists Barish's ear. "What's going on?"

Now Barish must come up with a smart, believable explanation so Scar doesn't get suspicious about all of us talking and getting along.

GC laughs. "Boss, there is nothing going on. The new boy is worried about getting sick himself."

Scar turns to GC and lets go of Barish's ear. "And the English-mouth? Why is he thanking me?"

"I . . . I mean . . . He wants to tell the whole world he knows five words of English. Clown!" GC snorts.

Amar's face withers. Is he fearful of punishment from Scar or confused about GC calling him a clown?

"You two must keep the group under control. Do you understand?"

"Yes," Barish and GC reply.

A popular movie tune comes on. We all look around. Scar has a smile on his face as wide as his belly. He pulls a tiny phone from his pocket. "Allo, allo!" he shouts into it. The person on the other end must be deaf.

"Yes. Right, Boss. The frames are done. I will bring them over as soon as I wrap them. Right away."

Pause.

"No, he hasn't. You're right. We can't have them all get sick."

Pause.

"I will send one of the boys to get it."

When he is done talking, Scar clicks a red button on the phone and turns to me. "Gopal, are you good at math?"

Is he thinking of sending me out? I am so stunned that all I can do is nod.

"Go to the pharmacy to get medicine for Sahil."

Bubbles of excitement tingle through my body. I can't believe my luck. An errand! Out on the street where I can be alone! But my happiness doesn't last long. "Stay with Gopal and make sure you both do your job right, or else you will be punished," Scar says to GC.

GC stands straighter. "Don't worry, Boss."

Then Scar puts his palms on my shoulder and squeezes them so hard that the pain travels down my arm. "Listen, if you try to run off I will take the skin off your back. If you get away I will bring you back, beat you up, and starve you. If you think you can ask someone for help, forget it. This city is big and no one has time to worry about a little worm like you. And if you even so much as talk to a stranger, not only you but your family will be punished."

His eyes bear down on me. "Do you understand?"

I'm afraid I might wet my pants. Somehow, I manage a faint "Yes."

"You have twenty minutes—fifteen to walk there and back and five to buy the medicine. If you take any longer than that I will beat all six of you and there won't be any dinner."

Scar gives GC the money. He tells me to count the change, get a receipt, and hand both back to GC. "Hurry now." He thumps Barish on the back. "Help me pack these frames. As soon as the two of them return, I want to lock up and deliver them."

A minute later, GC and I are on the street. I haven't been out in more than three months and the world has changed. It takes me a few steps before my eyes adjust to the bright and blinding sunlight. It soothes my bare arms and legs and I wish I could gather it up and take it to the attic. The air, even though it is mixed with traffic fumes, is fresher than the gluey smell, and I breathe in deeply. To walk out in the open feels like I am on a picnic. I am giddy with happiness.

Our one-story building stands a bit away from the other buildings and is at the end of a street that goes nowhere. They look newer and better constructed. When we get closer the noise picks up and people are hurrying along the street, going in and out of the buildings, and haggling with vendors. "Hurry or we will never make it back in twenty minutes," GC says.

"What if the store is crowded and it takes us longer?" I ask.

"Then we get punished."

GC walks so close to me that his arm brushes against mine. I try to distract him by saying, "Our building must be the oldest in the area," and take a step sideways to put a little distance between us.

He also takes a sideway step. "Yes. Many years ago there was a factory here before it got burned. Most of the buildings were damaged except ours. The land prices are so high that the owner thought it was better to sell the land and rebuild the factory farther away from the city. I don't know how Boss managed to get the old shack."

The traffic picks up as we turn onto a bigger street. It is as crowded as the one by the station or near Jama's house. GC keeps on blabbering. I read the signs, SWEDESHI MART, CHANDANI BANGLES, PIYUSH JUICE CENTER. None of them tell me where we are.

I glance at GC. If I take off, will he be able to catch me? He is taller than I, so he can probably outrun me.

A bus honks and an old lady moves out of the way and bumps into a banana cart. GC holds her arm to steady her. While he does one of the few good karmas of his life I keep walking, faster and faster. The street is crowded and I weave through people swiftly. If that bus stops I can get on it. I wish Scar had given me the money, but he is not stupid. If I get on the bus it might take the conductor a few minutes before he asks for the money to buy the ticket and by the time he kicks me off the bus I will be two or three stops away from here.

Have I lost GC? My heart beats louder and louder. I

236

hide behind a truck to catch my breath and scan the street. I don't see GC. Maybe I will wait here for a few seconds and when I see a bus coming down the street, I will make a dash for the stop to get on the bus.

Someone grabs me from behind. "Why didn't you wait for me?" GC's gray eyes flicker with anger. "I don't want to complain to Boss, but if you try to run away again, I will. Just stay with me."

"I don't have to."

"Yes, you do. If we don't return soon Boss will beat up Sahil, Barish, Roshan, and Amar. Do you want that? If you run away, not only you but your family will have to pay for it."

My hands are clammy and my throat feels like a withered *gorus-chinch*. I can hear the rubber tube coming down on my friends' backs because I took longer to finish my errand. Even if I run away Jatin knows where we live, so Scar will be able to take his revenge.

GC points across the street. "The store is right there."

He keeps his grip tight on my hand while we zigzag through the traffic. We buy a pack of *Sudarshan* pills and GC pays for it. When the storekeeper returns the change with a receipt, I count it carefully as GC holds his hand out. I give him the change.

As we walk back, I keep reading more store signs. One says INDUSTRIAL TOOLS COMPANY. Oh, how I wish it said SHREE TOOLS, INC., where Jama works! There is a ready-made cloth shop with a pink and purple dress displayed behind a glass window, which reminds me of Sita.

We walk in silence until I ask, "Why don't we both run away?"

"When you have been without family for as long as I have you can't run away, because there is no home to go to and no one to see."

GC's words cut like Scar's lashes on my back.

"What if I escape?"

"Like you did a few minutes ago? *Bilkul bakvas*," he snorts.

Someday, he will know my efforts are not absolute nonsense.

He gives me a sad smile where his lips curve up but his eyes stay blank. "Boss gives me a place to sleep and food to eat. It is not much, but it is better than being out in the cold and rain."

"Why didn't Boss send you alone to run this errand?"

"I can't read, write, or do math. Boss knows you're smart and will bring the right medicine and the correct change back."

GC is smart enough to buy the medicine himself. He must know that too. I don't know why, but for some reason he doesn't want to tell me that.

When we return, Scar is ready to leave. GC hands him the receipt, medicine, and the money. Scar counts the change, gives me a pill to give to Sahil, and puts the change and the bottle in his pocket.

He is ready to step out with a sack full of boxes when

he stops, turns around, and puts the sack down. Then he takes out the bottle and gives me a few more pills. "In casc he needs one more or someone else gets sick." Scar seems pleased with me and I hope he will send me out again.

"Yes, Boss."

"Make sure that lazy boy keeps on working."

"I will, Boss."

He lifts up the sack and leaves again.

The key clicks in the lock.

twenty–three

Over the next few days, I give Sahil the pills and Roshan gives him tender *nimba* leaves. Sahil's fever goes down. Roshan insists we also chew the *nimba* leaves to stay healthy. Amar protests. "I am not a goat or a cow. Why do I have to eat the leaves?"

We all laugh at his smart excuse, but we make sure he eats them.

Sahil returns to sticking beads. He rocks back and forth, back and forth. It is hard to tell if he has lost weight or not, because he was so skinny to begin with. His eyes don't shimmer like the pond at sunrise, though. Barish lets him sleep a little longer in the morning, and if Scar leaves during the day, Sahil takes a break.

Also, every night I tell a story. Not about what I used to do but a made-up one like the Giant and calves, Timid

Rabbit, or Akbar and Birbal story. GC has been good, but I don't trust him like Barish does. It is like giving monkeys a ladder. They will always climb it.

Every day, I wait for Scar to send me out for an errand. If he does I will talk to someone on the street and ask them to help us. I know Scar will send GC with me, but as long as I don't run away GC won't complain. And I know I can't run away alone. If I do my friends would be punished and I can't allow that. My freedom will be nothing if they are beaten and hurt. But if I get the chance to go out I can ask someone to help us. If I can get Scar's pencil I can write a note and slip it to someone. That way we can all be rescued together.

It has been three weeks since Scar sent me out to get medicine. Since then he has not asked me or anyone else to run errands. Sometimes I am mad at myself. Like a branch swaying in the wind my mind goes back and forth with thoughts. Scar may never allow me out again. I should have tried harder and not let GC catch me. Maybe I should have run away while he paid for the medicine. But if I had escaped, Scar would have punished the other boys. And maybe Sahil would have gotten sicker. Jatin knows where I live, so Scar would have come after my family and me as he said he would.

I am happy Sahil has recovered, and also thankful that none of us got ill. It is easy to take care of one sick person and divide up his work among five healthy ones.

But if three or four of us had gotten ill, I don't know what we would have done. Then Scar probably would have kicked the sick ones out on the street. No one has family in Mumbai except for me. Without medicine, money, and no one to take care of them, what would happen to them? The thought gives me goose bumps.

For the first few days after GC and I went out to get the medicine, I was worried that GC would tell Scar I tried to run away. But I know GC has not complained, because Scar has not punished me. He continues to call me by my name and in fact, since I ran the errand, Scar has given me other jobs to do. Sometimes he asks me to make morning tea and clean up after him. Often he wants me to count the number of frames and gives me multiplication to do. When I give him the answer he pulls out a pencil, writes down the number on a scrap of paper, and slips them both into his pocket. I do all the jobs carefully to gain his confidence and wait for him to give me another outside errand.

Slowly, GC has become part of the group. He hasn't told his story but he does listen to ours. All day we work, but at night when we turn on the flashlight and share the stories, it feels like we are a family, and I think about how we can all escape together. With GC on our side it should be easy to make a plan and carry it out. We will have only one chance, though, so we have to work this out so well that it can't fail. As I think of the ways to get out of here, a story I had made up comes to my mind.

"I have a new story to tell," I say when we are done with our work.

"What is it called?" Amar asks, clapping his hands.

"'The Ants and the Jackal.'"

"Hav-have you told it to anyone? Roshan asks.

"Yes, to my twin brother and sister, Naren and Sita, many times," I say.

"Oh, I like the title. Come, let's sit down and listen," Amar says.

When we get in a circle I turn the flashlight on. "Once there was a colony of ants who lived near the edge of a forest under a great big *nimba* tree. One day a jackal came and told the ants, 'Move from here and make room for me.' The ants were puzzled. 'We have been here for a long time. We don't bother anyone and no one bothers us. There is enough place for you to stay, too.'"

"I can guess what happens," Amar says.

Barish puts his hand on Amar's mouth.

"The jackal gave a smile, baring his sharp teeth. 'Are you telling me what to do? I like the exact spot where your home is, so scat, scatter, and stay out of my way,' he said.

"The ants were scared. 'There is nothing we can do against such a big enemy,' one of them said.

"'We will have to leave our home and find a new place,' others said. It was time to say good-bye to the tree and move away.

"When they thanked the *nimba* tree for letting them stay for such a long time, the tree asked, 'Don't you like it here? Why do you want to leave?'

"The ants told the tree about the jackal. 'He is big and we are little. If we don't obey his order he will crush us under his paws.'"

By now Amar is bouncing his bent legs. Like Naren he has a hard time staying quiet. "Then what happened?" he asks.

"The tree fluttered its leaves softly. 'It is true that the jackal is big and you are small, but he is one and you are many.'

"Puzzled, they asked, 'How can that help us?'

"'Think of yourself as one and attack together. You will defeat him.'

"The ants liked the idea and they made a plan. The next day, when the jackal saw that the ants had not moved, he was furious. He padded close to the anthill. The ants were ready. Before he could say or do anything, thousands of them crawled onto him and started stinging. 'Stop biting, leave me alone!' he screamed. But the ants kept on stinging.

"The jackal dashed forward, he walked backward. He wiggled his body this way and that way. He even tried to bounce but nothing helped him. 'Please, please, please! I will move from here, right now,' he pleaded.

"And that is how the ants drove the jackal out, and—"

"So we are the ants and Boss is a jackal, and we must sting him?" GC asks before I finish my sentence. There is something—like a challenge in his voice that makes me nervous.

"It is a story," I say.

"It is not just a story, Gopal. You want us to get rid of Boss."

Maybe I shouldn't have shared this story. My heart thumps with fear. What if GC tells Scar I am planning an attack on him? "You don't share your stories, and when I tell one, you tell me what it means? You want me to get in trouble with Boss, that is all."

"How can I do that? You have become Boss's *cham-cha*. He even calls you by your real name," GC says.

"I didn't ask him to."

"No, it is more like you wiggled your way in like a worm. Barish, now that Gopal has taken your place do you feel like a family?"

Barish doesn't reply. I wonder if he is also jealous of me. Even if he isn't, GC's pointing out that I have replaced Barish might make him angry with me.

"Why-why do you fight?" Roshan asks GC.

"You all have fallen under Gopal's spell. One day he will run away and leave us behind to be beaten up."

Roshan's lashes flutter in fear. "I-I don't want that."

Amar stomps his fist. "Gopal will never do that."

I go to bed, unsure of what GC might do. Ever since Sahil got sick GC has acted friendly, but tonight the way he reacted to my story makes me nervous. I don't know if he is on our side or not. He has scared Roshan and pointed out to Barish that I am taking his place.

Now I am worried about Barish also.

twenty-four

As soon as Scar comes in the morning, he claps and shouts my name. There is something in his voice that turns my mouth metallic with fear. Everyone looks at me. Sahil's fingers start tapping. GC hasn't even seen Scar this morning so it is not about the story I shared last night. I am puzzled.

Scar paces the room.

When he sees me he stops, picks up frames from his bench, and shoves them into my hands. "Look at these! They are messed up. Because of that, we may not get any reorders from the customer. Do you remember who did these?" All three have the same pattern—instead of blue flowers, someone has used bluish-green beads and they don't match the blue borders. Sahil did those.

"I made them."

"Are you lying?"

"No." I look him in the eye for a split second.

"Don't make such a stupid mistake again."

The weight lifts from my chest and I can breathe again. "I won't."

I turn around to go up and that is when something hits my bare legs. My knees buckle; I bang my head on the ladder and fall down. Scar stands over me with a sinister smile. His cross-eyed stare reminds me of the day I came here and fills me with dread.

"Stop wasting time!" he shouts.

I grit my teeth and amble up the ladder, rubbing my forehead to avoid a bump. It doesn't work. I can feel a painful lump. While I glue beads, pain and anger pulsate through my head. I am going to get to Scar and make him pay for this.

Scar calls GC and Barish to help him. Will Scar ask them about the frames? Maybe I shouldn't have lied. I try to listen but I can't hear anything—not even a word.

When they come up Barish tells Roshan, "Go down. Boss wants you to trim his hair."

Since I came here this is the first time Scar has asked Roshan for a haircut. At lunch I notice Scar's back hair short and trimmed while his front is long and sparse. He has combed it in such a way as to cover his bald spot, but it doesn't seem to work.

Scar leaves right after he gives us food, saying he will

return soon. When I go down to get some frames, I see a pencil beneath his wooden bench that he must have dropped. Quickly, I bend down, pick it up, and slip it into my pocket.

GC follows. "You shouldn't have done that," he says.

Did he see me take the pencil? I don't know. "Done what?" I ask.

"Lied about who did the work." He looks at the frames sitting on Scar's bench. "Those are Sahil's and I heard you say you did those. You are in trouble."

"I didn't think—"

"Boss knows. He always does. He was testing you."

"Did he ask Barish and you about it?"

GC doesn't answer me. A shiver weakens my spine. Even though he is quiet I'm sure Scar must have talked to them.

When I start work my hand shakes as I pick up the beads.

Clap! "All of you come down. I have something to show you," Scar says upon his return.

When we gather around him, he glances over to the back door. As always, it is locked. The windows are closed. Scar is holding the coiled brown tube he used to beat Sahil and me. I step back.

"Remember this? This is to keep you honest." He lets go of one end and the thing rolls open. He raises his hand and then brings it down. It makes a sound, *satak*, as it hits the floor.

My hands curl up in fists to trap what little courage I have left.

"You need a reminder, so watch this. Gopal, come here," Scar says.

One of my friends gasps as I stand before Scar. He raises the tube again. "Turn around, lift up your shirt, and bend over."

I follow his order and turn to face my group. I close my eyes and hold my breath. *Satak*, the tube comes down on my bare back. I whimper.

"*No!*" Sahil screams.

"The boy gets one more lash because you screamed."

Satak!

A ribbon of sting burns my back. Tears roll from my squeezed-shut eyes.

"Did Gopal make these frames?" Scar roars.

Silence.

"Tell me the truth or you all get punished."

GC takes a step forward. "Boss, he didn't make those frames."

Scar lifts up the tube. *Satak, satak*, I get two more lashes.

My entire back is on fire and it sizzles and throbs with pain. I feel something warm sliding down. Blood. When I open my eyes, blurry red and yellow spots dance in front of me. I hold on to a wall for support.

"You do this again and not only you but your family

will pay for it. How would you like it if I beat up your twin brother and sister, Naren and Sita? Or should I bring them here to work with you?" Scar shouts.

How does he know about Naren and Sita? It must be Barish or GC who told him that I have a brother and a sister. Why did I trust them and tell the stories to the group? How stupid, careless, and gullible I have been! Now I have put the twins in danger. If Scar tells them that he knows where I am they will follow him like pet monkeys. Oh, what have I done!

GC must have told Scar about my family. That is why when I asked GC he didn't answer me. Maybe it was Barish, because he is afraid I have taken his place. I wonder if they have told Scar about the ant and jackal story. I turn to glance at them to see if I can tell from their faces, but before I can do that, another *satak* whips across my back. I use all my strength to stop from falling.

The phone rings. Scar pulls the phone from his pocket. As he listens, he tosses the tube down. I breathe in relief.

"We can fill the order, and I will make sure he does them."

He clicks the red button, puts the phone down on the bench, and coils the rubber tube. "Get back to work. All of you."

I take a step. Scar grabs my upper arm. "Stay."

When everyone has gone up, he gives me a tumbler of water. After I take a couple of sips, Scar says, "I'll have

251

a new job for you tomorrow. Do it right and make me happy."

He asks me to make him happy after what he did to me? I want to throw the tumbler against his forehead, kick his belly, spit on his face. I want to draw his blood like he has drawn mine. I want to turn him into a cockroach. Instead, my eyes fix on Scar's polished sandal. I don't want him to walk out of here and go to Jama's neighborhood. Scar has hurt me, but he can crush me more, a lot more, by snatching Naren and Sita. I gulp down my fear and steady my voice before I reply. "I will."

Scar is watching me as I clutch my shirt and the tumbler. I climb up slowly.

When I bend over my wooden desk, my back screams with pain. I sit shirtless because I don't want it to rub against my raw skin. My heart feels even more raw. Scar hurt my back, but that will heal. GC has betrayed me. Why did he have to tell Scar I lied? Scar knew that anyway. Maybe GC wants to take my place and this is the way to do it. And GC or Barish—whoever told Scar about Naren and Sita—has hurt me even more.

None of us are happy today, except maybe GC. Sahil mixes a new batch of glue and it burns my eyes and stings my nose. My throat turns scratchy. Even the scent of *nimba* can't get rid of the stink. We breathe the gluey air and keep our hands busy. The room is stifling, and yet there is the chill of silence. Our sadness is as solid and stubborn as a buffalo sitting in the middle of a lane. It won't budge soon.

Scar turns on the TV. He watches a funny movie and his laughter rises up like smokestacks. "Ha, ha-ha, ha, ha."

After Scar leaves, Amar puts his arms around my neck. His tears wet my skin. He stares at GC. "Why did you tell Scar that Gopal lied?"

"I had to."

"No you didn't. None of us did, *sacch na*?" Sahil says.

"I-I want to-to . . ." Roshan is so upset he can't even finish his sentence.

I look GC in the eyes. "So when you know a secret you spill it out?"

GC shrugs and glances at Barish. Have they planned this together? I can't tell. GC stands like a statue and his gray eyes go blank. I want to yell, shake, and hit him.

Barish is the only one who hasn't said a word. It makes me believe that he and GC are in it together. Sahil spreads my jute sack on the floor. Barish covers it with his long-sleeved shirt. I want to fling his shirt away and ask him to tell me the truth, but I don't have strength left.

Tears roll down my face.

We turn the naked bulb off and go to bed. I lie on my stomach. We are not a group anymore. It feels as bad as the day Jatin tricked me and brought me here. There is no flashlight, no *kahanis*, and no laughter tonight.

Oh, why did I share my stories? I thought they would glue us workers together as a group, but instead they have spun a web and trapped me. I thought *kahanis* were my friends, but they are my enemies. They have ruined me.

Sahil combs my hair with his fingertips like Aai used to, to soothe me when I was upset. It always worked. Tonight, Sahil falls asleep before I do, with his fingers stuck in my hair. I gently move his hand away.

"Gopal, are you up? Gopal?" GC whispers.

Silence.

"If you are awake talk to me, please. I can explain everything," GC pleads.

Since the others are asleep, he can't shout. After asking the same question three times, he sighs.

In the moonlight that pours through the window, I see him get up and come to me. "Let's talk, Gopal," he pleads.

I stay quiet.

"I am so sorry Scar hit you."

Anger explodes from every pore of my body.

"You're not sorry. You didn't have to—"

"Listen," he says sharply. But his voice is soft when he speaks again. "I had to complain to Scar against you, don't you see? He knows Sahil and you have become friends and will protect each other. Scar was looking at everyone's expression when he hit you the first time.

Amar closed his eyes. Roshan put his hands on his mouth to smother a scream and Barish looked distressed. At least one of us had to speak against you to fool Scar. Even when I got you in trouble I knew what I was doing. I was saving us all from Scar's suspicion. The last thing I want is for him to know we are friends. He will scatter us."

He may scatter us anyway, I think. The *nimba* leaves rustle. I look out the window. Moonlight streams through the window in narrow bands, but my face is in the shadow. "You're lying."

"What? That the others reacted this way?"

I was bending over, but Scar would have noticed them.

"He's a lot smarter than he lets on," GC adds.

"Why would he want to act dumber than he is?"

"Because it is to his advantage. And it is better for us to let Scar think we are enemies."

That stops me. Is GC telling the truth? Did he try to protect us? It could be that GC is making me believe Scar is dangerous so he can get me in trouble again. He still might be playing a trick. GC has not mentioned Barish. And even if I ask GC if he told Scar about Naren and Sita he will deny it. There is so much more GC is hiding than what he is telling me.

He reminds me of the pond in monsoon—you never know where it is deep enough to suck you in, shallow enough to splash in. I don't trust him and it is best to stay away from him. "I'm tired," I say, and lie back down on my stomach.

He returns to his sack. Only after I hear his heavy and even breathing do I take out the pencil from my pocket, slip it into my folded raincoat, and close my eyes. But the pain in my back keeps me awake for a long time. I play over the talk GC and I had in my head as if I am reciting times tables for Mr. Advale.

I realize Barish probably didn't tell Scar about the twins because I know his secret, and he wouldn't want Scar to know it. So it has to be GC. I am almost sure.

The pain comes in waves and I have to shut my eyes tight to hold my scream in. When a wave subsides I try to think of a way to escape. If I could write a message asking for help and throw it out the window, will someone pick it up, read it, and come to rescue us? It is unlikely but I must try. When I get a chance I must get a piece of newspaper that has a lot of blank space. Maybe that is my only hope for freedom.

Finally, when sleep comes, it is dense and I can't find any dreams in it.

I wake up with blazing pain. I roll to the side, draw my legs up, and sit up slowly.

"Your skin!" Sahil cries. "It is redder than it was yesterday."

"And more raw," Amar adds.

GC goes down and brings back a tumbler of yellow water. "Drink this turmeric water. It will help you heal faster. It is my grandmother's remedy."

First he gets me beaten up and now he offers me his special medicine? I'm so mad I want to throw the yellow water in his face and stain his clothes. But I remember Aai used to apply turmeric paste if I scraped my knee, and she gave turmeric and salt water to Naren when he had a cough. It can't hurt to drink it. I take the tumbler and wrap my hands around it. The taste of turmeric-infused water is worse than Scar's tea.

Silently Roshan plucks *nimba* leaves, tears them in small pieces, adds water, and applies them to my back. It feels like a thousand bee stings. I sit by the fan so it dries quickly.

I put my shirt on and go downstairs to rinse my tumbler before Scar comes.

Today, Scar gives me a new batch of frames to make. They are made of better wood and the beads are even and clear. "If you do a good job with these higher-quality frames, you will be rewarded," he says.

I don't want to be rewarded. All I want is freedom.

"Did you hear what I said?"

"Yes, Boss."

"Work hard and fast."

Of course, so you can make more money. "I will."

I work as fast and as carefully as I can, which takes my mind off the pain. But I can't escape the weight of distrust and the grimness of our group. They gag me. What made this place bearable was to know we were a family who cared for one another. The stories have vanished as if someone put a curse on them. I miss them, and yet I don't want them.

One day I steal a piece of newspaper and stuff it in my pocket while I help Scar wrap the frames I made. When I get a chance I also take out the pencil from my raincoat and slip it in my pocket. There is only one place where I can write a message—in the bathroom. I wait until lunch when I am allowed to use the bathroom. I take out the paper and pencil and begin writing. It is hard to do because I don't have anything solid to rest the paper on. I manage to scribble a note in very bad handwriting. "We are children trapped in the building next to the *nimba* tree. Help us get free."

I finish my food quickly so I can be the first to get back up. Roshan follows me so I don't have to worry. Still, I don't want anyone to know about my note, so when I get up, I casually reach out to the *nimba* branch with my fist, open it up, and let go of the paper. It floats away. I just hope Scar doesn't see it. Will the wind carry the paper away until someone grabs it? Will it get away from here and close to other buildings, where people are? And if it does, there is so much junk on the city streets that I wonder if anyone will even notice it. Maybe this was not the best idea. Still, my heart flutters with hope that someone may see it, read it, and help us.

In the afternoon I look out the window. The paper

never made it down but is stuck on a branch. I pray for a strong wind to set it sailing. I hide my pencil back in my raincoat before going to bed.

The next morning the paper has disappeared.

For the next two days I wait for someone to come help us but no one does. Like one of my air palaces it was a foolish idea.

My only way out is if Scar sends me out on an errand.

If he does I should have only one aim: to get out of here and not worry about anything else or anyone else. The errand money Scar gives me will probably be enough to hop on a bus or a train and get away from here. I know where Jama lives, so it shouldn't be difficult to ask for the directions and find Jama's house. Aai, Naren, Sita, and Jama will be so happy to see me alive. If Baba is back, I can see him too.

The day I step out of this place, I will see my family.

twenty–five

With each passing day the air turns lighter and the sky looks clearer. Slowly, my back has healed. Amar's hugs have brightened my days. Roshan's leaf-paste has kept the infection away. Barish has lent me his shirt to sleep on. Sahil lets me sleep extra in the morning by filling my bead tray. And GC has brought me turmeric water every single day. Without them what would I have done?

Still, I don't trust GC. He has been quiet and avoids looking at me. But I know he is watching me. I am still afraid of what he can do to me, to all of us.

Scar has not asked me to run an errand but even if he does, I wonder if I will be able to walk out of here, catch a bus, and escape alone. In the last few days all the boys have acted like good friends. They have done so much for me! If I run away, Scar will beat them up. And I know how much it hurts. I hear the *satak, satak* of the rubber tube as if it is coming down on their backs. Scar will scatter them, maybe send them to do dangerous work. I can't let that happen to Amar, Sahil, Roshan, Barish—even to GC.

Is there a chance of getting all of us out when I am not sure about GC? But the way he has taken care of me makes me think that I must not count him as my enemy. My thoughts are like a tangled-up piece of string.

After many days of sun, we have a cloudy morning. Sahil's hair is curlier in the heavy air. It starts to sprinkle, and Scar is wet when he comes in. "This change in weather makes me miserable. I thought we were done with monsoon! It is rainy and damp again."

When I tell Scar my order is done ahead of time, he brightens up. "Make some tea for us, Gopal."

This is the first time after beating me that he has asked me to make tea for him. He examines each frame before he wraps it up in newspapers. "These are good. Really good. Have a full cup of tea with me."

I don't feel like celebrating with him by having more tea, but it is better to follow Scar's order than not. I add more milk and water and watch it come to a boil.

"How much is fifty-two times forty-four?" Scar asks.

I throw the tea in the boiling mixture while I calculate. Fifty-two times 44 is hard, so I break it up in my head. Fifty-two times 40 is 2,080, and 52 times 4 is 208. I add 2,080 and 208 and tell him, "That is two thousand, two hundred eighty-eight."

He smiles as he pulls out a silver pen, writes down the number on a scrap of newspaper, and tucks it into his pocket. Is he making that much money? He must be or else he wouldn't have replaced his lost pencil with such a nice pen.

Even with a stretch of overcast, drizzly days, Scar is in a good mood. Maybe it is because of the new frames I am making or because Diwali festival season is here. On the TV there are advertisements for sweets, saris, and jewelry. We don't get to watch the TV, but when Scar has it on, the sounds drift upstairs.

Two days before *Diwali*, on *Dhanteras*, Scar gets sick. His eyes are bloodshot, his face is flushed, and his temples shine with perspiration.

"Gopal." He claps weakly.

When I come down he points to the kitchen. "Make me a cup of tea," he croaks.

"Yes."

"It is an auspicious day, I must have sweets," he mumbles as I go to the stove to heat the water. All this time he gives us just enough food so we don't starve, and now he moans about needing sweets! He needs medicine more than anything else, but why should I tell him that? I'm not stupid enough to prick myself by hugging a thorny acacia tree. Let him have sweets if he wants sweets.

"Make sure you add enough milk so it doesn't taste watery."

Like ours? I think.

"And make a little extra so you can have a sip or two."

The master is so generous!

When I set his stainless-steel cup down, he grabs my hands. "Get me some sweets. It is Dhanteras and I must have some." He takes out a fifty-rupee note from his pocket, enough to buy a small box of mixed sweets. "Walk three streets down and take a left, then a right at the second corner. The store is three shops past the corner. Take a jute sack to carry it in so the whole world doesn't see it. Now hurry." He wheezes back and closes his eyes.

It is hard to stop grinning. Scar has given me the money and has asked me to go to the store alone. He must be delirious with fever, otherwise he would never have done this. It is my chance to flee. I bend down and pull one of the sacks out from the pile beneath his wooden bench.

"It looks like it might rain. Should I take my raincoat?" I ask. I am thankful for the cloudy day so I have an excuse to take it.

"Yes. Get me my sweets. Hurry."

I run up and grab my raincoat. All eyes are on me, but I avoid looking at them.

Now I have money in my pocket and I'm on the street. My heart thumps faster and faster. After I left, Scar may have asked GC to follow me. I look over my shoulder, but he is not there. A bus passes by, stops at the corner, and people get on. I don't know where it is going, but it doesn't matter. It will take me away from here.

I run down the street, cut into the line of people, grab the metal rod, and climb up.

The faces of Sahil, Amar, Roshan, Barish, and GC dance in front of me. How can I leave them behind? But this is my only chance, and if I don't escape now, I may never be able to do so.

People push me from behind and I must move forward to make room for them.

Scar will punish them. I will regret this. But if we can all escape together no one will have to suffer. I must ask someone to help us all.

I must.

I can't move forward. Someone jabs me in the ribs. I turn around and hop out.

"If you don't want to ride the bus, then stay away from it!" someone yells. I wipe my sweaty hands on my shorts, stick my hand back in the pocket to make sure the money is still there, and try to stop trembling.

The street is crowded and people are in a festive mood. Who should I ask for help? The man with the leather bag? Whom should I trust? The lady buying vegetables? If I can make eye contact with someone and they smile, then I can talk to them.

I look at men and women passing by, but they are hurrying along. Some men and women are holding their young children's hands and others are carrying shopping bags. By now I am at the sweet shop and no one has even glanced at me.

The place is mobbed with shoppers. The shopkeeper is handing out the boxes, taking the money, giving it to the man behind the counter with the cash box, and returning the change to the customers as fast as he can. I must talk to someone, but who would listen in this noise? Maybe if I can write a note I can slip it to the shopkeeper. Maybe he is as nice as the owner of the Deepak Food Store.

I remember I have a pencil tucked in my raincoat, but I don't have a piece of paper. Then an idea comes to me. I have a fifty-rupee note on which I can write. I glance at the street to make sure GC is not there. He isn't.

Quickly, I move away a few steps, take out the pencil, and fold open the bill and rest it on the raincoat. On one side is the picture of Mahatma Gandhi. I try to write on the same side. My hands tremble so much that first I have to take a few deep breaths. *Please rescue us. We are six boys in the old building three streets down by the nimba tree with the broken branch. Please hurry.*

I tuck my pencil back into my raincoat and wiggle between a man in milky-white *kurta-pajamas* and a lady wearing a red silk sari.

"Hey, you. Out. Get out."

I look to see who is talking.

"Don't act so innocent. I know why you have sneaked close to us," the lady in red yells at me.

"I want to buy sweets," I say.

"Buy or steal?"

"What?" My mouth tightens up.

"Leave the child alone on this auspicious day," the man in the white *kurta-pajamas* says in a deep, booming voice that seems to echo from the hills.

"Maybe you haven't looked at him. If I were you, I would worry about my wallet."

My face is hot with shame and I haven't done a thing wrong.

I take a step backward.

The booming-voice man puts his hand on my shoulder and moves me in front of him.

"What do you want?" he bends down and asks.

"A box of mixed sweets."

"One large mixed sweets," he orders.

Before I can tell him that I don't have money for a big box, the shopkeeper gives me a box and holds out his hand for money.

I have fifty rupees and I don't think it is enough for such a large, fancy box of sweets.

"I don't have enough money—"

"See, what did I tell you? Now who's going to pay for him?" the red-sari woman snarls.

The shopkeeper looks at me. He doesn't want any bickering on Dhanteras. It is the day of Goddess Lakshmi, the goddess of wealth. She would be displeased to see a fight on her special day, and if she is displeased, she might leave. The shopkeeper wants to keep her happy.

But he also wants money for the box he handed me. My throat tingles with shame. Like an ant in a landslide, I can't scurry into a crack fast enough to save myself.

He offers a solution. "Pay what you have now, and pay me the rest later."

What can I say? I can't ask Scar for more money.

"I . . . um . . . have enough money for a small box. Would you . . . um . . . mind . . . exchanging this for a small one?" I ask the shopkeeper as I hand him the money. He opens the bill and everything seems to stop for me. He pauses, his eyebrows go up, and his face becomes stiff. Then instead of handing my money to the man with the cash box he slips it into his shirt pocket.

He picks up a small box and gives it to me. "Don't worry," he says.

I don't know what to do because he doesn't take the big one back. Of course, on this auspicious day he wouldn't take the sweets back.

Before I can say anything to the shopkeeper, the booming-voice man says, "Didn't you hear him? You don't have to pay for it. Get going."

The woman in the red sari glares at me. Her nostrils are wide, ready to burst open.

I almost forget to thank Sweets-Man.

I turn around and say, "Thank you."

Sweets-Man waves his hand. *"Sambhalun ja!"*

The booming-voice man asks, "What's your name?"

"Gopal."

"Happy Diwali, Gopal," he says. "Share your sweets."

I slip both boxes into the jute bag and take off before the lady makes any nasty remarks.

On the way home I think about Sweets-Man and how he looked at the note. He must have read it and that is why he kept it separate. Like Aai, he told me to be careful—I am sure he is going to help us. I wonder if he will call the police. If he does we could be free today, or tomorrow, or the day after—on Diwali.

"Happy Diwali, Gopal. Share your sweets. Share your sweets. Happy Diwali, Gopal." The booming voice echoes in my mind until I realize these sweets are not for me. Scar will take away even the big box that Sweets-Man gave me. Scar won't believe I got it as a gift and will think I stole it, or worse yet, he might think I bought it with money I stole from him.

But why should I let him have the big box? It is not his. It is mine and I want to share it with all my friends—even with GC. I must think of a way to hide it from Scar.

Instead of going to the front door I check the back door, but the lock is secure. I could climb up the *nimba* tree and slide the package to one of the boys, but Scar

268

might hear the noise, open the window, and catch me. There is no way to save the sweets. I have to walk in through the front door and hand Scar both the boxes—unless he is asleep and doesn't notice me.

No such luck. Scar is sitting up. The tea has made him alert.

"Took you a while," he says.

"It was crowded."

He reaches out. "Give it to me."

I put my raincoat down, slip my hand in the bag, and pull out the small box. I hand it to him. He fumbles to untie the red string as I hastily fold up the sack and shove it under his seat and pick up my raincoat.

He flings away the string, lifts the cover, and brings the open box closer to his face. While he admires the sweets garnished with silver paper, I kick the sack farther under the seat with my foot.

He waves his hand to dismiss me, but first he grabs a diamond-shaped sweet and gives me a sliver of it. "Go," he says.

As I turn around, I see him pop the rest of the piece in his mouth. Scar offers me his sweet out of superstition. He probably thinks that if he shares the food with me I won't cast an evil eye on it and give him a stomachache.

There is a whole box of sweets for us to eat tonight. I just hope Scar feels well enough to go home.

And I hope he doesn't check under his bench.

∾

After my errand it is hard to concentrate on gluing and beading. Doubts flood my mind like rainwater floods the streets in monsoon. I have asked Sweets-Man to help us. What if he doesn't talk to the police? What if the policemen are as mean as the one who kicked me? What if someone talks to Scar about all this? Sweat breaks out on my face and as I wipe it I notice GC staring at me.

He smirks.

"What? Why are you smirking?" I blurt out.

"You tell me," he says.

Sahil, sitting between us, has stopped rocking.

GC suspects something, and if he tells that to Scar, I am doomed. We all are.

I wonder if GC will ask me questions tonight. I hope that when I share the sweets he will think that was my secret.

The idea of sharing sweets brings a smile to my face but it doesn't last long, because I again think about our rescue. I wonder if Sweets-Man has contacted the police by now. The way he looked at me I know he would. But this is a busy time for his business, so he may not do anything right away. And what if after a couple of days he misplaces the note, or uses the money by mistake?

He seems trustworthy, but a bead of doubt rolls around in my head. My heart wants to believe in him. I think Sweets-Man is a good kind of person. But what if he talked to the police and they don't do anything? What if Scar has bribed some of the police and they tip him off? Roshan said they were once moved hastily before. It could happen again. If Scar finds out about what I did he will split us up and send me far away from Mumbai. Then I will never see my family again. Barish and Amar will get separated too. Maybe by asking for help, I've put my friends and myself in danger.

All afternoon as I work, time mocks me by sauntering slowly. Finally, around seven, Scar gives us dinner and leaves.

Alone! At last! I hug my secret for two more hours. Before I share the sweets I want to make sure that Scar doesn't return. Finally, it is time to quit work.

"Tonight let's keep the light on and share stories," I say. I want to see their expressions when I pull out the box of sweets. "This is Diwali season."

"Yes, this is a festival of lights," GC says.

"Before we start I have to go downstairs," I say.

"Why?" Barish asks.

"You'll see." I skip down the ladder.

I feel around under the bench until I find the right sack. When I do, I grab the box and untie it. "Close your eyes and don't open them until I tell you to," I call to the boys as I climb back up the ladder. Amar has put his hands on his eyes while the others have just closed them.

"Can we open our eyes?" Amar asks when he hears me sit down.

"No. Wait."

I take off the lid and put the open box in the middle. "You can look now."

Amar's dimple lights up his face, Barish covers his mouth with his palm, Sahil hugs his knobby knees, and GC's gray eyes sparkle. Roshan's lashes flutter in excitement and his mouth is wide open. "Ar-ar-ar-are these for us?"

"Yes."

They all stare at me for a moment and I stare back at them. "I knew you were hiding something. I just didn't know it was this! How did you get them?" GC asks.

I notice he doesn't accuse me of stealing. I tell them about what happened when I went to get the sweets. After I finish, we admire the sweets. There are white and green diamond-shaped bars, yellow round *laddus*, orange honey-combed cubes. Some of them are covered with a thin layer of silver and some are garnished with nuts and dark cardamom seeds. I pass the box around and they each take one piece. When it is Sahil's turn, he picks up one, breaks off a bit and offers it to me. It is his way of saying thank you. Barish, GC, Roshan, and Amar follow his example.

We eat without talking. The sugary, nutty, spicy flavors fill my mouth and I let them play on my tongue.

When we are done, Amar wipes his mouth with the back of his hand. "We still have some more left!"

"Enough to last us for probably two more days," I say.

"You had money, you met a kind man, and you were

alone. You should have gone back to your aai," Sahil says.

Barish brushes his hair back. "I was thinking the same. Why did you come back?"

I am tempted to say, "I almost did." Why did I not stay on the bus? If I had, I might have been with my family. Regret washes over me.

"If Gopal runs away Boss will break up our group. He will make our lives miserable." GC's eyes darken with fear.

"So? Our lives can't get much worse. And Gopal would have been with his family," Sahil says.

Amar wiggles closer. "*Yaar*, maybe next time you can get away and then come back and help us."

"I do want all of us to be free," I say.

GC shakes his head. "It is never going to happen if you escape alone, because Boss will send us somewhere else right away. You won't be able to find us."

They all sit, glum-faced and silent. I wish I could tell them about my note to Sweets-Man. But I don't know if anyone would come to rescue us. Why get my friends' hopes up the mountaintop and have them come tumbling down?

Besides, I still don't trust GC completely.

"I promise, if I get out of this place, so will you." As I say this, my voice wobbles like a table with three legs, but inside I feel solid. With my promise I try to keep them hopeful.

"May we have some more sweets? Please?" Amar asks.

"Yes, let's eat some more."

We take a few pieces out.

"Where should we keep the box?" I ask.

"No-not here," Roshan says trembling. "This ro-room is so bare there is no place to hide the box. If-if Boss finds it he will beat us."

Roshan is right. This room holds nothing but our benches, jute sacks, pairs of clothes, and our towels. I have a raincoat and Roshan has a comb, but that's all. If Scar comes up, he will see the big, red box right away.

"Hide it in the same place you did before," GC says.

Sahil reties the string on the box.

I go down, slip the box in a jute bag and shove it way in the back under Scar's seat.

We sit and eat silently in the story circle with the naked yellow light off. "I want to share a secret with you," I tell them when I am done eating. "The first time I saw the Boss, I named him Scar-Man, but then he kicked and hit me, so I decided he didn't deserve *man* behind his name."

It feels good to talk about Scar.

Amar sits next to me. He says something, but even I can't hear it because he mumbles.

"Louder," Barish says.

Amar shakes his head.

Sahil goes next. "Gopal tells us about his family and it reminds me of my maa. I used to push her out of my thoughts, but now I let her stay with me." His voice sinks low and soft. "The more she stays with me, the more I miss her."

"How did you get separated from her?" I ask.

"It happened on a day when the earth shook, houses came down, and people got crushed."

I remember him telling me how his school building came crashing down. "Did your house collapse too?" I ask.

"Yes. When I ran home from school my home was no more. So I kept on running. I never saw my parents again."

Amar leans forward. "Then what?"

"There was a sandstorm and then, then someone came, I think. I don't remember." Sahil becomes distant. We know he won't talk now.

"I-I-I hate my father," Roshan declares. "I hate him for believing in strangers and sending me away with them. And, and . . ."

We wait for a few minutes for Roshan to continue. He doesn't.

"I was not bad," Amar says. "My stepmother wanted me out of her house, so she complained to my father about me. He knew it wasn't true. I guess he didn't love me, because he never, even once, took my side."

"Your mother loved you very much," Barish says.

"So what? She left me, didn't she? If she hadn't died, I wouldn't have had a stepmother in the first place." He starts sobbing.

Barish puts his arm around Amar. It takes a few minutes before Amar stops crying.

"Will you tell us how you came here?" he asks Barish.

Barish hesitates a minute before he begins. "One day I borrowed my uncle's bicycle without asking him. I didn't know how to ride well and I ran into a tree. The bicycle was banged up and I was scared to tell my uncle, so I ran away before he found out what I had done. It was a mistake.

"I hid behind a temple for two days and there I met a man who said he would take me to a city where I could work in his tea stall and make so much money that I could buy a new bike for my uncle. He was well dressed, wore sandals, and was not skinny like the villagers. For a few months I stayed with him and he treated me well, but then the man passed away. I had money saved up and I was ready to go back to the village when my money got stolen."

"Wh-where did you keep your money?" Roshan asks.

"Under my pillow in an empty cigarette box. Without money I couldn't go home so I found a new place to work, and the boss promised me he would pay me well. The promise was like a rose, but what I got was one big thorn of a boss. For two years, I served tea, washed dishes, swept floors, and cleaned the tables. One day a customer cursed me because his glass was not full. I told him it was not my fault since my boss filled up the glasses. The man argued with my boss, demanding his money back. Finally he threw the tea at my boss, smashed the glass on the wall, and walked away. That night my boss beat me up and I ended up here. Now I am afraid of Scar and what he can do to me."

GC is the only one who hasn't shared his story, but I don't expect him to do so. I am about to say that we should go to sleep when I hear GC's voice. "I loved my grandmother very much. We had three cows and a few goats and I used to take them to pasture in the surrounding hills. My grandmother packed me lunches of corn *roti* with garlic chutney. There were eight of us friends who went together, and while our animals grazed, my friends and I played, shared stories, and played pranks. Sometime we let each other's cows into the fields. The farmer would come running and shouting, chase the cows away, and catch the owner. When I returned in the evening my grandmother and I milked the cows and goats, and I delivered the milk."

I am afraid that if I interrupt GC the spell will be broken, so I keep my hands tucked under my feet like Naren did to keep myself from saying a word.

"Did you drink real milk?" Amar asks.

That doesn't stop GC. "Yes, we did. It was creamy, foamy, fresh, and warm. During the long winter my grandmother told me stories. Then one day she got sick, and even with medicine she didn't get better. One by one we sold our goats and cows until we had none left. We ran out of money. We were hungry and my grandmother needed medicine, so I stole money from a neighbor's house. I got caught. When she found out, my grandmother cried. She passed away that same night."

Sahil scoots closer to GC and puts his arm around GC's shoulder.

"My grandmother was the only person I had in the world and when she died, I had nobody. I killed her. I know I killed her," GC whispers.

I wonder if the old lady in the street reminded him of his grandmother. "Don't blame yourself," I say.

He wipes his eyes. "Once she died I left the village. I traveled without a ticket, and when the ticket collector caught me he kicked me off the train. But I just snuck back on the next train. Sometimes people on the train were kind and shared their food with me. This is how I reached Mumbai. I made friends with a boot-polish boy and started helping him. We traveled in the trains and slept in different stations at night. It was not bad."

"How did you end up here?" I ask.

"One day some *gundas*, thugs, came and asked us for money. We tried to run away. My friend got away but they caught me. They took all my money, beat me, and tied me with rags. The next day one of them told me he was my boss and I had to work for him."

"Doing what?" Barish asks.

"Pickpocketing. I wasn't good at it and I got punished a lot. One day a man caught me with my hand in his pocket. I begged him not to turn me over to the police, and he asked me if I wanted to make frames. It was better than pickpocketing, and I came here. By the time I realized Scar had trapped me it was too late. I wanted to get out of this place and I tried to escape twice, but you see me here."

"*Yaar*, I wish you could have run away," Amar says.

"Never get tangled in wishes and dreams, because they never come true." GC adds, "It is very late and we must go to sleep."

I guess he doesn't want us to ask questions, and we don't.

I wonder why GC doesn't tell us his name? He has told us everything else. As I spread my sack I think about how he has become part of the group. If we don't get rescued we could still be free if we come together and attack Scar. We can overpower him and tie him up, because he can't fight six of us at the same time. But will GC ever do that? As bad as this place is, this is like a home for him now. I remember how difficult it was to sleep on the footpath just when Baba, Aai, the twins, and I arrived in Mumbai. I can understand why GC doesn't want to end up living in the streets, alone.

twenty–six

The next morning, on Kali Chaudash, Scar arrives early. We're up but haven't started work. We scramble to set up our trays, but he comes up the ladder quickly.

"You filthy, ungrateful pigs! You haven't started work yet?"

He twists Sahil's ears and slaps him, then he turns to me, "You are the smart one. You should know better than to waste your time, Gopal." He jerks my arm behind my back and twists it. The pain shoots up to my shoulders. I bite my lip to stop a scream. He looks at me. "Keep an eye on them. I want the work done, and done right. If any one of them messes up, you will get a beating that you will never forget."

I want to hit him over the head with the bead tray. If we had all done that as he came up the ladder he would have collapsed. Why didn't I plan the attack with my friends last night? "Yes, Boss."

"I have brought some milk for your tea. Make it last for the next two days because I don't want to see your faces on Diwali."

"We will," Barish says.

"I'm talking to Gopal."

"Yes, Boss."

Scar is cruel and shrewd. Now that we have a big fancy order, he gives us tea. He wants us to be alert so we can do a good job. But that is all. I don't like the way he plays us against each other to make us distrust each other.

After I make tea, he tells me, "Start working on the new pattern."

I wait for Scar to give me the pattern while the others go up.

"What are you still doing here? The stuff is upstairs," he says.

When I get upstairs, there are stacks of frames and a pattern. I have done this one before so it is not new, but Scar must think it is.

My mind churns as I work. If the police come tonight I can be with my family on Diwali! How happy they will be. In my excitement I glue the wrong-colored beads twice.

I have to concentrate or else I will be punished. The only way I can do it is if I work faster than before, so my mind can't wander like a goat. It is easy to do the pattern since I have already done it and finished them quickly.

Before I take the frames down, I make sure I have not made a single mistake. Then I give them to Scar. He must have taken some medicine, because he doesn't look miserable like he did yesterday.

"It is nice you got done with this quickly, but what good does it do when you mess up? You donkey! You used the wrong pattern!" he screams.

"This is the pattern that was by the frames."

"Who told you to use that one? You careless, no-good, wandering dog!" he says, looking around. He shuffles the newspaper pieces and a piece of paper slips to the floor. I pick it up and hand it to him. "This is the one I gave you," he says.

It is a new one and I have never seen it before. "I—you didn't give—"

"You left it here, you cockroach."

How could I have left it in his pile of newspaper? "The frames and the pattern were—"

He slaps me across the face. The pain blows away the cover I have placed on my anger. I hold on to my words— *you never gave the pattern to me and now you punish me. You're a liar and a cheat*—with all my might and don't let them spill out.

It doesn't help. "You—you fat little worm! Who will pay for this? Wait until I send you to a fireworks factory to shut your smart mouth." Scar slaps me on the other cheek so forcefully that I stumble. "Get back to work. No food for you today."

When I get upstairs the rest of them are working away with their heads down just like they did when I saw them the first time. I fight back the lump that settles in my throat. Now before we are rescued, Scar will send me away and I will end up in a factory far away from Mumbai. I wish I could somehow send a message to Sweets-Man that we need help right away. At least he knows where we are trapped and maybe he will be here with the police, soon.

I don't get food but it doesn't matter, because we have sweets. After Scar leaves we make the tea because the milk would spoil by next morning. We drink our tea upstairs with sweets, come down, wash our tumblers, and hang them up. Barish turns the light off and I turn on my flashlight. I put it in the middle. "Who wants to tell a story?" I ask.

"You tell one, Gopal," GC says.

I begin my marble story. "One day a little boy went for a walk looking for a treasure. He didn't want silver or gold; he didn't want money or jewels. All he wanted was something beautiful. He meandered into a forest where trees as tall as a ship filled the land. Before long the boy saw something glint. It was under a pile of leaves, so he knelt down to remove it."

I stop to catch my breath. Before I can tell any more the flashlight starts to flicker. I turn it off. "What happened?" Amar asks.

"The battery is low. Until we put in new ones we won't

be able to use it. I can still tell the story in the dark."

Amar starts to cry. "What's the matter?" I ask.

"We will never be able to buy new batteries, and we will never have the flashlight again."

We fall silent.

There is something strange about this story because it remains untold. Maybe it is cursed and that is why I have never been able to finish it. Or maybe because it is the Kali Chaudash night, which bring evil spirits out and one of them have stolen my story.

Oh, no! I am turning superstitious like Scar.

It has been thirty hours or more since I gave my message to Sweets-Man and no one has come. I don't know how long I can wait. Maybe in a few days when I give up my hope completely I will feel better. But would I ever give up? To have no hope would be like the night of Kali Chaudash—dark and evil. But after every Kali Chaudash comes Diwali!

"Have you planned to get us out of here?" GC whispers just as I am falling asleep.

I am anxious and nervous inside, but my voice must not give it away.

"I thought you didn't want to leave this place. You told me that, remember?" I ask as calmly as I can.

"Yes. But at that time I didn't have anyone. Now I have all of you. If we escape together, then I am not alone. Am I?" His voice breaks when he says the last few words.

I am torn between doubt and trust.

"You believe me, don't you?" he asks.

There is something in GC's voice that tells me he is not lying, but I can't tell him my secret—not when he won't even share his name.

"Gopal, I trust you. If you are planning something, please don't say a word to the group. Amar will fidget, Roshan might not be able to keep a secret, and the others might also show their excitement."

"I'll remember your advice."

"Is there anything I can do?"

"Like before, let Scar keep thinking we don't get along."

"*Accha*, I'm good at that," he says. Even though I haven't told anything to GC, I still hope and pray he is on my side.

He has given me the right advice about not talking to the group. But one thing GC said bothers me.

What did he mean that Roshan might not be able to keep a secret? I think of the day Scar found out about Naren and Sita. It was the same day Roshan went down to give Scar a haircut. Maybe it wasn't Barish and GC who told Scar. Maybe it was Roshan. Scar's threats may have made Roshan tell my secret, and that is why he has been quieter than before. I sweat with new worries.

My mind whirls and I am awake, asleep, dreaming, thinking, floating, and falling, all at once.

Then a dream takes hold. The window behind Scar's

bench is open and does not have the iron grille on it. Scar is not there. All of us are huddled together and Amar is waving to someone. Why don't we just hop out of the window and run away? I move my feet and jerk myself awake.

twenty-seven

The day of Diwali comes and goes without Scar, policemen, or rescue. The only good part is that Scar has left some bread and lemon pickles for us. We eat that, banana chips, and then have sweets and enjoy a Scar-free festival.

"What should we do with the empty sweets box?" GC asks that night.

"We have to hide it," Barish says.

We all know that. The question is, where? The room is so small and the box is too big. If Scar finds the box, not only will he beat us up, but he'll know we have banded together. "Let's cut it up and throw the pieces out the window," Sahil suggests.

Cutting up the box makes sense, but I don't like the idea of a pile of red cardboard pieces right under our window. Scar might notice it when he goes to cut *nimba* branches.

"We can stuff it back in one of the jute bags," Amar says.

"No. That is dangerous. Scar has been sick and occupied by holidays, so it has worked for the past few days. The box has to vanish," GC says.

I agree with him.

"We-we can burn it," Roshan suggests. I look at him and he avoids my gaze by looking away.

"That is dangerous too," I say. Sahil nervously taps the wooden bench. It gives me an idea. "Let's cut it up and stick the pieces under our benches."

Sahil mixes up a batch of glue while we cut up the box with a knife. We turn over our benches and stick the pieces right onto the underside of the benches. The box disappears. Outfoxing Scar makes us giddy and we snicker. Sahil asks me if he can keep the string. When I say yes, he slips it in his pocket.

It has been a good Diwali, but I can't sleep. I shouldn't be having fun with my friends. My family must miss me. I wonder if Baba is alive and back with Aai, Naren, Sita, and Jama. Maybe they are still looking for me, or by this time they think I am dead. I wonder if they are still in the city. I hope they haven't gone back to our village.

The next morning GC's eyes are red as if he has chopped up a dozen onions. I wonder if he stayed awake last night.

"What's the matter with you? Don't get sick on me," Scar warns GC when we are down for tea.

"I'm fine, Boss," GC says. "Some people are worried about their health, and I want them to know I won't get them sick." When he says the last part, he looks at me.

Scar gets GC's message and gives him a nod. "As long as you do your work well, I'm happy."

"I will. You can always count on me, Boss," GC says smoothly.

GC is smart and sleek. With this short exchange he has told Scar that our group is divided. I grin.

"What are you so happy about?" Scar barks.

Quickly, I bend my head, stare at my feet, and clench my fist to stay quiet.

"No tea for you. Go work."

I climb up the ladder. Relief spreads through my body as I get away from him. It is better for me not to show him my face. That way I can't get in more trouble with him than I already am.

I work and think. If Sweets-Man has talked to the police they might have not been able to come because of Diwali, but they might come today and rescue us. I must behave as normally as I can until then.

Aai used to tell a story about a mighty tree and a tiny twig. The mighty tree used to laugh at and tease the tiny twig, saying it was going to blow away when a storm came. The twig would just bend in reply. After each storm, the twig looked miserable, but not the tree. It lost a few leaves and small branches, but it still looked tall and regal. Then one day a huge storm came. It brought winds that whipped, *zumzumzum zum zum, zumzumzum, zum zum*. The twig doubled over until the winds died out and it survived, but the great tree got uprooted and fell. If I want to live, I must act like a twig. Even if Scar shouts or hits me, I must stay calm, because the most important thing is to get out of here. Then I can be with my family again!

As I think of my family, I realize that my friends don't have families in Mumbai. I wonder what will happen to them. I hope the police will take care of them and help them find their families.

Once the other boys come up the ladder, Scar turns on the TV loud. We suppress laughter when we hear his off-key singing. But then his singing stops, and it is clear that Scar is upset. Even with the TV on, we hear him swear into the phone. He shouts such filthy things into the phone that I wonder if the person on the other end is using similar language. Then, suddenly, he turns off the TV and claps us downstairs.

The first thing Scar tells us is, "Take a bath one at a time, wash your hair, and scrub yourselves well." He points to Sahil. "Make sure your fingers and nails are glue-free. Don't mix more glue today."

We're so surprised that none of us moves. "Hurry up, cockroaches! I don't have all day."

It is such a luxury to have a whole bucket of water. I

wash my hair and scrub my body. I dry myself and put my clothes on. I am about to come out of the bathroom when I hear Scar's phone ring. I stay inside and press my ear to the door.

"You will like the boys. They are clean, healthy, and good workers. I'll bring them tomorrow morning," Scar says.

I lean against the wall so I don't fall. Scar is going to take us away from here. It is too late to save us. Someone must have tipped off Scar about our rescue.

When I gently open the door and peek, Scar is facing the other way. I walk toward the ladder without making noise, but I avoid looking like I am sneaking. If he stops me, my sweaty forehead, the prickled hair on my arms, my trembling knees will give me away. Once upstairs, I try to listen to Scar's phone conversations. It is difficult because he doesn't talk loudly like he did earlier.

My friends' wet hair shines and their spotless faces sparkle in the bright light. They don't know Scar has planned to send us away. If I had not said a word to the Sweets-Man this wouldn't have happened.

We are doomed.

For lunch, Scar gives us *dal*, rice, and two *rotis* each. It looks like he wants to fatten us up instantly.

"Hurry up and finish," he says.

"Yes, Boss," GC replies.

The phone rings. My heart jumps. Scar straightens up as he says, "Yes, I have made all the arrangements. The project will be done. No need to worry."

He clicks off the phone and gives each one of us a lingering look. "Make sure you stay clean." Clap! "Get up and finish those frames."

We stuff the last few bites into our mouths and go back to working in our smelly space.

I can't stop my mind from bouncing from one thing to another, and my anxiety grows until it is as tall as the buildings I saw from the bridge. I end up with one dreadful, miserable thought. If the police don't come tonight before Scar takes us somewhere else, I might be hundreds of miles away from here by tomorrow. I will be forever lost to my family, and they to me, unless we can plan an attack on Scar tonight. Then, when he comes tomorrow to take us away, we can beat him with the bead trays and tie him up.

Tonight I must share my plan.

Scar's phone rings and I press my ear down on the floor to listen.

Sahil stops rocking and Amar's eyes fill with questions.

I concentrate on Scar's talk.

"But they said tomorrow. Must be some mistake!"

Pause.

"I will hide them."

No more talk. Just as I sit back up, a loud clap thunders. We go down. Scar's expression is grim. "Listen, boys. Use the bathroom quickly if you have to. Then go

292

upstairs and stay there. When people come to make a delivery don't make a sound. If you do, you're as good as dead, because I will send you away with them to work in factories far away." There is a steadiness in his voice that makes me believe he would keep his word.

We use the bathroom and get back to work. He takes the fan and the pail full of *nimba* stems down. Then he removes the ladder.

Soon, we hear voices and something being dropped on the floor. Then the door shuts, the ladder moves, and Scar pokes his head up. "Follow me," he says.

When we go down, the place is full of large cotton bags. Colorful fabric peeks out of them. "Move these packages up," Scar orders. As we transfer them up, a sleeve sticks out or a leg of pants flops through. Maybe Scar is going to start a new business and find new kids to stitch buttons or hem garments.

"Put them all around the walls and leave a small place for you in the middle of the room," Scar says. We move our wooden benches to the center of the room and put the cloth bags around three sides. "You stay up and work, and if you hear voices, don't make a sound. You understand?"

I fight back tears. The group has become quiet.

We keep on working in silence. It feels like we are trapped in a hole. It is difficult to work with all these bags towering around us. I keep banging into someone's knees or an elbow. Our own stale breath suffocates us.

The sun will set soon and Scar will leave. If the police don't come today, it will be too late. With all these bags it will be too difficult to attack Scar tomorrow when he comes up. We are doomed.

"Gopal, put away your work and come down. Right now," Scar orders.

I stash my bead tray and go down. Before I know what is happening Scar stuffs my mouth with rags that he uses to wipe the frames. The taste of glue is horrid. I want to scream, but instead I gag. Then Scar wraps my mouth shut with a strip of material, ties my arms with strips of jute, and tells me to stand in the bathroom so no one can see me when they come down the ladder. One by one he calls the others and ties their mouths and hands up. All this takes only a few minutes.

Scar has planned this perfectly, and now I know there is no way out for us.

When Scar is done gagging and tying us up, he tells us to go up the ladder. It is difficult to climb with our hands tied behind our backs, but we manage to do it.

Once we sit down cross-legged on the floor he ties our legs up. "Don't move an inch. If one of you so much as squeaks, you are in trouble." Scar spreads his arms wide. "Big trouble."

We are huddled with our arms and legs tied and folded, our knees and elbows poking each other, our mouths stuffed and wrapped shut. There is no place to shift without the sacks tumbling down and smothering us. I am scared and soaked in perspiration. Amar's eyes are tightly closed, Sahil has a vacant look, Roshan's head is limp, Barish rests his head on his folded-up knees. GC looks from one sack to another as if he is not sure that this is for real. My eyes follow Scar.

"Stop staring at me. You evil boy!" he screams.

Oh, how I wish I had a real evil power to ruin him.

Scar unscrews the naked yellow bulb. Then he fills up the space he was standing in with more sacks. The room is pitch-black.

The ladder moves away.

I try to wiggle my hands free.

Even though it is not my fault that we are tied up, I feel guilty. Maybe it was a mistake to ask Sweets Man for help. He must have talked to the police and someone has tipped off Scar. Now we will be scattered. Maybe the police will show up after Scar takes us away tomorrow. The same few thoughts spin in my head.

I have no luck in freeing my hands.

It seems like we have been trapped for hours, but it has only been a few minutes.

Finally, there are voices outside the building. Footsteps rush, and someone knocks. Then silence. Silence like the pitch-dark night in this hole.

Then voices float up. Two or three people are talking all at once.

"Is this the only space? What is upstairs?" I hear a stern voice.

"Nothing, sir, it is a storage area," Scar says. His voice sounds like a screechy, trapped monkey. The police are here to rescue us! Tears trickle down my cheeks.

"Let's have a look."

"It is just clothes and it is quite stuffy up there. I think it would be a waste of your . . ."

"Move the ladder."

"Yes, sir. I will help you. Please have something to drink. What can I get you? Tea?" Scar says.

"We don't have time for all that nonsense. Are you going to show us what is upstairs or not?" The voice is not loud, but the words are uttered with force and anger.

The ladder moves. I hold my breath.

"Where are the lights? Flip on the switch." Someone is at the top of the ladder.

The switch turns on and off, but nothing happens. "There is no light there because I only get things down during the daytime. No reason to have a light there. As you see, there is nothing but our merchandise."

"I can barely see, but he is right. There is nothing but sacks full of clothes, Inspector," someone says.

"Are you sure?" the stern voice floats up.

"We're here," I shout.

No words come out.

"Come and look, Inspector."

There are sounds of footsteps on the ladder.

"Anyone in there? Speak up," the inspector's voice booms.

"Yes, we are here. We're here," I scream inside. No one hears me because I am voiceless, drenched in perspiration, shaking.

"Let's move these things out," Inspector says.

My palms are still bound. I try to rub them together, but it only makes a dull shuffle. Someone else is coming up the ladder.

The strip starts to come loose and I can move my hands a bit more. I am almost there.

Someone shifts things around and a bag tumbles down.

"He is right, Inspector. There is nothing but clothes here."

What if they leave without checking? It is difficult to breathe, but I have to get my hands free. Harder. Push. Pull. Loosen the bonds as fast as I can.

"*Accha, chala.*" I hear disappointment in the stern voice.

One of my hands slips free of the knot and I wiggle out my flashlight, flip it on, and point the beam onto the ceiling.

"What is that?"

I flash the beam back and forth in reply, but the light goes out.

"Did you see the flash?" someone asks.

"That was just—"

"Quiet," the inspector cuts Scar off. There is not a sound. I start thumping my hand on the floor. Others also must have gotten their hands free, too, because their thumping joins mine.

"They are here! Move those bundles out," Inspector booms. *"Now."*

"But sir—" Scar whines.

The man roars again like a lion. "Stay out of my way!"

Before we know it, the bags disappear. The policeman unties our legs and arms and we pull the cloth from our mouths before climbing down. There are four men in police uniforms, but one has three stars and a red-and-blue-striped ribbon at the outer edge of the shoulder straps. He must be the inspector. As he watches us line up, the vein in his temple pulsates.

"You kept these children upstairs as your slaves!" the inspector shouts.

"I, I am—"

He points at Sahil. "Look at him! You have starved him. And him," he points to GC. "He is so hunched over. You must have made him work like a donkey."

"I fed them and I never beat—"

"Sir, look at this." One of the policemen picks up the rubber tube. Scar's words die in his throat.

The inspector walks up to Scar. "You will pay for all your cruelty many times over. I will personally make sure of that."

Then the inspector turns to us. "Don't be afraid, children. No one can hurt you." When he looks down at our chapped hands, his face becomes hard again, and his eyes turn steely.

"I'll bring the children," he says to one of the policemen. He points to Scar. "I'll deal with him later." The policeman takes out handcuffs.

So far I have avoided looking straight at Scar. I feel that if our eyes meet, the nightmare will be repeated. But now I know he can't do anything and I glance at him. He has covered his face with his hands, but the police move his arms behind his back and handcuffs him. Scar's face is ashen—the color of a polluted city cloud. Perspiration rolls down his forehead, and the scar on his cheek is scrunched up. It reminds me of the day I came. But today his scar is puckered because he is panicked.

My friends are also looking at Scar. But it is GC's gray eyes that have darkened and speak most clearly. With his look GC is spitting, hitting, and punching Scar. His eyes tell of our pain, hunger, and aches. I wonder if Scar understands how much he has hurt us and how much we hate him. Maybe he does, because he averts his eyes from GC's gaze and looks down at the stone floor.

The inspector holds his hand out to Amar. "Come. Let's go." He wipes the tears from Amar's face and softly says, "I am here to take care of you." Then the inspector takes my hand and I extend my other hand to Sahil and we all walk out together. We don't look back.

Once outside I breathe in deeply.

"Who is Gopal?" the inspector asks.

"I am."

"You were brave to ask for help."

"Thank you, Inspector," I say. Then I blurt the words I have been longing to say. "Can I go home now? My family is in Mumbai and I know where they live."

"Yes, yes," he says.

It is so hard to be calm!

The inspector puts his hand on my shoulder. "It is time for you to say good-bye to your friends so you can go home with one of the policemen. We will take care of your friends until we find their families," he says.

"What if you can't find someone's family, or one of them is all alone?"

"We will look after them. I promise."

"When will I be able to see them again?"

"It is difficult to say, son. But I will try to arrange something." The inspector moves away a few steps.

The six of us make a circle. I don't know what to say.

Amar holds on to my arm. "You can't go. You have to be with us because we are a family."

"We'll always be a family," GC says. "Let go of Gopal."

I pull out the flashlight from my pocket and press it into Amar's hand. "Keep this. You'll need new batteries, but once you have them it will be like I am with you."

Sahil steps forward, puts his hand in his pocket, and

pulls out a string. It is the string from the sweets box. "There are six beads on here. Remember us."

"I'll never forget you."

"I-I am not a good friend," Roshan says.

I wrap my arm around his shoulders. "Yes, you are."

"No-no. Sca-Scar made me tell about yo-your family. He held the scissors to my neck and said if I didn't talk he would hurt me. So-so-sorry." More tears stream down his face.

I glance at GC and Barish. They both must have known it was Roshan who had told Scar about the twins, but they kept quiet to protect Roshan and me. "Don't worry now. We are all safe from Scar," I say to Roshan.

He pulls out a piece of newspaper from his pocket. There are pressed *nimba* leaves between the folded papers. "I kept this in my jute sack to remember my family," he says, and hands me one of the leaves. I tuck it into my pocket with the beaded string.

"You don't want to forget this," Barish says. He hands me a bundle. It is my raincoat.

"When did you get that?"

"I grabbed it before I climbed down."

"Thanks," I say.

Now GC and I turn to each other. "Gopal, I want to tell you . . . my name is Kabir."

I am too stunned to say anything.

"Is that your real name?" Barish asks.

"That's the name my grandmother gave me, but once

she died I didn't allow anyone to call me by that name. I should have told you my name a long time ago." GC squeezes my shoulder. "Call me Kabir."

"Kabir."

"Kabir," the others repeat after me.

Starting with Kabir, I give each of them a hug. In the dark I can't see my friends' faces clearly, but my cheeks are wet with our tears mixed together.

Amar gives me one more hug. "Gopal, come visit us soon."

"I will," I can barely whisper.

The inspector clears his throat.

It is time to go.

twenty-eight

The inspector takes my friends in his car and one of the policemen and I go to Jama's house in a taxi.

It is the day after Diwali, and the lights twinkle in windows and galleries. The mood is festive and it fills me with joy. The darkness has ended and I am free! My friends are free! It won't be long before the inspector sends Barish, Amar, and Roshan home. It might take a while to find Sahil's relatives, though. I hope all of the boys get back to their families. What will Kabir do? He doesn't have anyone. If Kabir lives in Mumbai I can see him. I will ask Aai if he can visit us. I know she will say yes.

Just like I thought of Aai, Baba, Naren, Sita, and Jama when I was making frames, I will think of Kabir, Roshan, Barish, Sahil, and Amar when I am back with my family. Six of us had come together, and now I am not with them. I take out the string with six beads and finger each of them. I pray to keep my friends safe and happy. Even though we will miss one another, I can't wait to go home and be with my family.

After a long cab ride we get off at the corner by Chachaji's shop. It is past nine o'clock and the shop is closed. I want to run down the street to Jama's house. I hold on to my raincoat and walk as fast as I can without breaking into a run. The policeman looks at me sideways and keeps up with me.

When I get close to Jama's my heart starts banging, my knees tremble, and my eyes tear up. The door is open and light from inside spills out. "Is this your home?" the policeman asks.

"Yes," I reply.

"Go," he says, gently stepping to the side. I rush in. Naren and Sita are lying on a mattress wide awake. Aai is sitting on the sofa, talking to Jama and an old man. I am stunned for a moment. It is Baba!

"Aai, Baba!" I cry as I run toward them.

"Gopal?" Aai opens her arms toward me.

"Our Gopal!" Baba is trembling, a shrunken, thinner version of himself, but his eyes come alive as he embraces me. Naren and Sita jump up and hug my legs, bouncing and shouting "Gopal! Gopal!" Jama wipes tears from his eyes. We are all sobbing, laughing, hugging.

I take a breath and let their familiar scents soothe me. "Aai, Baba," I whisper.

"Yes, Gopal," they whisper back. The way they call me by my name fills me with such joy that I can't reply.

I don't want to ask Baba where he was and I don't want them to ask me about where I have been. Not tonight.

name guide

Amar: Dimpled Chin
Barish: Thick Fingers
Kabir: GC (short for Gray Cloud)
Roshan: Night Chatterer
Sahil: Rocking Boy

glossary

Aaa jao (Hindi): "Come on," "Come over"

Aai (Marathi): mother

Accha (Hindi): okay, all right

Anamik (Sanskrit): without names

Baba (Marathi): father

Bahin (multiple languages): sister

Bajra (multiple languages): barley-sized grayish grain

Bakra (multiple languages): goat

Bakshish (multiple languages): bonus, tip

Bakvas bandh kero (Hindi): "Stop babbling," "Stop talking nonsense"

Bambaiya Hindi: Hindi dialect spoken in Mumbai; it includes a mixture of words from Marathi, Gujarati, Tamil, English, Konkani, and other languages.

Besan (multiple languages): chickpea flour

Bhai (multiple languages): brother

Bhaji (Marathi): fresh vegetable as well as cooked curried vegetable

Bilkul bakvas (Bambaiya Hindi): absolute or total nonsense

Bindaas (Bambaiya Hindi): carefree

Bindi (multiple languages): a dot many women wear on their foreheads in India

Bor (multiple languages): a small, tropical, berrylike fruit

Chachaji (Hindi): respected uncle; also used for elderly unrelated male

Chai (multiple languages): Indian-style tea with milk, sugar, and spices

Chala (Marathi): "Come," "Let's go"

Chamcha (Bambaiya Hindi, slang): sidekick

Chinch (Marathi): tamarind; the fruit pulp has a very sour taste and is used in cooking and making sauces and chutneys

Chota (Hindi): small, young

Chote muh, badi baat mat ker (Bambaiya Hindi): "Don't talk big with (your) small mouth"

Dal (multiple languages): lentil soup

Desh (multiple languages): home country

Dhanteras (multiple languages): a holiday two days before the festival of Diwali; it is considered an auspicious day

Dhotar (Marathi): a long piece of cloth worn by men; it is wrapped around the waist and legs and tied at the waist

Diwali (multiple languages): Hindu festival of lights that falls in October and is celebrated all over India

Dudhi bhaji (Marathi): curried squash

Faltu (Bambaiya Hindi): useless

Ganpati bappa morya, pudcha varshi laukar ya (Marathi): "Hail Lord Ganesha, return again soon next year"; a chant heard at the festival of Ganesha or Ganpati

Ghee (Multiple languages): clarified butter

Gorus-chinch (Marathi): a variety of tamarind with a sweeter taste than regular tamarind

Gundas (Hindi): thugs, bad people

Hamare baap ka bridge thodi hai? (Bambaiya Hindi): "Does the bridge belong to our fathers or what?"

Ho (Marathi): yes

Kahani (Hindi): story

Kal kere so aaj kare, aaj kare so abb (Hindi): "Do today what you plan to do tomorrow, do now what you plan to do today"

Kal-bal (Hindi): chatter

Kali Chaudash: the day before Diwali; it is considered the day of ghosts, goblins, and other spirits

Kanpatti (Bambaiya Hindi, slang): punishment

Khajoor (Bambaiya Hindi, slang): stupid

Khissa-khali (Bambaiya Hindi): literally, "empty pockets"

Kurta-pajamas (Hindi): men's long shirt and pants

Laddus (multiple languages): a dessert consisting of deep-fried balls of sugary dough

Ladki (Hindi): girl

Maa (Hindi): mother

Maha nagari (Sanskrit, multiple languages): big city

Mamu (Bambaiya Hindi, slang): stupid

Mayavati nagari (Sanskrit, multiple languages): illusionary city

Meri billi mujko meow? (Hindi): "Is my own cat going against me?"

Mi jato (Marathi): "I'm going"

Mumbaikar (Bambaiya Hindi): one who lives in Mumbai

Murga (multiple languages): chicken

Nalla (Hindi): stream

Namashkar bahin (multiple languages): "Greetings, sister"

Nimba (Marathi, Sanskrit): also called *kadunimb*, a tropical tree that has many medicinal uses

Navratna (multiple languages): nine jewels, the nine influential and wise people of the Mogul King Akbar's court

Oai ladka (Hindi): "Hey, boy"

Oui maa (Hindi, exclamation of surprise): "Oh mother!"

Oulta (Hindi): upside-down

Pakka (Hindi): real, for sure

Pakora (multiple languages): a kind of fritter containing potatoes, onions, and other vegetables; dipped in chickpea flour and deep-fried

Pav (multiple languages): bread

Pav-bhaji (multiple languages): bread with spicy vegetable

Pipul tree (Ficus religiosa): fig tree

Roti (multiple languages): flat Indian bread

Sacch na? (Hindi): "Right?"

Samazne (Marathi): understand

Sambhalun ja (Marathi): go carefully or be careful

Samman (Marathi): honor, self-pride

Shabash (Hindi): well done, great job

Shahanshah (Hindi): king of kings

Sudarshan (Sanskrit): an Ayurvedic medicine to bring fever down

Suna (Hindi): "Tell us"

Tea se jyada nai kitali garam hai (Bambaiya Hindi, slang): someone who thinks he is smarter than he is

Tera baap (Hindi, slang): your father (used as an insult here)

Thahro: (Hindi, Marathi): "Wait"

Tu bakvas bandh ker (Bambaiya Hindi): "Stop talking nonsense"

Tum acchi kahani sunate ho (Hindi): "You tell good stories"

Tumhi Marathi bolta ka? (Marathi): "Do you speak Marathi?"

Wah! (Hindi): "Wow!"

Xhun se laafa (Bambaiya Hindi): a hard slap

Yaar (Hindi): buddy, dear friend, pal

author's note

In recent years we have seen reports and stories about multi-national, brand-name, well-respected companies whose goods are made by child labor. Most of these companies are European and American. These stories set me on the journey to write this novel.

In my previous trips to India, my birthplace, I had talked extensively with young girls who worked as domestic help to try and understand their customs and why they had fled their villages, but in 2008 I decided to travel to India once more to learn more about child labor. As I traveled I talked with many poor children and adults. I learned how children worked, lived in slums, and how rural poverty pushed people to the big cities and changed their lives. On a train station in Jaipur, a boy around eleven years of age, dressed in clean clothes and with combed hair, stepped forward to help our taxi driver load the luggage without our asking him. I gave him money and then made sure our driver knew which hotel we were going to. When I turned around to talk to the boy, he was gone. I was disappointed. His bright eyes and friendly smile stayed with me. My protagonist, Gopal, is fashioned after him.

I also traveled to Matheran, a hilltop resort near Mumbai, and met a couple there. The man worked in our hotel and his wife carried our luggage. Some of their relatives had moved to Mumbai to look for work. They were such a delightful couple—happy, content, and hard-working. They left their home in the valley at four thirty in the morning because it took them almost two hours to climb up the hill to Matheran. I thought of my main character, Gopal, having those kinds of parents and family.

In Matheran I talked to one of the men who owned two horses. His livelihood depended on them, and he too was from the valley below Matheran. He had a teenage daughter, and even though there were marriage proposals for her, as is their custom, he refused to let her get married. "My daughter is smart and always comes first in school, so I want her to get a good education and have a better life," he told me. I also read heartbreaking stories about onion farmers from this area and how the good crop season had ruined them. I put all these people and stories together to create Gopal and his family. So Gopal comes from the state of Maharastra, and Marathi is his mother tongue. (It is also the official language of the state, and Mumbai is its capital.)

On our railway journey to Rajasthan, a boy around eight or nine dressed in soiled clothes stepped into our compartment at one of the stations. He began to clean the floor with his hands. When he spilled some tea one of the passengers had left behind in a paper cup, he took off his sweater and used it as a rag. Then he asked passengers for money. He was extremely shy, and when I tried to talk to him he looked scared. I was shocked to find out he was twelve. When I asked him about his parents and family, he hesitantly told me he lived with his maternal grandmother. He was nervous and glanced out the window as if he was afraid of someone. Then the train whistle blew and he left before I could ask him more questions.

I also talked with a nonprofit organization in Mumbai that works with children who run away from home or are lured into coming to Mumbai to find work. The challenging work they do provided me invaluable insight about what is being done to help these children.

In the affluent and industrial nations children earn pocket money by babysitting, mowing lawns, or helping with household chores, but in many other countries children work every single day from dawn to dusk and beyond for very little money and under unhygienic and cruel conditions. Some of the factories, shops, and farms exploit children, deny them education, and trap them in a cycle of poverty. Sadly, the problem is widespread.

During my research I found that child labor is more widespread than I had thought. An article on child labor in *Forbes Magazine* (February 25, 2008) reports:

The UN International Labor Organization guesses that there are 218 million child laborers worldwide, 7 in 10 of them in agriculture, followed by service businesses (22%) and industry (9%). Asia-Pacific claims the greatest share of underage workers (122 million), then sub-Saharan Africa (49 million). Noteworthy offenders: Cambodia, Mali, Burkina Faso, Bolivia, and Guatemala.

These children work in carpet weaving, garment industries, fireworks factories, as household help, in restaurants, and even as soldiers. The goods and products they make reach the far corners of the world and some of the biggest markets. The products range from cheap hand-embroidered and beaded purses and tops to garden statues, handwoven carpets, coffee, sports equipment, and more. These goods made by children are inexpensive and well made, but those who make them are denied education, their childhood, and sometimes their freedom.

Even in the United States there is child labor. Many children, mostly illegal immigrants, work all day doing farm and garden work and household chores instead of attending school. These children do not get an education and have no health insurance.

Where does this end? Child labor will persist as long as there is widespread poverty and children must work to feed themselves and their family, and as long as there is a market for cheap goods.

Here are some articles and websites about child labor:

Child labor article from *Forbes*:
www.forbes.com/forbes/2008/0225/072.html

UNICEF:
www.unicef.org/protection/index_childlabour.html

Antislavery website:
www.antislavery.org/homepage/antislavery/childlabour.htm#what

International Labor Rights Forum:
www.laborrights.org/stop-child-labor

Bachpan Bachao Andolan, Save the Childhood Movement website:
www.bba.org.in

acknowledgments

In the fall of 2007 my agent, Charlotte Sheedy, called me and asked me to consider writing a book about child labor. I thank Charlotte for her ideas, insight, and support, and Meredith Kaffel for her help.

I am fortunate to have friends in India whose homes are always open to me. The love and hospitality of the Dani and Gandhi families make going to India a pleasure.

Thanks to Altaf Shaikh from Saathi for talking to me about the organization. The work they do is incredible and inspiring. Please visit Saathi's website: www.saathi.org/index.htm.

My daughter Rupa Valdez was my first reader. Over the past year she and her sister, Neha Sheth, read and edited my manuscript. My son-in-law, Joey Valdez, is my technology problem solver. Without him a slightest glitch would stop me from doing my work. I am thankful to all three of them as well as to my husband, Rajan.

I extend my deepest thanks to my fellow writers and friends Georgia Beverson, Judy Bryan, Emily Kokie, and Bridget Zinn for their insightful critiques, suggestions, and comments. I also thank my critique-group members and friends, Rosanne Lindsay, Michael Kress-Russick, Julie Shaull, and Melinda Starkweather, for their generous help.

My sincere thanks to Sanjay Joshi, who has background and expertise with disadvantaged children, for his thoughtful and thorough reading of the manuscript.

I had no idea how much work was still waiting for me once I accepted the offer from Balzer + Bray. I am indebted to my editor, Donna Bray, for challenging and encouraging me to write the best book I could. And many thanks to Ruta Rimas and the rest of the team at HarperCollins.

Without my mom's blessings and love nothing would have been possible for me.

Over the years so many dear friends and family members have made this journey possible for me. I am grateful to them all.